TH

THEM
and other stories

Xosé Luís Méndez Ferrín

translated by John Rutherford, Xelís de Toro,
and Benigno Fernández Salgado

PLANET

First published
in Wales in 1996
by Planet

PO Box 44
Aberystwyth
Ceredigion
Cymru/Wales

Designed by Glyn Rees

Printed by Gwasg Gomer,
Llandysul, Ceredigion

The publishers gratefully acknowledge
the financial support of the
Consellería de Cultura e Comunicación Social
of the Xunta de Galicia

Esta obra foi subvencionada pola
Consellería de Cultura e
Comunicación Social, Dirección
Xeral de Promoción Cultural na
convocatoria de subvencións para
1996.

ISBN 0 9505188 4 0

Contents

Introduction

To introduce Xosé Luís Méndez Ferrín (b. 1938) and his writing is not a straightforward task. He is regarded in Galicia as a modern classic, and his work spans more than thirty-five years. He has produced both poetry and narrative fiction that have proved to be turning points in Galician literature. Furthermore, his resolute political stance has become so intertwined with his writing, a large part of which was published under Franco's dictatorship, that neither can be disregarded when considering him. His work embodies the political struggles of Galician nationalism, and he has been arrested and imprisoned on several occasions for his links with nationalist organisations.

Ferrín started to write during a difficult period in Galician history, characterised by the repression and censorship of Franco's dictatorship and by the weakness of the Galician publishing world; a period aptly described by the Galician poet Celso Emilio Ferreiro as "a long night of stone". Ferrín's generation not only had to contend with a political system that denied any notion of Galician identity and dismissed the Galician language as a parochial dialect, but also had to relate to the existing literary tradition, fragmented and interrupted by the Civil War. Ferrín's work can be understood as a compendium of answers to the uncertainties of this period. He incorporated and reflected literary tradition, and converted past experiences in order to renovate and modernise Galician literature.

Modern Galician literature started, after more than three centuries of silence, with a Romantic revival in the mid nineteenth century that coincided with the political affirmation of individual Galician identity as opposed to Spanish homogeneity. The practice of writing in Galician and the defence of our national identity continued throughout that century and into the present one. In the 1920s a new generation of intellectuals, the "Nós Generation" (the subject of Ferrín's story "Sibila"), asked new questions about what it meant to write in Galician, and changed the way in which Galician literature would be understood in future. Literature should not only reflect and reaffirm identity but also strengthen bonds with other cultures (particularly Celtic ones, for Galicia saw itself as a Celtic nation) in order to produce a universal literature. The dictum "Be from your land, and from your time" represented these new attitudes towards literature. This cultural, literary and political revolution lasted until the Spanish Civil War broke out.

Ferrín incorporates his work into this tradition in a dynamic way, reviewing and reassessing past experiences. His work has to be understood both as a reaction against the politics of his times, and as an endeavour to reconstruct, enlarge and modernise the literary tradition. On the one hand, he denounces the machinery of power and the repression of Galician identity in the narratives belonging to the cycle of Tagen Ata, which provide a mythical setting for the Galician struggle; and he depicts the fascist repression that followed the Civil War in stories such as "Them" and "Elastic Boots". On the other hand, he absorbs European traditions and develops a variety of styles: novels such as *Arrabaldo do Norde* draw from the French nouveau roman, "Artur's Love" deals with the "matière de Bretagne", "The Old House of Arranhão" takes a new look at Goethe's *Elective Affinities*, and the cycle of Tagen Ata opens an imaginary space that reminds us of Tolkien in books such as *Arnoia, Arnoia*. Ferrín has also reworked popular literature in a variety of ways, such as the ghost story in "A Family of Surveyors" and science fiction in "Labyrinth" and "Partisan 4".

One of Ferrín's finest achievements has been mastering the art of combining politics and literature. He has been seen as the prototype of the political writer. But it would be a mistake to try to confine Ferrín within a definition, for his work constantly transcends definitions.The relationship between literature and politics in his writing is complex and elusive, with a multiplicity of internal links that come to the surface and then hide themselves away, hints that we can follow but which then become misleading. As the narrator of "Cold Hortensia" says, after literature we are "on our way back to days of sorrow and certainties".

Written while he was in prison in 1970, Ferrín's "Return to Tagen Ata" has been singled out as the story in which literature and politics work together most openly. The mythical land of Tagen Ata is readily identified with Galicia and the Azerrata language with Galician, while Spain is represented by Terra Ancha. The plot revolves around two different parts of Azerrata or Galician nationalism: after the Spanish

Civil War a major division developed within the latter when political exiles in Latin America pursued a policy of political resistance against Francoism, while those nationalists who still lived in Galicia saw cultural resistance as the only way forward. But even in "Return to Tagen Ata", where politics and literature are most closely connected, Ferrín does not indulge in presenting a simple relationship: history, myth, memory and aspiration are mysteriously mixed. The protagonist's certainty about politics merges with her longing to be certain about politics; her desire to follow the right path and reject the nationalist leader merges with her sexual desire for him. "Return to Tagen Ata" is readily interpreted as a representation of the fight between an oppressed nation and its oppressor, but we should never expect such a struggle to be depicted by Ferrín as a simple one.

The mythological places and characters deployed in "Return to Tagen Ata" reappear in stories such as "Cold Hortensia" (1982) and in the novel *Bretaña esmeraldina* (1987). But whereas in "Return to Tagen Ata" we find a modern conflict taking place in this mythical setting, in "Cold Hortensia" it has become a part of the memory of oral tradition. Some critics see this strand in his fiction as Ferrín's greatest achievement, as it is here that he creates his own mythological world which is revised and rewritten with each new story.

Whether Ferrín is constructing a mythical world or describing the brutality of fascist repression, we are never far from the process of writing as a theme in itself. In Ferrín writing does not just aim to communicate, tell stories, construct myths, represent Galicia's identity. The reader is constantly aware of the extraordinarily eclectic nature of Ferrín's vocabulary, and of his meticulous construction of complex sentences. Bernardo Atxaga has described his experience as a Basque writer in terms of the impossibility of using a language which he calls invisible, because many of the words he employs are exclusively literary and not known to readers whose use of the language is primarily oral. The language's lack of transparency defines the experience of both the Basque and the Galician writer. Yet Ferrín's language consciously displays this lack of transparency to such a degree that his writing could almost be called exhibitionist, since the language and the process of writing are exposed in total nakedness. Ferrín's prose is on occasions almost opaque, and then the process of reading goes together with another process, that of questioning the words, wondering about the secret corridors of the syntax. Words in Ferrín not only bear meaning but are physical objects that we can observe and almost touch, reminding us constantly of what is natural and what is artificial in language. Ferrín's language is the struggle *for* language, a demonstration that it is impossible to take language for granted.

In this sense Ferrín not only inserts his own work into the Galician literary tradition, but he also summarises the latter and puts it on show. He does not hide his devices, and this is what makes his work so powerful. He displays the contradictions and the strengths of our literary tradition. Ferrín openly performs the act of converting oral stories into myth and then into history. He exposes the act of constructing a literary language, of choosing and organising, of appropriating words from memories, from old sayings, of recovering the words we once had or would like to have had.

In this anthology we have tried to reflect the variety of Ferrín's writing, from his first short stories such as "The Gate", "Grieih" and "Philoctetes", published in 1958 when he was twenty years old, to his most recent work included in *Arraianos*, published in 1991. We have tried to choose at least one short story from each style and to combine this with our personal preferences. For this reason the reader will find more stories from his most recent books *Amor de Artur* and *Arraianos*, where we believe that Ferrín's language has most fully realised its potential. We shall, of course, never be sure whether we have made the right choices, but we hope that the reader will gain as much pleasure from reading the collection as we have derived from compiling and translating it.

Xelís de Toro

A Note on the Translations

These translations were prepared under the direction of John Rutherford, assisted by Xelís de Toro and Benigno Fernández Salgado, at the
Centre for Galician Studies, The Queen's College, Oxford University.
They are the result of a new venture in group translation, and an
unusual number of people have been involved. A certain prejudice
exists against such an approach, but this is, we believe, because it has
been most notoriously followed in biblical and other religious translation, where the need to settle for theological and doctrinal com-
promises has often prevailed over literary considerations. In the case
of non-religious fiction it is less difficult to identify the author's
ideology and agree to respect it, letting literature prevail. To those who
deride all "translation by committee" we reply that the performance
of an orchestra of talented musicians under an energetic and forceful
baton can be as individual and exciting as that of any soloist. Each
member has so much to offer to the whole, and the combination of
different experiences, backgrounds and age groups must, if it can all
be held together, produce a more complete translation than could be
managed by any individual working alone.

John Rutherford and Xelís de Toro worked with Michael Shaw on
ten stories. Helena Buffery, David M. Clark, Sílvia Coll-Vinent,
Charlotte Eimer, Benigno Fernández Salgado and Carlota Eiros, Xosé
María Moreno Villar and Sara Walker, Emma Oram, and Richard
Peters prepared first drafts of individual stories. Several translations
received their final shape at our *Obradoiro de Traducción*, or Trans-
lation Workshop, led by John Rutherford, Benigno Fernández Salgado
and Xelís de Toro, whose other members at various times have been:
Helena Buffery, Sílvia Coll-Vinent, Claire Daniel, Charlotte Eimer,
Carlota Eiros, Manuela García Méndez, Nigel Knight, David Long-
rigg, Richard Peters, Michael Shaw, Marilyse Turnbull and Kathryn
Tyson.

Translating Ferrín has been an exhausting and exhilarating experience for all of us. Ferrín's attitude to language, like his attitude to

politics, is one of uncompromising radicalism. In his writing there is a constant determination to describe experience exactly as it is, rather than as it might be comfortable to regard it, or as conventional language likes to represent it. And so Ferrín dares to force his language, the Galician language, to do precisely what he is resolved it must do for him, however reluctant it may be, however much twisting and turning and distorting this may sometimes involve. Hence the extraordinary power of his writing. We decided that translators should be bold and radical too, and that our translations would resist the current tendency to tame that which is challenging in the original by, for example, splitting uncomfortably long sentences, fusing uncomfortably short ones, diluting weird combinations of words — which, in Ferrín, give such sudden startling insights — into bland commonplaces; and thus both making our job much easier and betraying our author. At the same time it was important never to forget our duty to our readers to produce texts that they will enjoy. These, at least, were our aims.

We are indebted to Xosé Luís Méndez Ferrín for his kind assistance with many problems of detail; to Nigel Knight and David Longrigg for their very special contributions; and to John Barnie, for being such a painstaking yet patient and tolerant publisher.

John Rutherford

Them

The Porter turned the crank and Fernando, who was seated at the wheel, adjusted the choke until the engine fired. We pulled away through a thick fog, which appeared milky in the cold light of dawn. The heavy crowing of birds sounded out from the moors as we chugged along in Fernando Salgueiro's cream Ford, the four of us sliding around along the sharply winding track down from the Alto do Furriolo to Veiga and Verea.

We were resting our rifles between our legs except for Fernando, who had left his sub-machine gun on one of the spare seats in the back, as if it were a box of chocolates to be presented to some distinguished lady.

We always used to drink brandy before and after this kind of business.

The Porter pulled out a bottle of "Tres Cepas" from inside his greatcoat. Fernando shook his head and fingered his thin black moustache. The rest of us drank. The Porter belched.

"That made you feel better!" said the Caballero.

The Porter's eyes were puffy and their lids were heavy and drooping, with bright red lower rims. Whenever he looked sideways it seemed to me that the effort must have hurt him. The Caballero was looking at the Porter, sitting next to him.

"We'll take the Porter home now," snarled Fernando distantly.

I had always thought that Fernando Salgueiro must have Filipino blood in him. At that moment his skin glowed brown, as if he were sweating; there were pimples on his narrow forehead.

"We'll take the Porter home so that he can screw his wife tonight," Fernando added, stroking his cheek as if to assure himself that hardly any hair grew there.

The Porter had a huge head, dark stubble and a triangular moustache which made him look like a radical or a Moroccan. He opened his mouth wide to laugh, showing his gums, and teeth which seemed to be covered in some sort of green lichen. But, almost at once, he bowed his pig-head, resting his brow on the barrel of his Mauser. I was in the front seat and, as I looked back at him, the Porter seemed the very picture of desolation. He said:

"She'll need some persuading to let me have my way!"

I'd known Fernando since we were kids.

"Well, well, well," he said, and I knew at once that he was sniffing around, nosing out some way of ridiculing the Porter.

We had been brought up together, Fernando Salgueiro and I. One day we went for a picnic by the river, in Vilazo, and he put earth and a dead blackbird into the paella that the Toubes girls had lovingly made for the group. And they'd just finished convent school in Chaves and were so excited about getting together with the old gang again, because we were like family, we were, back in Verín!

We were all scared of Fernando Salgueiro. He always had his own way; always ordered us around.

"We could stop off for breakfast in Bande," the Caballero suggested suddenly.

Fernando smirked. The Caballero was known for his greediness and I thought of the rolls of fat beneath his combat jacket, bursting out over his belt and the badge with the Spanish emblem on it. The lardy rolls, squeezed by the strap that girthed his chest. The red cross of those old-guard Fascists, the Caballeros of Santiago, was so rumpled up it had almost disappeared beneath his sagging left breast. He was older than the rest of us, was the Caballero.

"Go on, we always do," I meekly begged Fernando Salgueiro.

The tarmac road was broken in a hundred places, and had a number of deep potholes. A cloud of clay dust surrounded the car as we drove along. We climbed up to the Alto do Vieiro and the fog faded away. I looked to the right and saw the endless wasteland, the barren desert that, by Égoas Hill, extends to the marshes that stretch as far as

Portugal and that the herdsmen use as pastureland. The hill that could be seen in the distance must have been Penagache.

Fernando stopped the car and put the handbrake on. He gravely opened his leather jacket and took a packet of cigarettes from the breast pocket of his blue shirt. He mechanically flicked out a fan of cigarettes. He offered them to us and I was the only one to accept. Fernando Salgueiro always smokes Chesterfield. We lit them with his gold Ronson.

Then we got out of the Ford, making as much noise as we could, slamming the doors, shouting, joking and spitting. We tucked our pistols into our belts. Adjusting our caps, first to one side and then to the front, we felt the merry dance of the pompom, so deeply and so dearly Spanish. We slung our rifles over our shoulders. We looked at each other and wanted to be seen and admired by the people of Bande, who seemed not to be out on the streets at half past nine in the morning.

The Caballero de Santiago was a sorry sight in his khaki uniform and his jodhpurs, tight around his fat calves. The Caballero looked like one of the old faithfuls of Primo de Rivera's time, even though he was a doctor in Cualedro. The Porter had squeezed into a boiler suit, complete with strap and ammunition pouches, open at the front to show his blue shirt. Over his shoulders he sported a greatcoat. I myself left my top-coat in the car so as to show off the yoke and arrows on the breast pocket of my combat jacket, and using my middle and fore fingers I flicked the cigarette end into the air with the clean trajectory of a mortar shell. In his gleaming riding boots, breeches and black leather jacket, his sub-machine gun over one shoulder, our beloved Fernando Salgueiro seemed far taller than he really was.

A few windows closed; and various figures which we had glimpsed hanging out clothes on the balconies of Bande disappeared. Turning a corner, our squad came across a man of about forty wearing a corduroy jacket and trousers, the black button of mourning on his striped shirt, and a small beret, cocked to one side. He paled — I saw in his eyes a boundless look of fear — and moved off to the middle of the road, showing, by the speed of his steps, total submission before us. He thrust up an arm to hail:

"Arriba España!" with hoarse humility.

"We didn't hear that! Louder!" Fernando Salgueiro barked, with the most savage look in his repertoire.

"Arriba España! Arriba España!" the man shouted immediately, in a husky voice deformed by terror.

We exchanged glances and burst out laughing, as we continued on our way towards the inn.

Of course, we comrades always used to have a bite to eat after the dawn purges.

A small group of us from Verín had gone out that day in Fernando's cream Ford, up to the Furriolo. The Caballero, who lived in Cualedro, had wanted to come with us. Before sunrise, the squad from Celanova had marched six men out of the monastery and taken them up to the Furriolo, in a van that had been requisitioned from Celso de Poulo's family, after he had been killed in the first few days. We rubbed out all six of them there, in a ditch.

The owner of the inn was happy to see us.

"Long live the Camisas Viejas!" he exclaimed, laughing.

Fernando cut him short. "Shut up, you fool!"

"Shall I go and let the others know?"

"Not a word! We're travelling incognito today..."

The Falange from Verín had got it in for the worst elements who were working on the railway. Wherever there was work, the poison was there too. That morning our comrades from Celanova had brought us a nice present. Four trade unionists from Vilar de Barrio, one of the heads of the Sociedade de Corrichouso and the cross-eyed Sevillian who had been the right-hand man of the Marxist mayor of A Gudiña (the Devil take him!)

We had a round of coffee liqueurs while we were waiting for breakfast.

Because those of us who formed the squad from Verín — Fernando, Otero, Pazos, Pepe Taboada — had been together before the Alzamiento. When the innkeeper called us Camisas Viejas I thought my heart would burst. That's what we were, except for the Caballero. And our families had been ridiculed and suffered outrages in Verín. All of them had paid or would pay with their lives, those Marxists. Fernando especially hated the contract workers on the Zamora-Corunna railway; those affiliated to the union.

"That trash!" Fernando said, his mouth curling as, taking a swig of the coffee liqueur, he remembered the shootings of that morning. "The one from Corrichouso cried like a little queer. The others tried to look brave but I could see the fear in their eyes."

"And in their mouths," said the Porter. "Surely you can see the fear in the mouths of those Reds, Don Fernando? Can't you, sir? I can spot it immediately."

Fernando was beginning to enjoy himself.

"It would seem your wife doesn't want any fun and games with you, Porter."

Fernando was a demon for prising information out of such peasants.

"What's up, eh? Do tell — you're among experts. Go on."

"She's out of sorts, Don Fernando. She's in a terrible state with the worry."

The yellow-check oilskin tablecloth was riddled with holes from the cheap cigars and cigarettes smoked there by thousands of smokers on the 13th and 28th of every month, which were market days. Upon it our host placed our plates and glasses, a carafe of red wine and a loaf of white bread.

"I want a mug!" the Caballero insisted.

The innkeeper dutifully changed his unbreakable glass for a small white mug.

"Look at the Porter!" Fernando said, as if to himself, while turning his glass in his hand.

Fernando tapped his diamond ring against the thick rim of his wine glass, breaking the sudden moment of silence. And then the Porter spoke. His wife was sad. Everyone at home was, over there in Gustimeaus. Great sorrow had come upon them. Their seven-year-old son was poorly, as white as sperm. His face was burning up. A plague of lice was consuming him and nobody could cure it: not with potions, nor with constant changes of clothes, nor by shaving his head.

"Lice? Lice?"

"Lice, Don Fernando, I swear it. By the respect that I have for you and that my father had for your father, as a servant who served him well. Headlice and those other bigger ones that infest clothes. He's not got any crabs, though, because he's still only a lad, my little one."

The innkeeper told his wife to bring the cooked breakfast. Two big round serving plates; one with boiled potatoes, the other with eggs and fried sausages, covered in oil; and all of it sprinkled with paprika. Another smaller plate arrived with chunks of ham.

We served ourselves. The Caballero first, by courtesy of Fernando. Then me. We had to insist to make the Porter eat.

On the smoke-stained wall of the dining room there were prints of lakes and snow-covered mountains. On one side there was a screen with blue and red glass at the top, separating us from the kitchen. The Porter's eyes roamed absently from the pictures to the glass panels and from the glass panels to the pictures, whilst he mashed the potato and egg together with a fork. Since it was morning, the place smelt of bleach.

The Caballero said, his mouth red from the spicy pork sausage:

"If you like, Porter, I could have a look at your boy."

"Doctors can't do anything, sir. We've already taken him to Don Ildefonso Santalices, here in Bande. Don Pepe Barros came to see him at home. Thanks for offering though, sir. God bless you for it."

We ordered more wine.

"Look here, Porter."

I knew Fernando well. When I heard him say "Look here" in that tone of voice I knew that he was up to something, and I started to tremble. I know all about my friend's tricks. He's incredible.

"Look here."

And Fernando continued in a low voice, showing his tiny teeth in the cunning smile which announced mockery.

"And it wouldn't be that someone in the village resents you and your woman, would it?"

The Porter stood up and pushed back the chair. He spoke, running his eyes over everyone; but not as before, for now he was speaking only for Fernando.

"I didn't want to say anything but I am sure one of our neighbours envies us. I am sure of it, sirs. One day she came to ask my wife for some wine because her son, who was working on the railway, was due home and she hadn't a thing to give him for lunch."

I noticed Fernando tense up like the band on a catapult before the stone is fired.

"On the railway? A son on the railway? You say she's got a son working down on the tracks?" he burst out at last.

"Yes, sir, she has. At the moment he's in hiding, he's run away. He was one of the CNT crowd. Son of a witch, and herself the daughter of a witch!"

"Blimey!" the Caballero shouted jokingly, laughing his head off, his double chin trembling like an earthquake. "Burn the witches!"

Fernando Salgueiro can leave you cold with no more than a gesture of his hand, with just a frown, with just a look. He doesn't need to get angry and put the barrel of his gun to your belly to give an order — though he knows how to do that, too. With the Caballero a mere smile, one finger poised in ambivalent reprimand, was quite enough.

The Porter continued, nervously wringing his hands:

"She already resented us, that witch, because of my job in the spa down in the valley. When she came to ask my wife for the jug of wine, she didn't give her one. She was sick of helping her out all the time. 'Some other day. God bless you!' she said coldly. As for our neighbour, she had hardly got out of the front door when my little boy started to moan and throw up (begging your pardon!). It wasn't long before the lice came. She'd put the evil eye on him."

We asked for more wine, in Bande.

A circular clock, with mother of pearl around the face, struck eleven o'clock. The Caballero's eyes looked even more bloodshot than usual. Fernando bowed his head as if meditating, and the morning light made exactly the same reflections on his boots as on his brylcremed hair, which was parted down the middle. The Porter closed his eyes and a fly landed on his triangular moustache. I stroked my cheek. All of us had grown stubble. The ham was from Coriscadas, a village in Castro Laboreiro that produces ham all year round.

"Let's go and see that witch," Fernando ordered when the car started, after three energetic turns of the crank from the Porter.

"She's a poor woman," the Porter kept telling us en route. "That's why she's jealous of us and gave us the evil eye."

This time, the Caballero prudently limited himself to screwing his face into some sort of smile.

Fernando suddenly became very high-spirited. He took several cigarettes from his packet, with one hand, in the time it took us to get to Gustimeaus. He puffed smoke through his nose and smiled a half smile, as film stars do. I knew he was getting ready for a party.

We followed a winding road up a steep ravine. My ears were buzzing. As we started to descend we could see, in permanent shadow, an ugly little valley scattered with small water-meadows, their outlines defined by low rough-stone walls, and a stream without a single tree along its banks. Here and there stood houses, cowsheds and thatched maize-garners.

"Gustimeaus," announced the Porter.

The woman's house was the most isolated and stood nearest to the tarmac road. Smoke was filtering through the roof. The car could get as far as a wretched yard in front of the house.

Fernando looked back at us and showed his ferret teeth.

"Go and tell her to free the boy from the evil eye," he commanded the Porter, with a touch of arrogance.

"Bring your tools," Fernando ordered everyone.

We got out of the car.

"Come on, Porter," Fernando insisted. "Come on, move yourself."

I then saw how the Porter became as pale as wax. He opened his mouth a little and his triangular moustache trembled. I can spot the fear in the mouths of those Reds, he had said earlier.

Suddenly he got out and staggered towards the house. He kicked the door open and went inside. I heard a woman scream and indistinct shouts from the Porter.

The three of us went in, and there he was beating, with the palm and the back of his hand, a tangle of rags huddled near the hearth, by a rock that formed the back wall of the house.

"Neighbours, neighbours, help me!" the black thing screamed, merging with the wisps of dense smoke that the wind had blown around the kitchen.

When he saw us coming in, the Porter moved to one side, awaiting orders from Fernando. The Caballero started coughing and rushed out of the house. The woman straightened up and the light from the doorway fell on her face. I swear by Christ on the cross I thought that clean face, those clear eyes, as big as saucers from fear and perplexity, could not belong to anything but a good woman. She was wearing a black headscarf and she had gone down on her knees with her arms outstretched.

"I haven't hurt anyone! I haven't hurt anyone!" she said over and over again, between sobs, like a litany.

A feeling of tenderness and mercy welled up inside me.

"Fernando...," I begged.

Fernando looked straight through me with disgust. He spat on the dirt floor.

"Continue, Porter."

On hearing this, the Porter snatched the scarf from the woman's head and a golden hairgrip shone in the light of the fire. He grabbed her by her plait, shook her backwards and dragged her towards the hearth, towards the flames. She writhed on the floor and screamed.

"Shut up, child of Satan! You bewitched my son!" he bellowed.

"No! For Holy Mary's sake! Have mercy on me! I swear on the graves of all my loved ones! I never hurt anyone!"

"Take away the lice, you witch! Give my son his health, you God-forsaken woman!"

At this, Fernando Salgueiro goes mad. He barks out in the piercing, imperious voice which I know so well and he reserves for important occasions, that that's enough and everyone be quiet.

"Now it's my turn!" Fernando shouted.

He picked up my Mauser and slid the bolt back and forth to see if it was loaded.

"On your feet, witch!"

She obeyed. Her legs were shaking. The woman was about fifty and still had a fine figure. She crossed her arms and thrust her chin down against her chest.

It was then that Fernando rammed the butt of the gun into her guts, causing her to double over and fall in a heap on to the floor. He threw me the gun and I caught it as best I could. She writhed around in the dirt, sobbing and moaning her heart out.

"Now you're going to tell me where your pansy-boy of a son is hiding! Tell me now or else I'll kill you!"

He went down on one knee. In his high boots, Fernando Salgueiro looked like a lieutenant presenting arms during a military mass on Corpus Christi Day.

He seized the woman by the neck, unmoved by her muffled groans.

"You'll strangle her! You'll strangle her!" shouted the Caballero, coming back into the hut.

"I'll do worse than that!" answered Fernando.

With his right hand he drew his nine-bore long-barrelled Astra. He cocked it with his teeth, as Fernando Salgueiro always did when he wanted to act the hero and frighten people. Without letting go of the woman's neck, he tried to push the barrel of the gun into her mouth. She clenched her teeth and he broke a few of them with a single blow. Then he pushed in the entire barrel. The woman looked as if she was about to explode. Her eyes were popping out and her face turned purple. Blood was pouring out of her mouth and nose.

"Are you going to tell me where your son is hiding? I'm asking for the last time."

She moved her head slightly. It was impossible to tell whether she meant yes or no. Between them, the Porter and the Caballero sat her down on a bench against the wall. There she remained, crushed, with her legs wide apart and her apron and skirt crumpled between them. She must have been a good-looker once.

I knew Fernando only too well and I knew what he was like when he was in a rage.

"For the last time!" he said.

The Porter went up to the bench. He crouched down by the woman.

9

It looked to me as if he was about to defecate.

"Come on. Take the evil eye off my little boy," the Porter begged.

She tried to speak, yes she did, but all that came out of her mouth — now grossly deformed — were indecipherable sounds and a kind of bloody slime.

The woman lifted a hand, very slowly; a hand which I noticed was long and slender and white, like that of a nun from Chaves. She held up her index finger. We all waited in suspense, as if spellbound. The woman continued to gag and expel slime. Then she moved her finger from left to right and from right to left, again and again, in an undeniable gesture of negation.

"Daughter of Satan!" the Porter shouted, his hands clinging to his Mauser.

"You pile of shit!" Fernando growled with contempt, his hand shaking as he pointed the automatic at her head.

The woman stared at us all. One by one. In her clear eyes I saw simplicity and a boundless sadness, as if the whole world seemed horrible to her at that moment. She didn't stop producing inarticulate sounds. Her mouth had swollen even more.

Then Fernando hit the woman hard over the head with his pistol. There was a dull thud. Her body slumped along the length of the bench, and remained there, vanquished and still. The Porter picked up his rifle with both hands and smashed the barrel down on her ribs. Woman and bench fell on to the floor.

"That's enough, Salgueiro! That's enough!" the Caballero had said, as if apologising for his audacity.

"Everybody out!" bellowed Fernando, more furious than I had ever seen him.

We went out into the yard.

Fernando went to the car and took two big cans of petrol from under the bonnet. He entered the house. I reckon he must have poured petrol over logs and tinder, furniture, and the body of that witch. Over the stable and the straw inside. Over the barn. The remains of one can ended up on the thatched roof. Then he set fire to the whole lot with the help of his Ronson and a faggot made up of that day's newspaper.

Very soon, the flames sang out with joy and looked as if they wanted to swallow everything. A crazy furore of lambs, piglets and hens bombarded our ears. They didn't want to burn to death.

"To Verín! All of you!" Fernando Salgueiro, our superior, ordered with a triumphant guffaw which, as the car started, we all echoed in chorus as if we wanted to get something out of our systems, something strange which we could feel inside us and, at the same time, on the surface of our skin.

As we reached the top of a hill, I spotted the witch's house, consumed by flames, and a column of pale smoke which the wind was blowing towards the heights of Xurés.

Then I saw Fernando run his fingers through his hair, separating the stiff, gel-matted strands. We all made similar movements; we unbuttoned our combat jackets and our blue shirts to scratch our bodies. We could feel an itchiness which spread to our heads, to our backs, to our chests. The sun beat down on our faces.

It was then that the lice took us over for ever.

(From *Arraianos*, 1991)

Philoctetes

Nokao, a short-story writer, received a strange and remarkable letter which left his whole being in suspense. He read it a third time, aloud now, pulling occasionally at his pipe. It said:

"Mr. Nokao.

Distinguished Sir,

Please forgive, first of all, my effrontery in writing to you. I do not wish, in any way, to steal your valuable time. But there is a powerful reason: my immense gratitude. The purpose of this letter is my wish to make you aware of it. So that you can understand everything (you will understand everything, you are a short-story writer), I shall give you some information about myself.

My name is Philoctetes and at the present moment I am a political prisoner. I am fifty years old. When I was eighteen I was a revolutionary. One day somebody saw me handing out sheets of paper on which something very beautiful was written, but which I cannot remember. The person who saw me did not remain silent. Then they had me put here, on this side of the bars. I became a political prisoner, on this side of the bars, thirty-two years ago. I ought to have been used to it, I keep repeating to myself that I ought to have been used to it by the time of the wounding, almost a year ago. I had requested an interview with the Governor. It was granted many months later. I had forgotten what I had in mind to say to the Governor when I finally confronted his hateful face, with its thin moustache and narrow eyes, on the far side of the great desk. But I was unwilling to waste the chance of speaking clearly to the Governor, and I improvised a request. I said:

'I was once a widely-read man, sir. And I don't think it would be too much to ask to be allowed to receive books and newspapers from time to time.'

His little moustache quivered as he retorted:

'It is against the regulations. Besides, you would be the last to receive books. You are a revolutionary, an enemy of the established order.'

He spoke coldly, from behind his broad, smooth desk. To conclude he comes out with:

'I have your file here. Your number is underlined in red. You may go, "Philoctetes".'

I would have accepted everything apart from the measured tone of scorn with which he pronounced my name. I was cunning, but not cunning enough. I make as if to turn and go away. I see out of the corner of my eye that he is standing there, far from the alarm bells. Then I throw a chair at his head. It was marvellous! I had hit him, but only a glancing blow. In one bound I am at the door. At the same time he presses a button and the two sections slam together trapping my foot..., wounding it, crushing it. I lay on the floor screaming, with my foot trapped in the door, and I saw him coming towards me, slowly, wiping the blood from his head. I pondered on the fact that I had only wounded him slightly, and had intended to kill him. He comes up to me, as I lie on the floor, and when he reaches me he boots me in the face. All consciousness was swept away from me. I awoke in the punishment cell. I must tell you, Mr. Nokao, that the punishment cell is in total darkness. I touched my foot and realized that it was a lump of raw flesh. Some bones were probably broken as well. I removed my sock, or rather I tore it off, for it was stuck to the flesh. As a result I felt it was bleeding copiously. Then I washed my foot with drinking water and left it uncovered, resting my leg on the bedboard, with my foot in the air. I wiped the sweat from my brow with my sleeve and breathed deeply.

I do not know how many days passed before the stench came. I realized that my foot stank. I was not worried about it because I felt light-headed and was sweating profusely. When the Governor became aware that I was not eating, he sent the Doctor to see me. What a great man! A true idealist. He examined me and went away without a word.

I later learned from Nossos, the prisoner who acts as the Governor's orderly, that the Doctor had demanded I be transferred to the infirmary.

'Impossible,' he replied, 'Philoctetes is confined to the punishment cell. He cannot be let out of there.'

'He will die!' the Doctor shouted — as I was later informed.

'He cannot be let out.'

Then the Doctor, very calm, stood up and was almost out of the room when, like one who has forgotten something, he turns to face the Governor and says:

'I am going to bring this directly to the attention of the health authorities.'

The Governor — Nossos told me all about it — struck the desk a mighty blow and snarled through clenched teeth:

'Take Philoctetes wherever you want.'

Indeed, Mr. Nokao, the Doctor was very good to me, a true idealist. A wonderful person! From the punishment cell they took me to the infirmary half-conscious. I was distraught and hallucinating. My head ached. One morning I awoke in full possession of myself. I lay between clean white sheets. The Doctor took my pulse and said to me, very jovial and down-to-earth he was:

'You're on the mend. Your foot hurts, doesn't it?' (And it did hurt.) 'We had to cut it off. The Governor told me about the incident. If you want to read, go ahead. You'll be under my orders for a long time.'

And he gave me a book. He didn't give me any old book; he gave me your book, Mr. Nokao, the unique and enthralling book signed by your own hand. When thirty-two years have gone by without reading a book and then one reads a book like yours, it brings a feeling of breathtaking fullness in which extraordinary things happen, such as most people wouldn't understand, but you will, Mr. Nokao, because you are a short-story writer. Imagine me, first of all, with my morale undermined, defeated, and destroyed, from its very foundations. And then I see all the characters that your imagination gave birth to, in a fantastic ballet, approaching me and whispering in my ears sonorous words, brilliant hopes, the suggestion of a wonderful world. But I was far from this world until I made the attempt.

The attempt was a desperate one. Let me tell you that I tried to share with the characters in your book that atmosphere of freedom in which they were moving. I chose a story. Its title is 'Fear'; you know the plot, you sculpted the plot. I come in when the old woman realises that she is locked in the cathedral. I stood and stared, it was thirty-two years since I had set foot inside a cathedral. But I was soon aware that my role in the story was to prevent the old woman from dying of fright. The lamps in the sanctuaries were giving out a feeble light. I noticed how, little by little, the old woman's fear was growing, thanks to that extraordinary art of yours, Mr. Nokao. I let her beat on the locked and bolted north door, on the locked and bolted east door, and I decided to intervene when, possessed by terror, she was hurrying to beat on the massive main door. I heard her clattering down the nave, it was like the flight of a panic-stricken horse. I knew that, on finding the last door firmly shut, she would begin to see apparitions, her heart would fail and she would die. Thus it was written in your story, Mr. Nokao — predetermined. But I had just one fixed idea: not to let the old woman die. The truth is, I was not aware of the futility of my efforts. It would have meant taking all the tragic power away from the story. And it was all foreseen. I knew that the old woman was going to die and I went towards her. She was beating on the great iron-encrusted door and her hands did not make a sound, there was only an intense, excruciating pain. She heard my footsteps and saw me approaching her. She looked wild-eyed at me and screamed, once, twice, as was foreseen in the story. And I realize that my role in the story is that of a vision, the old woman thinks I am a vision. She inclines her head to one side, then downwards, in a manner as automatic as a spring. She dies. All this was foreseen in the structure, in the perfect ordering of events in your story. And I leave the story.

And I left the story. I found myself once again in the infirmary. I had a feeling of complete happiness, of fullness. Picking up your book I kissed it. I didn't say anything to the doctor. All I did was take a piece of paper and write you this letter, this long letter, which thanks to the doctor's kindness will not be submitted to the censor. You already know that my first attempt to place myself, among your characters, within your created world has brought about good results. So I will try to place my individual self within each of your stories, even though I know this will run up against the lofty walls, cold and upright, of your technique.

I would like to conclude this letter, this long letter, with the vigorous affirmation of my profound gratitude. Thanks to you, after thirty-two years I was able to emerge from this side of the bars into an unknown, free world. I think you will be able to understand: when thirty-two years have gone by without reading a book, and then one reads one like yours, extraordinary things happen. Yours in deepest gratefulness, Philoctetes."

Nokao finished reading the letter and, at the same time, his pipe went out. He emptied the ash. Then he began pacing up and down in his office. He was perplexed.

(From *Percival e outras historias*, 1958)

The Old House of Arranhão

All right, he had said. Now you can go and see the Old House of Arranhão. For years and years my godfather and guardian had been telling me, with the critical, ironical aloofness that was one of his main characteristics, all about the mysterious Manor House near the border with Galicia, until he finally succeeded in obsessing me with the spell of its legend. You are twenty years old, my son. Now I can hand the key over to you. Go there and take a look at the scene of the events. The Captain, my godfather told me after removing his cigar from his lips, was, at the beginning, just an opportunist who was taking advantage of Eduardo's enthusiasm and generosity. He was the villain of the tragedy. I received the huge, rusty key and noted, with some apprehension, that the iron weighed more than its size suggested. It was as heavy as if someone beneath the floorboards were trying to wrest it from my grasp. But who really was the Captain? I asked, relaxing in my favourite armchair (a South-American one, of finely worked leather) in my godfather's study, where the walls, the sofas, the mantelpiece and even the floor were covered in books. His name never even reached my ears, he replied. And if I did know it once, I have since forgotten it. João Wolfgang, perhaps? I asked. My guardian was gazing at the ceiling, as though dreaming of something far away, perhaps to be found in the lonely borderlands, in Serra Ruiva, in Grama de Corno Dourado, in Corga dos Enforcados, or in any of the places surrounding the damned House in which it had all happened a hundred years earlier and which now, for the first time, I was about to visit. Why João Wolfgang? my godfather suddenly asked. And even if that was his name, forget it immediately: in this tale the Captain can only be called "the Captain". Then he gave me the key to the Old House of Arranhão and determined that I would go and see it in November, so as to be back home in Arcos de Valdevez in December, on condition that I first handed over to him the translation of Hoffmann's writings on music for which he had been asking me for some time. Among the many gifts that God has granted me, he had said with a smile, he did not include the gift of tongues, my son. My guardian was not, in fact, the owner of the Manor and House of Arranhão, although he was closely related to Eduardo. The owner was a cousin from Lisbon whom I did not know and who, unwilling to have anything to do with the House because of the horrific legend associated with it, had left the overall management of the property and of the agricultural stock in my godfather's hands, neither asking him for anything in return, nor remunerating him for his work, in view of the fact that he lived in Arcos de Valdevez. So my godfather cynically restricted himself to looking after the key. He left the lands fallow and kept the House locked, not allowing anyone to approach it. But now he was going to make an exception for me, granting me entry because of my insistent requests to be allowed to inspect the places where such terrible events had taken place several generations earlier. Or perhaps it had been my godfather himself who, inflaming my imagination and my sensibility by narrating the tragedy, had taken care to arouse in me a passionate interest in visiting the House. The truth is that I have heard someone in the family say that Eduardo had invited the Captain to the House for two reasons, my godfather was telling me as he lit a cigar. First, so that he could take charge of modernizing the House and designing and creating the new gardens that Eduardo had decided upon having; and second, so that Eduardo would not have to spend so much time alone with Carlota, in the Old House of Arranhão. But did Eduardo not love her? I asked with lively interest. Did he not love his wife? Don't forget, my godfather pointed out, that she was older than him. And indeed Eduardo, a wealthy man who had retired to the Old House of Arranhão to enjoy life, does seem to have been younger than his spouse and, perhaps for this reason, he felt for her a tranquil, sedate affection that bordered on nausea. The fact is that my godfather and guardian seemed to know a great deal about this fidalgo, not just because of family oral tradition but also because he had read accounts, written by Eduardo himself, of his sufferings, and knew that he had been, by nature, a fickle man, a worrier and a hypochondriac. Bruises often appeared on his legs, suddenly and without his having received a single blow. They would be preceded by a burning sensation, and then a dull pain. Sometimes even bleeding stigmata would appear, going away again as unexpectedly and suddenly as they had come. And so, when November arrived, I diligently packed my sparse lugage into my saddlebags. But sometimes Eduardo was anguished to find, when he relieved himself, that he expelled, along with his urine, a thick, sticky liquid. He suspected syphilis. He would send for the doctor. Eduardo himself would clean the glasses and the crockery with meticulous care for fear of infecting Carlota or the Captain or, later, that fragrant flower of the winter springs, Otilia. He was desperate at that time, was Eduardo. He would wander around the garden: sandy paths and rustic stairs and charming summer-houses that the Captain was distributing around the estate, after presenting exquisite sketches of all this scenography on the upper storeys of the House. He would run with his head in his hands, casting the tails of his blue dress coat to the winds, his yellow waistcoat shining in the sun. He would splash in his hunting boots at the edge of the Olho Pond. He would even go down to the village and have a glass of something to drink. He was a strange fellow, our ancestor Eduardo, I would comment. He was inconstant, capricious, and impetuous, my godfather would say, standing up and pacing his study, a flat hand wedged between his prominent abdomen and his loose belt. I chose Garrão, the brown horse from Barroso, a splendid courser and climber, and trusty over rough terrain, as tough as a mule. I whistled to Laboreiro, whose tongue lolled out with happiness when he saw that I was mounting my horse and that we were going on a journey. Standing in the enclosed balcony, framed behind a window — as coloured and capricious as a kaleidoscope — the bulky figure of my godfather looked like a strange sphere as he wished me goodbye. I saw lightning flash on his hand. As I crossed the bridge and began to climb the slope, leaving Arcos de Valdevez behind, I felt a heaviness in my guts. Down the mountain came clouds of an old grey colour that made me feel frightened. But the weather soon cleared; the clouds soon turned white; and soon the horse was pricking up its ears, happy that the wind was no longer blowing the cold into our souls. To the left of the road the stark course of the River Limia began to show itself, with its beaches of pristine sand and its islets, timbered with alders and willows, trembling elms. Beyond those torpid, sluggish waters the sliver of the sun lit up a crag. The sky had darkened again, but a chink had opened in the heavens and a cylinder of light had fallen, like a lighthouse beam, on the crag. The shock bristled my back. Upon the crag a man reined in his horse: a restless bay. The horseman was wearing a uniform. He was far away. I thought I could make out a three-cornered hat, the green dolman of the Corps of Engineers, and the insignia of a captain. The oblique sunlight blinded me and I rubbed my eyes with my right hand. When I opened them again, man and horse had disappeared. My godfather was an admirable man. Lounging in his study in Arcos de Valdevez, buried in books containing a thousand dispersed pieces of contingent or superfluous information, he had been reconstructing the sides of the quadrilateral: Eduardo, Carlota, the Captain and ... Otilia! First of all, and certainly with indifference, he had picked up the domestic versions of the tale for, even when he was a young man, people had insisted upon cloaking in decorous explanations those shameful events that had taken place in the Old House of Arranhão, one hundred years earlier. But then my godfather, developing a passionate interest, determined to reveal the truth in the story by peeling away the wrappings of hypocrisy with which shame had tried to contain it. He found legal documents, deeds, written declarations, references in memoirs, verse of the period, satirical May-day songs and recollections of brutal burlesque serenades tenaciously transmitted on the benches surrounding the open hearths of the border folk. Little by little he peeled the wrapping away from the tragedy, so that I could be present at its retelling, given that I had missed the performance. Otilia was unique, my godfather would tell me as the multicoloured skylight made cinders fly from the diamond on his ring. She was tall and slender and her brown eyes would linger with concern upon the eyes of anyone talking to her, regardless of sex or age. Then, startled by her own audacity, she would lower her gaze to the silver-embroidered tips of her satin slippers, peeping out beneath the hem of her sky-blue skirt, beneath the Bruges lace that, with unconscious coquetry, insinuated itself into those folds. She had enormous, narrow feet, did Otilia, upon which she paddled along like a delightful duckling. Yet she could enter a room without anybody hearing her footsteps. She could enter the drawing room of the House of Arranhão and, in that instant, all conversation would come to a halt. Yes indeed, a group of people might be performing allegories and ballets, acting out pantomimes in imitation of the opera of Orpheus and Eurydice, or discussing collections of engravings, coins, or watches, or talking about such subjects as the grafting of fruit trees, extensive agriculture, the rescue of shipwrecked sailors, or antiques. Well, as soon as she, Otilia, entered the room, all activities were immediately interrupted. All looks converged upon her.The pianoforte and the flute would make disconcerting pauses, scientific speeches would take on shades of doubt, the most authoritative voices would hesitate. The attention of all would be drawn as by a magnet to the somewhat lanky, slightly stooping figure — hands clasping and unclasping as though craving something — of Otilia, embarrassed at the disturbance her entrance had caused among the esteemed gathering. Otilia also suffered from sporadic but violent nervous attacks. The Captain learned of Otilia's powers one day when she was seized by a sudden headache as she stepped on to a piece of land in Arranhão where the subsoil was known to contain exceptionally pure iron ore. She altered the movement of pendulums. In the days before the catastrophe, Otilia went into a cataleptic state in which, reduced to total immobility, cold as death, she could hear and see with perfect clarity. So there were a lot of people in the House? I asked my godfather and guardian, surprised by so many goings-on. No, they were always alone, face to face, the four of them, captivated, trapped in their geometrical hell, in their permanent equidistant temptation. But when the volcano finally erupted, Eduardo invited fashionable people to the House and other people who, by contrast, were wise and prudent; and amusing assistants, and experts in epigraphy and the local history of those borderlands. His intention was that such companions should lessen the anguish suffered by the four protagonists of this story. But soon, horrified, the guests left and dispersed. Indeed, just as my godfather had predicted, I set foot in Soajo that evening. I put up at the inn and, after having dinner in the company of some priests who were there for the market that was held on the first Sunday of the month, I went outside to stretch my legs, numb and bent from the ride. Otilia, Eduardo, Carlota, the Captain, my godfather said to me in a bitter, suggestive, ironical tone. Outside, electricity was gathering above the town of Arcos de Valdevez. I could feel that my nerves were about to explode. What did explode was the thunder. The lightning rattled the windows and blinded me, sitting there in my godfather's library. I was afraid. The black cat leapt up, toppling a pile of books. The Captain had been called to the Old House of Arranhão by Eduardo. To supervise the tasks of landscaping, gardening, architectural restoration and agricultural renovation. Carlota, Eduardo's wife, felt a pain in her heart, she had a premonition that she did not confess even to herself. The three of them, out there, on the border, in Arranhão, in the solitude, in the serra. In that landscape that is defined, in the distance, by the peak of Mount Penagache. Let my sweet little niece Otilia come too, from that convent school in Chaves where she is a boarder. Let Otilia come, Carlota had said. Let Otilia come, in her innocence, to place herself between the equestrian silhouette of the versatile Captain and the humdrum conjugal harmony of Carlota's life with Eduardo. So now all four of them were together, godfather. Yes, he had said, lighting his cigar with a brand from the fireplace. Yes, all four of them. I suppose that adulterous passion developed between Carlota and the Captain, and between Eduardo and Otilia, I said, very proud of myself, playing the man of the world. Another flash of lightning lit up the silver coffee service among the papers and official documents upon my godfather's writing desk. Do you really think that life is so simple? he asked me, just before the thunder split our ears and shook all the windows in Arcos de Valdevez. And I was thinking about the innocence of my assumption on that stormy evening, as I paced up and down the square in Soajo, my faithful Laboreiro at my heels. Suddenly I saw the dog drop its tail between its legs, lower its ears, stare into space for a moment and creep away, its belly almost scraping the ground. Laboreiro, come here, come here, I shouted. With a howl, Laboreiro disappeared among the maize-garners, into the shadows of the vineyards and the vegetable gardens, between the ashlar-work staircases, down the alleyways where the water channels sing. A carriage suddenly caught my attention. Drawn by two white horses, it passed close to me, and left a frozen trail of vapour behind it. Inside it, by the light of the moon, I had clearly seen a lady, elderly and very pale, smiling at me. The coach, driverless, made a clean turn, the horses arching their necks with bridles taut, around the pillory in the square, and disappeared down the street from which it had come. Terrified, I realised that neither the carriage's wheels nor the horses' hooves had made any sound upon the stones. I ran in a frenzy to the inn, jumped into bed fully-dressed, covered my head with the sheets and remained awake for many hours. In a nightmare of sweet and disturbing dreams I tossed and turned, fluctuating between forgetfulness and unbearable remembrance. She was beautiful and neurasthenic, my godfather had told me as, from one of the drawers in his desk, he produced a letter from a relative who referred to Otilia as the youngest, purest element in the quadrilateral. "Whenever Otilia is struggling with some strong, unsettling emotion," my godfather read to me, "the struggle reveals itself in an uneven colouring of her face. Her left cheek reddens, whereas her right one pales. There are even times, although they are rare, when she finds a way to refuse what is required of her. She does this with an elegance that, for anyone able to interpret its true meaning, is irresistible. She joins her palms, raises her hands on high, and then places them in front of her chest, as she leans slightly forward and gazes at the person pursuing her with his demands in such a way that he willingly renounces his every last request and desire." An enchanting girl! I believe that these exact words came to me in the darkness of my room in the inn at Soajo, as though, instead of evoking the melodious voice of my godfather, I myself were reading the old document that spoke of the tragedy. Suddenly the dogs stopped howling at the moon, or maybe they were wolves. This is all I remember before falling into a deep sleep. I thought that I woke up later when someone outside the room turned the door-handle. The moonlight was shining through the window, free of the clouds that had been sullying it. I heard the door creaking as it inched open. I felt a terrible fear; my head was cold; my body bristled all over with goose-pimples. The door was flung open. I tried to get up, but a strange power had paralyzed my muscles. A feminine presence entered the room with a rustling of silks and a brushing of soft-soled shoes against the floorboards. Surrounded by a nimbus of moonlight, the figure stopped facing my bed. It seemed to me that she was pressing her hands to her heart, thrusting her beautiful, round face at me — each cheek a different colour — in a pleading, imploring gesture, like someone who rejects or longs for something more than anything else in this world. I felt infinite disgust when, on my visitor's face, I saw sores or wounds or blotches or signs of rotten flesh, teeming with maggots. I managed to shut my eyes for an instant, and, when I opened them, the moon was hidden, the door was locked and there was nobody to be seen in my room in the inn at Soajo. I managed to sleep a little more, and in the morning I galloped out of the town, down narrow streets flanked by houses with outside staircases and high roofs next to granite maize-garners in military formation. Galloping towards the highest serras, longing to reach the Old House of Arranhão. It is true that a mad passion had sprung up between Eduardo and Otilia, sealed with feverish kisses beneath the branches of the lime trees. And it is also true (continued my godfather, incessantly pacing the library, his body as round as a tortoise) that, when the mature, prudent Carlota discovered the fatal attraction that existed between her husband and her pretty niece, she realised that she had fallen in love with the Captain on the day he had been riding down the Cruz Alta road and had found her in the rose garden, armed with scissors and gloves, cutting majestic flowers with which to bedeck the table vases at lunch. Carlota looked up at the horseman, a placid smile upon her ample mouth. Her poise and renown captivated the Captain who, well aware of what he was doing, displayed his teeth and narrowed his dark, worldly-wise eyes, stabbing his stare with full intent into the noble eyes of Carlota who, flustered, bade him good afternoon and, as she removed a glove, dropped her basket, scattering the sandy path with roses, damask roses, as red as desire. Without dismounting, the Captain brought the tip of his whip close to Carlota's cheek. Her hair being gathered into a beautiful blond plait, the Captain's whip first caressed the nape of her neck, then a place under an ear. Carlota could only laugh nervously, and she ran away towards the farmyards, towards the balconies, towards the New Room and the Old Room in the House of Arranhão, towards the kitchen where she drank deeply from one of the pitchers on the dresser that hold the coolest essences of the well that never runs dry. All this is true, my godfather told me, his chubby little hands clasped behind his back. But it is also true that Eduardo and the Captain had been close friends during their shadowy adolescence on distant spring afternoons in Coimbra, and that all their violence and intimacy in the sad city and in houses overlooking steep, wet streets were reborn in the memories of the two men during their infernal reunion in the borderlands. Yes, said my godfather, yes. Once the adulterous liaisons between Carlota and the Captain and between Eduardo and Otilia were established, there came a bitter day, which the gods should have stopped from ever dawning upon the world. The day when Eduardo, vexed and furious at not having found an opportunity to be alone with Otilia, who was now his, walked with the Captain to his rooms in the shadiest, coolest wing of the House. There was a good fire burning in the hearth and the two men took off their dress coats, loosened their waistcoats, unbuttoned their shirts and sat down by the fireplace. They began reminiscing about their student days while drinking carafes of the dark, acid wine of the serra, made from the grape known by the disturbingly feminine name of "Mencía". They remembered their games and passions among frightened freshmen and seasoned veterans, the lords and masters of all, governing their Republics with an iron rule of absolute power. Once again, Eduardo felt like a shy novice, and the Captain like a brave superior who inflicted offences and laid down the rules of the world. Coimbra seemed to come back to life between the two men in that room, and the sparks of desire were almost rekindled in master and slave during that hour spent far from the world, in Arranhão, while Otilia and Carlota lay sleeping, unaware of the barbarities that the two men were feeling and discussing over the goblets of their symposium. When they said goodnight, the Captain gave Eduardo a slap on the cheek, a firmer and harder slap than one of simple camaraderie, and Eduardo lowered his gaze, smiling like a slut. And when Eduardo went out on to the balcony, the cold of the night did nothing to quench the intense passion aroused in him by the session with his former master of masculine games. Eduardo's desire had been aroused: desire for Otilia, for the Captain. He ran to his wife's room, Carlota's room, and knocked on the door. Carlota had thoughts only for the Captain. She could think only of the Captain that night, it was as though the Captain were on the prowl. The Captain filled the entire house for Carlota. Eduardo knocked three times upon the door of his wife's room. From a secret drawer in the desk, my godfather took out another contemporary written declaration, attributed to confidences — highly indiscreet ones — of Eduardo himself. My godfather read this immoral text: "He knocked a third time, louder, and Carlota heard the clear echo in the still night; startled, she came to herself. Her first thought was: It might be, it must be, the Captain. The second: But that's impossible! She took it to be an illusion, but she had heard it, she wished and feared that she had heard it. She walked into her boudoir, and hurried to the panelled door, locked and bolted. She chided herself for being afraid... With all the serenity she could muster she asked: Who's there? A low voice exclaimed: It's me." It was her own husband! I exclaimed in my turn. Don't interrupt, the best is yet to come, said my godfather. He inhaled the cigar smoke and continued reading with a smile, stressing the rises and falls in intonation. "Who? Carlota asked, not recognising the voice. For her, the figure behind the door was the Captain. A louder voice answered: Eduardo. She opened the door and her husband stood before her. She greeted him with a pleasantry. This allowed her to continue in the same tone. The enigmatic visit became embroiled in enigmatic explanations." The Devil! I cried. This sounds like a passage from some pornographic novel, godfather. An eccentric who wants to sin with his own wife! Be quiet, it is much weirder than that, my godfather commanded before reading on. "But I am going to confess to you, Eduardo finally says to Carlota, what I have really come for. I have made a promise to kiss your slipper tonight. It has been a long time since you had that whim, says Carlota. So much the worse and so much the better, replied Eduardo. Carlota had sat on a truckle-bed to hide her flimsy nightgown from his sight. He knelt before her, and she could not stop him kissing her slipper and, without releasing it, seizing her foot and tenderly pressing it against his breast. Carlota belonged to the class of women, temperate by nature, who retain when married, without any premeditation or effort, the behaviour and habits of courtship. She never refused her husband even when, with a simple request, she could have deflected his attentions; yet without coldness or wanting to repel, she was always like a loving bride who feels deep shame in the face of even that which is right and proper. And that was how Eduardo found her that night, in two senses." The December twilight fell upon Arcos de Valdevez, with a gloom of snow and sadness. Even though the room was in deep shadow my godfather continued to read from the yellowed pages, or perhaps he was reciting from memory a text he had gone over a thousand times before. It spoke of Carlota's desire. Of how Carlota was beside herself, the poised, the prudent, the temperate Carlota. The Captain's spirit was in her and seemed to be reprimanding her for what she was about to do with her husband. Emotion was welling within her. She had earlier wept, and she was one of those strong people, those energetic people, whose charm is not dissipated by tears, but who instead acquire the nimbus of atrocious, unexpected attractiveness. Eduardo was so solicitous, so gallant, so insistent! He was asking for a welcome in her bed, without any conjugal demands. In the end it was a simple little oil lamp — once the great rationalistic paraffin lamps had been extinguished — that induced intimacy. Imagination created a pleasant farce. Eduardo felt that his comrade, the Captain, was a part of his own being, and Carlota felt little Otilia, whom her husband loved, inside her skin. My godfather's tones became clipped, with icy pauses. "For Eduardo it was Otilia he held in his arms; Carlota felt herself possessed by the Captain, and thus those who were absent and those who were present were intertwined in a marvellous, delicious and exciting way." It was true, by all the devils in hell, that he who was present (Eduardo) was not going to be denied his legitimate conjugal rights, and he demanded his lover's body merged with the tepidity of his wife's. They indulged in their fun and games, their crude and sinful words whispered into the ear, did Carlota and her husband. "They spent part of the night in all manner of sweet nothings and gambollings which, unhappily, became all the freer as their hearts played a smaller and smaller part in them." In the morning there was a huge, strange sun, to quote the words of the Galician poet. They both felt that a crime had been committed there. They had not granted each other their canonical marital dues. Quite the contrary: on that bed four people had cohabited, contained two by two in the feverish minds of those who were united in matrimony and who had, in thought, flouted its law. Carlota was the harmony of the cosmic spheres, the order of the nations of the world, the principle — incarnate in eyes of heraldic blue — of the continuity of family values. And despite all that, she had succumbed to the volatile temperament, to the butterfly heart, to the fickleness of her husband. They both knew that they had been under a spell that night. Higher powers had bewitched them. Otilia burned with love for Eduardo and he for Otilia. Carlota knew that she was the prisoner of the Captain, and he had come to Carlota with all the cynicism of a man of the world. He had decided to dominate the husband and the wife. To seduce them both. To become, as a guest and informal administrator of the House of Arranhão, the master of them both, of their possessions, of the farming and engineering works, of the landscapes and the account books. And, indirectly, the master of Otilia, of little Otilia. But then the Captain fell in love. He loved with an excessive, violent anger directed against himself, directed against the plan to humiliate the owners that he had harboured in his self-seeking mind. Sitting on my horse, I felt the great key of the Old House of Arranhão pressing against my stomach, between my cummerbund and my waistcoat. The barrel of one of the travelling pistols was grating against it, setting my teeth on edge. My godfather's eyes were empty, dead. He was motionless, with the old document in his hand. That night Carlota conceived a child who would have Otilia's dark eyes and the Captain's angular face, said my godfather. The road climbed among wild crags, through a country that heralded the steepest peaks of the serra. First there was a cascade of purest light as the rain stopped. I recognised a distant peak as the Rock of Anamán, above which a pair of eagles bent their wings and coasted through the sky. My horse, Garrão, seemed thoughtful as he advanced at walking pace, careful not to slip on the worn stone surface of the road, grooved by a thousand years of carts. Lindoso lay to the right, its blackened castle tower invaded by cawing rooks. Now there were no more *canizos* (which is what we call maize-garners in the borderlands) in the villages, and these were large and far apart, thatched with dark, damp straw. Laboreiro, my faithful dog, walked by the horse's side with his tail between his legs as though scenting something, or sad. My godfather was pacing up and down his study with his chubby little hands intertwined behind his back. His cigar lay abandoned, smoking in an ashtray shaped like an oriental dragon. How did the events progress, godfather? I asked him. He then began narrating in a low voice, monotonously, as though hurrying to finish a tale that was too obvious. Eduardo and the Captain, at a given moment, came face to face and stared at each other with rage. They considered a duel, they hated each other. Then they fused in an emotional embrace which encompassed their entire past life of camaraderie and student pranks, both imagining, in a muddled way, a future of mutual love in which their manly friendship would be preserved, and in which each would forever obtain the favours of the woman he desired. Eduardo wept and ran to the lavatory. He sat himself upon a tall Sèvres porcelain bowl decorated with garlands of flowers, and dissolved into diarrhoea and viscous, torpid ejaculation. The Captain picked up an iron crook and prepared himself to carry out a tour of inspection of the new dam. He had built it to increase the water level in the Olho Pond, my godfather had explained. A little island had been constructed in the middle of the new lake, with its tiny toy-like kiosk. They called it "O Passatempo". One reached the island in a boat capriciously designed to resemble a gondola. It suddenly went dark and the serra seemed even more of a serra. I took my riding cloak from the saddlebag and put it on just as dense rain began to fall, casting gloom into my heart. Laboreiro was walking close to the walls and the rocks, his nose to the ground. For a moment, by the roadside, I saw a lake and, in the middle of it, a sort of island upon which I thought I could glimpse a beached gondola. On the waters, rippled by the northeast wind, bobbed a grey cap of the sort worn by upper-class children a hundred years ago, with a velvet bow and all the rest. I wiped my rain-blinded eyes with a handkerchief and, when I looked again, some faint light that came trickling down allowed me to see dank bogs stretching away towards the south in vague expanses of sedge, rushes and reeds. Misfortune, or perhaps a blessing, had come to the Old House of Arranhão with that child, my godfather had told me, and I remembered his words as I drew rein and looked at the waters, clouded with mud and devoid of any island, gondola or bow-bedecked cap. Misfortune, because the

28

child was the son of all four of them and their communal sin; a blessing, because he could have broken the charm that held them all bewitched. But the situation soon changed. It changed when Otilia, taking the baby out in the gondola, was unable to prevent him from falling into the water and drowning. The boy would not come back to life no matter how much Otilia raised his inert little body to the sky, begging the Supreme Creator for the miracle of a resurrection. With the death of the child, Otilia submerged herself in sorrow, fell prey to loss of appetite, settled into silence, despite Carlota, in her infinite goodness, doing everything possible to absolve her of blame. In fact, it was Carlota who felt responsible for her son's death, which she took to be a punishment for her own waywardness. For many days Otilia was as if dead, although it was known that she could see and hear everything that was happening around her. Then she sleepwalked all through the building. When she finally made for the divan sofa upon which she was to give up her soul, all the clocks in the House stopped, even the one that the Captain had installed in the chapel tower. A wild wind blew all the windows open and Otilia — her legs daringly crossed, reclining upon the fashionable couch, wearing the innocent, contented expression of a young lady at a soirée, each cheek burning in its own colour and a dull glint in her brown gaze — summoned everyone, summoned the other three. Forgive me, she said. She gave the Captain her hand to kiss. She tried to throw herself to the floor to embrace Carlota's knees, but they all stopped her from doing so. She pressed the trembling Eduardo's head to her small, delicate breasts. Promise me that you will live, she said to him. When Eduardo answered that without her he would not, Otilia's charming little soul was leaving her wasted body. She was the first to die, after the baby, my godfather had told me, in Arcos de Valdevez, that year during which he had gradually unravelled the various acts of the tragedy. The second one to die had been Eduardo, who killed himself as a result of a violent attack of melancholia. My godfather had a documented account of this event, too. It read: "Someone saw the sudden flash, followed by the detonation; but he did not pay any attention to it. At six o'clock in the morning the servant comes in with a lamp. He finds his master lying on the floor in a pool of blood, the pistol next to him. He calls him, he shakes him; no response — just a faint death rattle." Of course everyone in the Old House of Arranhão appeared on the scene. His pulse was still beating, but his limbs were already stiff. "He had fired the gun above his right eye; brain-matter was oozing out in a thick paste. From the bloodstains on the arms of the chair, it was easy to deduce that he had been sitting at his writing desk when he had fired the shot; he had then fallen from the chair and rolled back to its side in his last convulsions." That feeble spirit was lying there, in his Chantilly boots, blue dress coat and yellow waistcoat, elegant as if to seduce, with his last gesture, either his friend or his wife, or both of them, now that he had lost his lyrical lover, slim and neurasthenic. As for Carlota, her life became a serious cause for concern when the Captain, suddenly sensing that the Old House of Arranhão was no longer, and never again would be, his to control, left to place himself in the service of Wellington, and to die a hero at Buçaco. And what about Carlota? What became of Carlota? I asked, intrigued. She never left the House again, my godfather affirmed. She lived for many years more, dedicated to the constant care of the old chapel in whose crypt lay Otilia and Eduardo, the two lovers, side by side, mechanical victims of the law of elective affinities. The servants and relatives apprehensively noticed the semicircular smile upon her mouth, similar in every way to the smiles on the statues of ancient Greece. As an old woman, she would wander through the rooms of the House and grumble into the air, into corners, or even while she sat at one end of a sofa, her forehead tilted attentively, as if listening to an invisible person on the armchair next to her. Or sometimes, in her room, Carlota would chant long monologues interspersed with silences in which replies could have been divined, if there had been people there, people called the Captain, or Eduardo perhaps, or Otilia. Oh yes, godfather and guardian, you can see, sir, that I am beginning to understand everything that, with the tortuousness which is said to be characteristic of the people of the borderlands, you had decided to instil in me during those long, evocative sessions in the furnace that Arcos de Valdevez had become that unforgettable summer, and in the cruel winter that had preceded it. Because some time ago now the rain, thin and cold as it can only be at this end of the earth, turned into snow. And the snow is falling now, softly, like a gift from hell to celebrate my presence in the serra and to soothe me on the eve of my downfall. Everything is soft, beneath the gentle falling of the snowflakes, and Garrão, who, like me, has never been here before, is quickening his pace, perking up as though sensing his own stables ahead, the stables of the Old House of Arranhão. Godfather, you knew, when you sent me here to visit the theatre of those century-old horrors, that the story you were telling me was not complete. You knew, sir, that it had not only been Otilia and Eduardo. That it had not only been Carlota and the Captain, her husband's close friend and companion in mutual adolescent affection, nor had it only been Otilia and Carlota, aunt and niece fascinated by each other's natural charms, who had danced the steps so clearly traced in your narrative; but that there had been other patterns, other movements. That the Captain and Otilia, Otilia and the Captain, had perhaps shared the stormiest idyll and passion in this whole tale, and you, sir, had hardly even permitted me to glimpse it in the wretched girl's final act of giving the Captain her hand to kiss upon her death bed. You did not let me know the whole story, godfather, because you wanted me to come here, to the Old House of Arranhão, to see these things with my own eyes, to see their shadows and the people's shadows, to see the embers of the passion that had once burned here and that, no doubt, smoulders still. It stopped snowing and, on a bend in the old road, worn away by centuries of coaches, carts and innumerable cattle, by quadrupeds like cows and goats, by horses and by people's clogs, the Old House of Arranhão loomed before me. Silence and tranquillity had followed the great snowfall. The cold had gone away. Laboreiro pointed his nose and remained motionless, like a dog in a tapestry hunting scene. On the House the tiles were gleaming in the afternoon sun with a chilling, steely glint. The old, derelict chapel had been eaten away by brambles and charlock. Buried under the blanket of snow what had once, no doubt, been gardens and labyrinths of myrtle was a desolate landscape of white hillocks. The peace was that of a nightmare dreamed a thousand times before. I felt far from Arcos de Valdevez and from all confines of lands inhabited by human beings. As I made my way up the main avenue, my boots sinking up to my knees in flaccid snow, the key in my hand, I knew that once I crossed the threshold of that door, all the dead who had been there for one hundred years, glutting their desires in a repeated, polyhedral pattern, would try to take possession of my nights and my days. I knew that the company of whom my godfather had as carefully as insufficiently informed me would come to meet me and try to destroy me because, once the child had been drowned in the lake — either by accident or by design — only I could threaten their depraved, multiple attraction. To begin with, great caution and not to trust those four friendly smiles beginning to appear through the windows of the central balcony.

(From *Arraianos*, 1991)

31

Coffee Liqueur

Vilar de Rei, 1910. Through the narrow skylight and a narrower window the pale dusk sinks on to a womanless kitchen. Elbows pressing on a heavy chestnut table, three old men bow their heads, smooth or grey, and clutch glasses of coffee liqueur. They talk, and dark, sugared silences hover under the tiles of the roof.

Martiño dos Rousos, recently returned after fifty years in South America, smiles under a fair moustache as he gulps his drink down. He is a full-bellied, bounteous host on this cold evening in Vilar de Rei. A fine vicuña-wool poncho is wrapped around his shoulders. He offers hard, twisted cigars as the faint light plays on the gold and ruby rings adorning his fat hand.

Invited by the returned emigrant to the old shack that had belonged to his father, two men sit and talk with him in growls: Xosé Coello, withdrawn, fastidious, with aquamarine eyes and high cheekbones, and Camilo dos Fandelos, a smiling man, hard and erect, still with a touch of the arrogance of youth. Drops of fiery sediment filter from the corners of their mouths. The coffee liqueur dilates the old men's pupils and their gestures become more and more frequent and gratuitous. They sternly contemplate the painfully resurrected events of former times. They talk in stammers, without interrupting each other.

"I left because I had to leave," asserts Martiño, stroking the soft fabric of his poncho with his fingertips. "I guess neither of you knows what really happened. I'm going to tell it to you like it was."

Martiño, faced by the silence of his old friends, uncorks the flask of coffee liqueur and, as he fills the glasses with the thick, dark liquid, starts hammering out the story of the events they all remember.

He was just a lad in that distant year. Regarded as an odd character, who even had eyes that flashed with sporadic compulsion and that knowledgeable people took to be the first signs of that terrible affliction, the gout, Martiño had loved Rosa in Vilar de Rei. Rosa, a golden-haired, pallid, languid creature of twenty-five, with dark eyelashes and quiescent pupils that could lose themselves in the farthest meadows, feeding on bliss and on silence.

"I became blind, you see, and I thought she was mine," mumbles Martiño, bringing the cigar to his liqueur-sticky lips.

Martiño dos Rousos does not know for sure if, at the beginning, he had thought of Rosa, the second wife of his father, old Celso dos Rousos, as a sort of special little sister brought by the fairies. A sister with a constant, vague smile, like the smile of a china doll, which had suddenly appeared on her mouth as the old widower came hand-in-hand with her into the lean-to in the Extramural Quarter, where he lived with Martiño and with loneliness, where he made clogs from morning until night, and where the three old men now sit drinking, watched over by the ghosts of memory. Martiño dos Rousos had kept his eyes open to observe how the china doll — without changing her expression, almost without moving, it seemed — would make the beds, do the dusting, cook, bake, go to the woods and return laden with firewood and kindlings, never fail to wash the clothes, put every little thing in its place, and finally sit in silence outside the door, listening to the human sounds of the farm labourers' carts returning to town, during the sowing season. Martiño dos Rousos loved the presence of that woman, whom he called "auntie". Celso, an embittered old man, gazed at him with the eyes of a stricken goat.

"My father always looked down on me," growls Martiño, spitting into the fire.

With a permanent scowl on his toothless mouth, with a piercing look that expressed disapproval of the puny youth's every action, with pitiless criticism of the way he nailed the leather to the wood of the clogs, or even with yells and slaps across the face that plunged Martiño into embarrassment and confusion in Rosa's presence, the father saw a devout passion for his young wife in the lad's bewildered eyes. Silent hatred was born in the clogmaker's withered breast.

"I don't believe she ever loved him...," the American quietly asserts, with a smile that tries to be spiteful, raising his hand to his temple in a quivering, hesitant gesture that expresses all the uncertainty in the world.

Did Rosa respond in any way to the deep, dreamy homage that the lad paid her? In the dying evening, before the faces of Camilo dos Fandelos and Pepe Coello, half-hidden in the shadows, the American vehemently defends the proud and lofty theory that Rosa had seen him as a faithful suitor, a choice caprice.

Yes: when rain had opened the doors of Heaven that wild, brutal autumn, tipping a flood of lead on to the town, Rosa, accompanied by Martiño, had gone to Celanova with the urgent task of collecting a large delivery of leather that had arrived from Ourense in old Rexo de Maside's five-mule wagon. Martiño, gripping the handle of the great blue umbrella, noticed, as it whirled and blurred above him, the contact of her firm breasts on his arm when she drew closer with a look in which mourning eyelashes fluttered a simpering apology or something similar. Oh, wasn't this perhaps the sign of the love of a woman for a man? And what was one to think of the special way in which she would serve him an extra slice of horse mackerel or pilchard on his rye bread at midday, once the clogmaker had gone off to his labours? — and in the kitchen, that same feebly lit kitchen where the three old men are now silently evoking a past brought back to them by the bitter sweetness of the coffee liqueur, Martiño and Rosa were left, passionate and alone?

"I couldn't take Rosa's death; my father never recovered; I thought I'd go crazy."

To round off two months of consumptive fever, Rosa gave up the ghost. She had gone as white as sperm and there was no flesh left on her cheeks, just a huge, dark, gaping mouth and opaque eyes of polished jet. On the long night of the funeral wake, the shoemakers of Vilanova, that is to say of Vilar de Rei, had crowded into the room in the lean-to outside the wall and had slowly emptied demijohns of coffee liqueur. They were tall thin men, rapid in gesture; the drink put flashes of insanity into their small eyes, alight with Sephardic fire; they laughed openly across the dead woman's bed; they wore their Sunday-best ankle-boots, and round their necks they had white silk kerchiefs, the insignia of their trade. They exchanged muttered words and maxims with country folk in clattering clogs and clean black-buttoned collarless shirts, who were haloed in an odour of cowsheds and oats that cleared the air of its stink of belches and cheap cigarettes. With their forearms pressed to their chests and their shawls pulled over their heads, old women and young women wept and wailed and picked away at the beads of endless rosaries. In the middle of the room stood the ascetic iron bed, covered with the five-stitch shawl, made in Astorga and purchased in Simeón's, that old Celso's first wife had so often proudly worn when young. Upon the enigmatic circuit of the Cashmere design, wearing cream-coloured slippers, with a sheet pulled up to her chin and a veil deforming her face, as pinched as a lark's, lay Rosa's unbelievably shrivelled body, shrouded to resemble some white sausage. On low benches either side of the bed, bolt upright, hands on knees, Celso and Martiño dos Rousos sat stiff and stony, staring and staring at the dead woman's face. Suddenly old Celso staggers to his feet and out towards the row of maize-garners that rest on Roman slates; he goes up to the town wall to urinate. When he returns he pours himself a glass of coffee liqueur and sees his hated son dancing at the other side of the dead woman. Martiño is grinning like an idiot as he looks at the corpse. Absently he lets fine trickles of saliva run from the corners of his mouth. The father drops his glass of coffee liqueur, which shatters on the wooden floor, and a fluttering of black cloth and rustling skirts converges to mop up the sticky liquid. Celso and Martiño are left alone by their guests, who reverently withdraw to the corners of the room. Face to face, with the corpse, which seems to be wearing a smile of mockery, between them, father and son glare at each other with terrifying, piercing flames in their eyes. At first, Celso sits down sideways, to conceal his intentions, on the edge of a chest. He starts to goad Martiño with words charged with venom that he fires from his blackened mouth, yet the expression on his pallid face does not change. A certain smile on the old man's lips offends Martiño like a slap on the cheek and, in anguish, he wipes the saliva from his mouth, he looks through tear-flooded eyes at the irate figure of his father, he runs into the workshop for a shoemaker's knife, and he returns with the knife in his hand. As the two of them stand on opposite sides of the dead woman, Martiño threatens his father with a prolonged growl. The old women wail with their heads in their hands and their black shawls pulled down over their eyes. With dead Rosa between them, father and son confront each other in boundless hatred. Celso smiles and places a hand upon the dead woman's sunken belly. His, only his, he seems to be saying with his gesture. And he falls upon her like a bull, in a torrent of tears, pressing his lips, sticky with coffee liqueur, to the dead woman's frozen cheeks, to her eyes. His son throws down the knife and runs from the shack. He goes out into the cold dawn; he wanders along the stone streets; he walks around the castle; he stumbles down the Barronca road in an endless sob; he weeps as no one in the world has ever wept before; he hastens towards A Merca, towards Ourense, towards the complete liberation of a Montevideo crowned with the smells of meat and of leather and of infinite carriages, adorned with peaceful mercantile progress, and vibrating with the incessant sound of drums beaten by bands of negroes drunk with nostalgia, in the grey sadness of the River Plate; and there he stays for fifty years, working like a galley slave.

"America saved me; I got strong. I could have killed my father that night!" concludes Martiño dos Rousos, pressing his chin against his chest.

Señor Xosé Coello comes to his feet in the silence and, deep in thought, he passes a hand over his bald, pale pate. The old master shoemaker shakes his head in hidden annoyance as he places his glass of coffee liqueur upon the table.

"I have never lied to you, Martiño," says Señor Xosé, taking dainty steps up and down the kitchen.

The sun has disappeared, and Martiño lights two gas lamps, hanging them from pieces of clog-iron wedged into the rubblework wall. Intense shadows invade corners of faces like bats. The old men's eyes disappear into black wells. The illuminated parts of their faces vibrate in a quivering oscillation. As Señor Xosé Coello steps up and down in silence, the other two men slowly refill their thick blue glasses with coffee liqueur.

"It wasn't like that, it wasn't as you've described it..."

Señor Xosé does not agree with Martiño, and he sternly shakes his head to emphasise his dissent. Because you need to know what Rosa was really like: a true rose, if ever there was one. She had gone as a little girl to Santa María with her parents, from where they had been brought to work as housekeepers. They were as poor as the magpies of the hills. They had appeared one day, after a long journey from the border mountain of Mugueimes. Two black-faced cows pulled the cart, in which there was a heap, precariously secured with ropes, formed of pots and pans and a trunk of clothes. Trudging in front of the wagon, the landless labourer lowered his face in shame as he entered Vilar de Rei. Behind the wagon, a consumptive peasant woman, her headscarf covering her face and a threadbare shawl tied behind her back and forming a cross over her withered breast, was holding the hand of a little girl with wide-open eyes and long eyelashes. Rosa entered the town, driven by gnawing hunger. Ah, how everything had come together, had fitted into place, as if it had been written that it should!

Rosa grew, and soon she was more adept at running the house than her mother, that snivelling, whining owl of a woman who spent her evenings drinking raw brandy and smoking cigarettes. But when Rosa was still little more than a camelia bud she was raped by her father on the solitary track across the moors of Os Montiños. The housekeeper, his lip quivering and his eyes agape, laid her down among some young oak trees. Rosa, sobbing her heart out, let herself be taken by the brute that rocked and squealed on top of her like some foul-smelling boar. From that moment on, the girl was silent, melancholy and withdrawn.

"That evil brute perished from a twisting of the guts, and his owl of a wife soon followed, vomiting bucketfuls of black blood," Xosé Coello tells them as his slight body sways about the kitchen.

That was when Celso dos Rousos' eyes fell upon Rosa, the housekeeper's daughter. The widower's imperious loneliness had driven him to her, and she meekly allowed herself to be led to San Salvador Church one cold, clandestine morning, to become the new wife of a tireless master clogmaker, living in a wretched shack built up against the town wall of Vilar de Rei. And, in the twilight of his years, Celso entered frenziedly into that temperate yet suffocating love, entered into that peace that set him on fire like a colt and made him redouble his incessant production of clogs, hiding beneath his cheeks of impassive myrtle an impossible joy that nobody had ever given him before. As severe as a boxwood image of St Roch, the reticent Celso dos Rousos hid his passion from the people of Vilar de Rei. As the two of them went to market, Rosa would follow a few paces behind, her eyes lowered beneath her large crimson headscarf, walking bolt upright on her soft, bare feet over the slates that paved the old Allariz road, bearing on her head the large basket containing pairs of clogs packed in straw and covered with a Castilian blanket. Before her, Celso walked stiffly along country lanes, along ancient hollow ways, along tracks in which cartwheels had gnawed deep ruts, along proud highways that bore coaches and progress, knowing that the good, demure woman with sad, downcast eyes was meekly following in his footsteps. And he adored Rosa as a kite could adore the prey it has seized, with the all-encompassing emotion of someone who makes a splendid, gigantic conquest. That love, blind to his enamoured son's raging fires, was sweetly returned by the young bride. Rosa the housekeeper's daughter, hurt as no-one else had ever been hurt, driven to the edge of madness on the moors of Os Montiños, clung with vegetable tenacity to the powerful, amorous current of the reborn old man. And neither Rosa nor Celso knew it...

"That's a lie!" exclaims Martiño dos Rousos. He jumps to his feet, knocking his chair over. The vicuña-wool poncho flows back over his shoulders. He slams his open hand down on to the table.

"I am telling you my truth," is Xosé Coello's calm, quiet reply, and as he takes up the thread of his words Martiño slips back into his chair, pours himself some more coffee liqueur and submits to the story being told by his good old friend.

Rosa had never loved any other man than her husband. The sickly young Martiño, eaten away by his love for her, had nurtured an immense hatred for his father. A hatred that led him into endless confrontation and provocation. Rosa was unaware of this secret, burning love. Perhaps her attentions and shows of affection towards the weakling were taken by him as signs of something quite distinct and far removed from the faithful wife's intentions. When Rosa lost her foothold in life and relinquished her long-suffering soul with a timid goodbye, Celso dos Rousos realised that few words other than those strictly necessary had ever issued from that mouth, the mouth of an image of Our Lady of the Incarnation. In the old room in the lean-to by the town wall, Celso closed his eyes and without weeping he reflected on his immense misfortune. He drank deeply of coffee liqueur throughout the interminable evening and the boundless night of the funeral wake. Clutching on to that flower with the utter despair of impossible happiness, old Celso was drowning in love for the dead, white girl, for the white dove, for the gust of white light that had joyfully braced his tireless old labouring shoulders. As she lay there dead, her lips pursed in a curious, cold grimace, her beauty strangely lost, all the solitude and all the overwhelming sadness of the town of stone fell upon Celso's heart, just as the lean-tos ranged along its wall sometimes collapse in the depths of the cruel midwinter. And it is at this moment that he is roused from his melancholy dream by a silence of fire, and he looks up at his son, standing there with a knife in his hand and with hatred flashing from his eyes. And then he understands the situation to which he had been blind, and he covers his eyes with his hands to weep at his double misfortune. He does not speak. He allows Martiño to spit unrepeatable insults across his young, beloved wife's bed of sperm and starch, until the wounded son is lost in the night with a cry that contains promises of revenge and fierce, bitter rancour for his lecherous father. A bewildered father, who is soon to lose heart, health and even sight. In the end, as the three men in the kitchen knew, Celso dos Rousos had hanged himself from a beam, beneath his chin a slip knot formed in clog-lace leather.

The three old men do not move. In the night of Vilar de Rei they drink deep of the coffee liqueur, as that far-off day in 1860 keeps returning to them. They fill their glasses again and again, and they are beginning to feel themselves throbbing, losing control. The one who drinks the least is Camilo dos Fandelos. Tall, slender, tough, he is, of the entire Hebrew tribe of Vilar de Rei, the shoemaker who had most stylishly folded his soft hat, best tied his white kerchief, and most elegantly undone the bottom buttons of his black waistcoat. Camilo dos Fandelos hardly raises the rim of his glass to his distant, indifferent smile. He remains cool (he has hardly spoken) and his voice has an exact, rigid, domineering sound to it.

"Every man tells his own story," he says, laboriously lighting a cigar as gnarled and knotted as his neck.

His words are bare and brief. According to him, Rosa hated Celso dos Rousos, and a gesture of protest from Xosé Coello, weary under the burden of coffee liqueur, is immediately quashed by Camilo's strange, nostalgic laughter. Because what happened was that Rosa, a young girl forced into an unwelcome marriage, rejected the love of the jealous old guardian of his own honour, who kept watch over her daily trips to fetch water from the Fonte de Baixo, the only respite she was allowed, apart from Sunday mass and the novena in the church of A Virxe do Cristal. She had been married, because she was poor, to the least poor of the shoemakers, and a dull yearning for revenge had grown in Rosa, the housekeeper's daughter. And then it was that the young wife noticed a pale, slimy presence that hardly took up any room in the shack. She becomes aware of Martiño and his forlorn devotion. Rosa winks at him, she pokes the tip of her tongue out at him behind the old man's back, she sways her buttocks at him in the kitchen. And so the lad's passion becomes public knowledge, the whole town talks about it, and even his father learns of it. Celso dos Rousos' deep, melancholy jealousy sours his blood, he grows dejected, and he extends his labours in the workshop into interminable sessions so as to climb into bed numb with exhaustion. That hussy Rosa primly lowers her eyes of honey in the presence of her lord and master; in his absence she keeps Martiño's blood forever on the boil. Her galloping consumption summons father and son to her bedside, in a truce broken — by both parties — when one of them rests his hand on Rosa's white forehead for too long. When she dies, demijohns of coffee liqueur appear in the laying-out room. The father hardly touches it, while the son gulps it down. After a while he is harshly and bitterly reproved by his father.

Camilo dos Fandelos fixes his eyes on Martiño dos Rousos, whose large fair moustache is trembling. He tells him:

"The truth, my good lad, is that your father reprimanded you because you were drinking too much. Just cast your mind back."

The son's response had been a violent one. He screamed insults and his eyes bulged out of his head. Men rushed to hold him back but, somehow, Martiño seized the shoe knife and pointed it at his terrified father, who bowed his head and wept meekly on the pillow of the dead whore. And it was then that Martiño dos Rousos wandered off into the Vilar de Rei night, towards Ourense, Vigo, America.

"That isn't true!" Martiño shouts in fury.

"Indeed it is true!" replies Camilo with a dispassionate smile, his cigar wedged into the corner of his mouth.

"How can you know for certain that Rosa hated the old man and fired Martiño's lust?" Señor Xosé Coello slowly asks.

The lamps seem to grow dimmer, a troublesome silence hovers over the kitchen. All three companions place their glasses on the table and rest their heads in their hands, as though overcome by fatigue. Camilo finally answers:

"Many years have passed; I shall never forget Rosa's kisses in the haystack; she told me everything as we embraced, especially towards the end of the summer before she died, under an enormous moon that drowned us in light..."

Martiño dos Rousos' head falls on to the table as though made of lead and his hands knock over the flask and the glasses of coffee liqueur in a sudden mechanical movement.

(From *Crónica de Nós*, 1980)

The Gate

Everything I am about to write happened because he — O. Phea, a factory worker — had to go, year after year, eighteen of them, the same way, along the same road, riding the same bicycle. If he hadn't been a factory worker and hadn't lived in the grey city outskirts, by the main road — a tarmac one — he would never have had to ride along the stretch between his front door and the factory door. It was because of all that coming and going to and from the factory — always the same cypress tree, like a knife — that everything that happened to him happened to him. And it happened like this:

O. Phea hung his lunch-pot, well wrapped in newspaper, on the crossbar of his bike. He looked at his wet clogs and at the blue sky, smiled and thought:

"How lucky I am! It isn't raining today: yesterday I ended up like a drowned rat..."

Then he started off pedalling slowly — which is how factory workers ride bikes — down the asphalt road. And, suddenly, that cypress on the right. He tutted and thought to himself that it was shocking that cypresses didn't stand on their heads every so often, for a change. He carried on cycling and reached the factory, as he always does, after the ruined house, the saw mill, the miserable garden...

On another day, any other day, O. Phea got back on to his bike. He was in a bad mood, he had quarrelled with his wife. Halfway down the road he said:

"That's outrageous!"

He said this because, on turning that particular corner, he should have come to the low wall which, years ago, had been bare and which, now, was becoming bare again, with the death of the great ivy plant, that plant which had stopped the sun from licking the stones of the wall for eight summers. Right here, on turning the corner, he should have come to the low wall, as usual. But... O. Phea braked and put his left clog on the tarmac: the wall was no longer there.

"But it was still here yesterday...!"

Never mind, the wall wasn't there today. It had been, yesterday, but the wall wasn't there today. And in its place was a narrow track of white sand, firm and compacted; on either side of the track the great eucalyptus repeated a hundred times the image of its species.

"I wonder where that track leads. Who could have made it?"

That night O. Phea wrote a letter to his son. He had written him many before, but they must have all got lost in the post because he — O. Phea's son — hadn't replied to any of them. The letter said:

"My dear son,

Today I went to work and I couldn't find the ivy wall. I don't know how it happened, but now there's a track there, really nice and neatly done. When you were little you used to love playing in the road, but I didn't let you, because of the cars. That's why it came to me that if you were little and you were here, I'd take you to play on the..."

O. Phea tore up the paper. From their bed, his wife had shouted to him:

"Come to bed, do you hear? You're wasting loads of electricity for nothing."

On the next three days the worker stopped his bike by the track, and on these three days the worker went on to wonder where this sandy track could lead, this sandy track that ended in the great tarmac road at the front, in two rows of eucalyptuses at each side, and at the back... Where did it end at the back? On the fourth day he decided to find out. O. Phea turned resolutely, and pedalled down between the rows of eucalyptus trees. They were tall, and getting taller, and the light was getting dimmer. The worker pedalled furiously on, obsessed, he had to reach the end... the end of the track. And, on turning a corner, the end was before him: a gate. Yes — O. Phea slammed on the brakes

— that was all it was. An old, rotten gate. The bars crossed each other, not knowing that they formed a cross. The bars of the gate were rotten, and a great humidity was rising from the damp earth. Behind the gate a dense forest could be seen. A forest. Great heaps of broken leaves or stripped bark, not a rustle or a murmur. O. Phea saw all this, his hands clutching the brakes, some twenty metres from the gate. He was afraid of such desolation. With a sudden movement he turned and went back the way he had come. That day he reached the factory very late and was not allowed to work.

From then until the day — until that day when all was revealed — eight days went by.

That morning, while O. Phea was having his glass of firewater — it was the morning of the eighth day — and his usual hunk of maize bread, he wrote his son another letter.

"My dear son,

I know this letter will get lost as it crosses the sea, like all the others. You too got lost one day when you crossed the sea. And today I'm going to go through the gate to have a good look at the forest from the inside. Today I'm not going to work. Look after yourself. Even though your mother says you must have died, I think you read all our letters. Or maybe you don't read them. But if you do, don't be too upset, because we are getting used to being without you. Don't feel upset, because we know that if you don't write there must be a reason. Love from your father, O. Phea."

He got on his bicycle, reached the track, rode down it. He thought:

"Today's the day. I'll find out what's on the other side of the gate."

And indeed he would find out, but that knowledge was going to hurt him. And this is what he was told by an old man with a chest-length beard whom he met on the track:

"Don't go, O. Phea, it will hurt you."

"Who are you? I don't know you."

"Don't go through the gate."

"I shall."

"As you wish..., going through that gate always hurts; I should know, I'm the one who made it. I'm the artist who..."

"I shall."

And O. Phea was determined. And he arrived. There stood the rotten gate. Beyond, the piles of dead leaves and the grave, hieratic trees. He stopped his bike. His chest was trembling over his heart. He left his bike on the ground, it looked like a dead bike. There was a smell of damp. He took one, two, three steps forward. He tried to grasp the latch of the gate. He became strangely nervous, feverishly he ran his hands all over the gate, tried to reach between the wooden bars... He stepped back, his eyes staring. He stammered:

"The gate and the forest..., they're paintings! It's all an enormous picture. Behind the gate there's only a canvas. The gate and the forest are paintings. They're a painting..., a picture! An enormous picture! Behind the picture there is nothing!"

The old man was right, it hurt him — O. Phea, a factory worker — that the mysterious forest was not real.

Yes. Everything that happened to O. Phea happened because of too much coming and going, for eighteen years, along the same road.

(From *Percival e outras historias*, 1958)

The Monk of Diabelle

At dusk, the condemned man made up his mind and lit the candle, alleviating the gloom in the cell. He banged on the door, calling for the guard.

"Do you want another cigar?" the guard asked as he opened the door, with a crunching of rusty metal.

That afternoon they had given the prisoner some sweet wine and a little cake. The chaplain had brought him a gift of a bundle of cigars, since this was the last night that the prisoner would spend in this world.

"Whenever you want another cigar, ask the guard for one; you smoke as much as you like," the priest had said.

The following morning the prisoner was going to be garrotted in the Main Square of Ourense, which would be full of people just as on bull-running days. From beyond the cell door, along the dank and foul-smelling corridor, whispers of conversation and the odd laugh came to the prisoner. It must be the Brothers of Peace and Charity, the Executioner from Burgos, the President of the High Court, the Chaplain and the Prison Governor, who were going to spend the night as the prisoner was, without sleep.

"I'd like some writing materials," requested the prisoner.

"Don't you want another cigar, then?" insisted the guard with the pallid face, grinning stupidly at him and revealing black teeth and whitened gums that looked as though they were full of pus.

The prisoner sat down. The candlestick stood on the thick-topped table. The candlelight shone into the prisoner's face from close up. He had deep blue eyes that sparkled like stars. His hair fell, straight and carefully combed, down to his shoulders. He was simply clad in a white silk shirt with a delicately frilled front. The prisoner was close-shaven and had skin even whiter than his lace-trimmed shirt. He accepted the cigar and left it on the table, unlit. Again he asked for paper, pen and ink.

"I want to write a letter," he explained.

"Who's it for?" the guard demanded.

"Do I have to tell you that?"

"I'm not sure."

"Well then: I want to write a letter to Engineer Guilherme António da Silva Couvreur, who lives in Lisbon."

"I assure you that I shall make your wish known to the authorities," said the guard, suddenly looking serious. And he left, bolting the cell-door behind him, with a clanging of locks, bars and latches.

The prisoner was a tall thin man. He came to his feet and began to pace up and down the cell, his hands crossed behind his back. He was wearing black riding boots. As he paced and paced the condemned cell in Ourense prison, his heel-caps drew penetrating sounds from the stone floor. Sometimes he passed a long and bony hand across his domed forehead and turned his eyes to the ceiling. He was smiling imperceptibly. He had a narrow face and prominent cheekbones.

To write to Couvreur in the last hours of his life: such was the fervent desire of that man a little over forty years of age, with a hard chin and curved nose, in whom it was still possible to sense the energy and ardour of youth. To open up his heart to the man he had loyally served right up to the moment of shared failure and the loss of the disputed border area of the Couto Mixto through the odious skullduggery of Spanish liberalism. To tell him, first and foremost, hand on heart, of the respect he felt for him.

"I should like Your Excellency to know," the prisoner would write, "that in these last moments of my life of adventure, I thank the heavens that they gave me the honour of having been able to serve such a gentleman as you in the capacity of agent and personal spy. That throughout my Legitimist activity as a volunteer in the service of those august cousins the true Kings Carlos of Spain and Miguel of Portugal, and in the service of the Holy Faith and of God, from the moment I was forced to leave the cloisters of Celanova monastery and the

Benedictine Order as a result of compulsory secularization, I have never been as happy as I was when I decided to place myself at Your Excellency's command at the time when Your Excellency came to the border to carry out the functions of Secretary to the Portuguese Section of the Boundary Commission, of which Brigadier Leão Cabreira was such a despicable President, may he rot in Hell. By Your Excellency's side I fought honourably, and when Your Excellency had to leave the borderlands, a victim of the machinations of the man we know only too well, it was with my mind set on Your Excellency that I resolved to do what I did, which would cause me to end my days on the scaffold."

It is true that, after years of frenzied activity, fighting like a wild boar up hill and down dale, the Monk of Diabelle had acquired a reputation as a relentless fiend. Following the Treaty of Vergara, he had withdrawn to his ancestral possessions in Diabelle and in Rubiás dos Mixtos and, after the end of Miguelist activity, had become a lone horseman of the moors, aloof and silent. Without giving up the orders he had received, he had renounced the Divine Office because he did not consider himself worthy of exercising it in those testing and revolutionary times, as they were described on the occasion of the pastoral visit of the Bishop of Ourense to Tourém, that is to say, Turei. The Monk of Diabelle put his decision into practice by exchanging his black Benedictine habit for a dress coat, a frock coat, satin-trimmed trousers or, more frequently, riding breeches and riding boots. The villagers respected the bulge of his pistols in his cummerbund and doffed their caps to him as they left mass. An orphan and sole heir because of the death of his elder brother, the Monk of Diabelle lived in the enormous tumble-down house through whose rooms strutted the chickens and the turkeys which in the evenings roosted on the beams in the dining room like vultures. An old gossip cared for him, having looked after him as a child as she had looked after his deceased father. The Monk of Diabelle was exigent only as to his clothes and his weapons, and their cleaning so concerned him that such niceties took up most of his time.

With his middle finger he flicked the wick of the candle and, as if liberated, it gained new strength to light up the cell, as black as the place on the border known as the Pit of Hell, which the prisoner now remembered with a smile, thinking of that day when his band had slit the throats of a patrol of six soldiers and sent them toppling into the dark mouth of the abyss, and nobody had ever found out what had become of them. Into the Pit of Hell of Sendim da Raia.

The prisoner would never forget the moment he met Engineer Silva Couvreur, on the Privileged Road, the custom-free highway which, connecting the villages of the Couto Mixto starting at Meaus, passes between Randín and Picoña to end up across the border at Turei.

"I shall never forget the day I was presented to Your Excellency," the prisoner would write as soon as the guard brought him what he needed. "I shall never forget the evening when the Judge of the Couto Mixto introduced us so that I could help to guide the Commission in the establishing of parish limits, of watersheds, and of the route of the Privileged Road. Meanwhile, the infamous Leão Cabreira rode on ahead, puffed up and stiff in the Infantry Brigadier's uniform that he did not take off even to go to bed, alongside the man who dominated him by the means which Your Excellency and I too know full well, Fidencio Bourman — the most cunning and sagacious of the servants of the Queen of Spain and of the depraved clique that attends her. For some unknown reason, my horse and Your Excellency's were lagging behind, preceded by the retinue formed by the other members of the Commission and the village elders and leaders of the Couto Mixto who, repugnantly servile, accompanied them. As we forded the river at Ourille by the side of the stepping-stones, where there is a bend in the track, the entourage disappeared from view and Your Excellency and I entered into a lively conversation about the final destiny of the Couto Mixto. "Its freedoms will be violated by the anti-Catholic despotism of the tyrannies in Madrid and Lisbon," I had said to Your Excellency, revealing my deep pessimism. At that moment, Your Excellency's horse was standing next to one of the age-old marker-stones which signal the Privileged Road in the free lands of the Couto Mixto. I remember that Your Excellency fixed me with a stare. "Portuguese federalism can guarantee a canton here!" Your Excellency exclaimed, shaking a fist in the air.

Everything depended on the Portuguese Revolution, in which Engineer Guilherme António da Silva Couvreur believed fervently. The Monk of Diabelle, his heart wounded by the defeat of Carlism and the failure of Miguelism, was carried away into a dream-world by the conspiratorial words of his brilliant Portuguese friend. In order to survive in the face of the uniformist tendencies which threatened from

Spain and from Portugal, the Couto Mixto had to come under the power of the latter kingdom. An oral protocol between the Monk of Diabelle and Silva Couvreur guaranteed on their words of honour — given beside the megaliths that mark the Privileged Road, in the presence of Him who for one of them was the Supreme Being and for the other simply God — that the enclave which had been independent since the beginning of the world and since the beginning of all kingdoms would once again be free under the protectorate of the Federal Republic of Portugal, when this came into being. It was imperative, therefore, to ensure that the Boundary Commission assign the Couto Mixto to Portuguese authority, and to frustrate the ambitions of the Spanish by whatever means were necessary.

"As soon as I put myself at Your Excellency's disposal," the prisoner intended to write to his illustrious friend, "I set to work on the Conspiracy and I revived my network of informants and guerrillas in the border area, not trusting, for the reasons I am about to mention, the authorities of the Couto Mixto. As a result of this, I soon discovered some very surprising facts. For example, that in the first session, celebrated in Vigo on board the schooner 'Neptuno', the President of the Spanish Section, Ambassador Fidencio Bourman y Carvajal, all smiles and flattery, had proposed Brigadier Leão Cabreira, the Head of the Portuguese Section, as President of the Boundary Commission. I immediately smelled, with the nose of an experienced conspirator, that the Spaniard wanted to gain control of Cabreira, and was making a start by playing to his vanity. It seems that, at that moment, they toasted with sherry, instead of doing so with a glass of madeira, something I considered, once I knew of the episode, to be a joke on Bourman's part and a good example of Cabreira's idiocy. With time, and especially after the arrival on the scene of the shameless Lula Ares — as well we know, Your Excellency and I, your servant — the Portuguese representative's submission to the interests of Spain was complete. After our meeting at the Rock of Anamán, everything became clear, as Your Excellency will not have forgotten."

The prisoner ran his fingers through his hair and stood for a moment with his hand on his head and a bitter smile on his lips. The prisoner, when he was still a free man, the Monk of Diabelle, had had a secret meeting with Couvreur in the summer pasture beneath the Rock of Anamán. The August sky was a mantle decked with diamonds and a festival of lights. On that ridge of the border mountains one felt so high up one could touch the stars. The heavenly glow lit up the last thatched huts of the herdsmen of Curral Vello. Corga dos Enforcados Ravine was alive with sound and in the surrounding foliage a nightingale chattered away. An occasional heap of charcoal was smoking and its smell of burned heather tickled the nostrils. Salmonde Hill was dark and Couvreur soon crossed it, stealing along narrow passes under the guidance of a servant in the Monk's confidence. The Monk himself had come on foot from Montalegre leading his stallion by the reins.

The condemned man was remembering that moment and thinking that he would mention it in the letter he was going to write to his friend the federalist Engineer.

"As soon as I saw Your Excellency's face in the resplendent light," he would say, "I perceived your profound concern. It was not good news we had received, Your Excellency on the one hand and this your friend and servant on the other. Our worst fears seemed to be confirmed. Don Fidencio Bourman y Carvajal had set his heart on the annexation to Spain of the Couto Mixto. He was lord and master of the will of the Portuguese plenipotentiary, Frederico Leão Cabreira, and he hardly had any other opponent than Your Excellency. Spain's main interest was the Couto Mixto, once the submission of Mount Madalena to Madrid's authority had been agreed. Cabreira was slowly turning into a puppet in the hands of that astute and perverse Bourman. Your Excellency can no doubt clearly remember how the Boundary Commission caravan always included a wagon carrying barrels of sherry with the sole purpose of filling the belly of the Brigadier, who was ever more immersed in torpor and in the pleasures that the lascivious Lula Ares offered him. Proud as he was of his titles and his military rank, Leão Cabreira had lost all strength of character and willpower, if he had ever had any, dominated by generous wine and conquered by apathy and vice. I am certain that Your Excellency will remember our meeting beneath the Rock of Anamán, my favourite place on the border. There we came to the conclusion that, in exchange for the Couto Mixto, Bourman was prepared to cede to Portugal such trifles as villages like Lamadarcos, Cambelo and Souteliño. It was therefore necessary to thwart his manouevre by taking expeditious measures.

What had to be done, then, was to impede such cessions and insist on Portugal's rights to the Couto Mixto. So the Monk of Diabelle went down to Ourense to ask the Town Council for money in the name of the Cause, and to Braga to collect contributions from the Miguelistas. In both enterprises he failed, and he returned to the border with his purse full of air. Relying solely on his own means and a little help from Couvreur, although in the hope of backing, which never materialized, from the lodges in Porto, the Monk of Diabelle nurtured the seeds of faction around Oimbra, mobilizing sworn Legitimists who organized assemblies and riots, burned public property and planted explosives in the Town Hall of Verín and the Courthouse of Xinzo. The word was spread that the perpetrators of the damage were the inhabitants of certain villages who did not wish to become Portuguese citizens and who threatened even greater devastation. Next, the Monk encouraged the people of Castro Laboreiro to protest, and incited them to revolt for their rights of pasture in the Kingdom of Galicia. He also stirred up the people of Sabucedo and of Padroso. In the midst of all the confusion, Silva Couvreur proposed to the Boundary Commission that the Couto Mixto should be ceded to Portugal and that the five villages of the Monterrei valley should be incorporated into Spain, with a recognition of the summer pasture rights of the people of Castro Laboreiro. Bourman's refusal was so categorical that a severance of diplomatic relations was threatened. The Couto Mixto had to be Spanish, he asserted.

For a moment the condemned man stopped pacing his cell. He sat down, put his elbows on the table and rested his face between his hands. He gave a great sigh, the imprisoned Monk. His reminiscences made his pale eyes cloud over for an instant. Soon the guard would come with the paper and a pen and he would be able to write the letter he owed to Engineer Silva Couvreur.

"My dear sir," the Monk would write, "the combined effects of my factious borderers and Your Excellency's articles in the Porto Press, which told the truth about the culpable attitude of Leão Cabreira, should, according to our plans, have favoured the incorporation of the Couto Mixto into Portugal. But this did not happen, and Don Fidencio Bourman used his influence in Lisbon so effectively that, with the help of Cabreira's insidious reports, Your Excellency was replaced and had to leave the Boundary Commission. Neither you, Your Excellency, far less I, your servant, will ever forget the dramatic consequences of our failure."

They had pitched the camp in Ourille valley, with the wagons of the

Boundary Commission arranged in a circle. Sitting on a coachman's seat, legs spread wide, the shameless Lula Ares was combing her long blond hair in the sun. A horse at full gallop could be heard in the distance as it approached the encampment. Thundering along the Privileged Road, a horseman arrived, his broad cape of rough cloth flapping in the breeze. He drew rein before the main tent. "Bourman! Bourman!" exploded the voice of the Monk of Diabelle. And the echoes in the mountains repeated with crystal clarity "...man..., man," and scaled the peaks and reached the houses of the traders in the village of Meaus.

"My misfortune, Señor Enxeñeiro Guilherme António," the condemned man would write to his friend, transferred now to Lisbon, "my misfortune began at the very moment when a red cloth of anger covered my gaze as I was informed of Your Excellency's discharge and dismissal. As Your Excellency will remember, I presented myself before Don Fidencio Bourman to challenge him to a duel. Even though the Couto Mixto enjoys the privilege of arms, and the Spanish and Portuguese laws against duelling therefore do not apply there, the Spanish Ambassador disregarded me and refused to fight, slighting me as I had never been slighted before. It was then that I took the decision to declare war against the crowns unlawfully held and usurped by those unworthy women, liberals and Bourbons, Dona Maria Glória and Dona Maria Cristina, and I rose up in arms together with a pride of lions of mine who were prepared to fight to the end. Your Excellency, far away in Lisbon, could no longer be the object or victim of serious intrigues or be accused of any complicity. I knew for certain, señor, that the conclusion to my campaign of honour could be none other than death."

Fidencio Bourman left the tent in his own good time. He was wearing a jacket of brown velvet with crêpe edging, and neatly checked trousers. He had a goatee beard and a long pointed moustache. He was of low build and his hair was grey, and everything about him suggested moderation. "I have come for Your Excellency," the Monk of Diabelle had shouted as he sprang from his stallion. He slapped Bourman across the face with a glove. Gold-rimmed glasses flew through the air. The hint of a frozen smile appeared on the Spanish Ambassador's lips. From the tents, surprised and muttering, came the commissioner, the assistants and the servants. Leão Cabreira, his dolman unbuttoned and his hair ruffled, showed his puffy face under the awning of the wagon of the shameless Lula Ares. "Stop! Stop!" shouted Couvreur, who was already wearing his dust-cloak over his travelling clothes, ready to leave for Vila Real. "Bourman, I have come to challenge Your Excellency in order to put paid to you and to your intrigues," cried the Monk of Diabelle. "In the Couto Mixto we are exempt from the ban on duelling," he added in a hoarse voice. Bourman paled, but did not change his mocking grin. "I do not recognize in you the quality of a gentleman," he said in a sharp, calm voice. "Besides, my good fellow, duelling is a savage practice," he added after a heavy silence. When the Monk was about to draw his cavalry sabre, his blue eyes ablaze with anger, people stepped in between them with pistols cocked. The Monk of Diabelle looked daggers at Bourman and left at a gallop towards Picoña Hill. Poised there, by the castle ruins, between the sun and the people who down below were watching him, overcome with fear, he brandished his sabre over his head and its blade shone like a bolt of lightning. "Death to the Liberals! Long live the Canton of the Couto Mixto!" he cried before disappearing like a fatal shadow towards the valleys of the south, towards Mota de Maria Sacra, towards the solitude of the serra and towards the avenging of betrayed freedoms.

"A whole life dedicated to the restoration to the world of a lost order has culminated in defeat and execution," the condemned man was thinking as he donned a black overcoat over his silk shirt, for the cold of the prison had penetrated his bones. He arranged his long hair over the high woollen collar and buttoned up the double-breasted coat, which followed the contours of his waist and his chest. The prisoner was thinking about the death he was going to be given before dawn, and he was not afraid. He had so often killed without compassion that he did not dare feel pity for himself! He would die as he had killed: with a steady hand and with his head held high. "And that honourable freemason of the ancient and esteemed Scottish order was a loyal ally," thought the prisoner, pacing the cell again. The last hopes for the Couto Mixto were still in Couvreur's hands, depending on whether the word Couvreur had given in the border mountains had an influence some day on the decisions of the republic of cantons that might or might not come to be in Portugal and that might or might not agree on federations of free and privileged lands with the sister revolution that might or might not break out in the Kingdom of Spain. The condemned man felt the vulture of pessimism pecking at his heart.

"Señor Enxeñeiro," the Monk of Diabelle would say to Silva Couvreur in his letter: "I know that, from the moment Your Excellency left the Couto Mixto as a consequence of the despicable moderatist machinations of Don Fidencio Bourman and of the weakness of Brigadier Leão Cabreira, his trained puppy, my behaviour was that of a blind, mad, furious beast of the mountain crags. Bereft of hope and charged with rage, I brought together a band of murderers and suicides; I know it well. I brought together Mad Costa Alves from Lindoso and that evil brute the Barber of Guntumil; I brought together Celso of the Mules, the wily horse-thief operating for years in the woods of Aparecida, and the Farrier of Lobosandaus; I brought together that prig the hall porter at the Xurés Spa, and Zé Vilarinho, the sexton of Nosa Señora da Peneda Church. When I appointed Fonsito Arias, the youngest son of the lady of the manor at Ribas, near the Virxe do Cristal Church outside Vilanova, as my lieutenant, the group was complete whose members were well known in the Legitimist faction for their courage, for their resistance to hardship, for their determination and, why not admit it, for their cruelty. We became a feared band of implacable burglars and highwaymen, never straying far from the border. We settled many scores pending ever since the treachery at Vergara and the rebellion in favour of the grandson of King Carlos, in 1847. I hope that Your Excellency is not ashamed of this his servant," the prisoner would say in his letter to Silva Couvreur, the good freemason.

Before a year was out, the Monk of Diabelle's band beheaded an Isabeline informer, using a wagon-pole as a block, in the parish of Sarreaus. On the road from Santo André to Randín it robbed at gunpoint the cloth merchants who come from Lisbon. It went down to Celanova to attack the house of the priest of Alcácer de Milmanda, fleeing across the Chaira moors towards Mount Penagache. It burned a shed with thirty cows in it, in Baltar itself, the shed and cows being the property of the court clerk Texada, of liberal persuasion. It shot the secretary of the Chamber of Commerce of Montalegre, Diogo Peres Feijó, up against the pillory of Soajo, in front of all the people at the fair on the first Sunday of the month. It cut open the belly of the parish priest of Fondo de Vila, Don Fagundo Mobilla, as pigs' bellies are cut open, and hung him from an oak in Terrachán, for having presented Bourman with a carafe of coffee liqueur. It set light to the fields of

Coto dos Cravos, Sesteiros dos Bañadoiros and Verandas near Castro Laboreiro, because those who farmed them had shown themselves favourable to Spanish rule.

But on 14th January, a large search-party managed to surround the band in a cowherd's hut on the plains of Pedra da Loba, near Grama de Corno Dourado. Three of them were shot dead. The rest fled in all directions, apart from the Monk, who gave himself up with his arms raised and a smile of indifference on his handsome pale mouth. The outdoor life had never prevented the Monk from caring for his long hair or dressing in accordance with rural aristocratic etiquette. He shaved every day. At the time of his capture, he was wearing pearl-coloured breeches, black boots with silver spurs and a short jacket of green corduroy. His demeanour made a deep impression on his captors. But this did not prevent him from being condemned to death by garrotte.

Since the guard was taking such a long time to bring the writing pad, the Monk of Diabelle prepared the conclusion to his letter to Silva Couvreur. "Here you have," he would say, "the conclusion to this long letter, dear sir. I trust that, if it were one day possible, Your Excellency will do what must be done to return its privileges to my unfortunate Couto Mixto, as a canton founded in the Federal Pact. Since the end of this letter will more or less coincide with the end of my life, I wish to assure Your Excellency that I go to the scaffold ready to accept whatever the hereafter has in store for me. I have made my peace with God, whom I always set above all my acts, even those which could be considered the most reprehensible. He knows of my Faith and my Love for Him. Receive now, sir, fond memories of your spy, confidant, and faithful servant."

The condemned man heard footsteps in the corridor and looked up towards the cell door. It opened and in came the guard with the stupid grin and the blackened teeth.

"The authorities do not grant you permission to write any letters," he said.

And he added:

"Won't you be wanting another cigar?"

Note. Don Xosé Benito Brandón e Elices was born in the Manor House of Diabelle, in the parish of Randín, in 1818, and he was christened in the parish church of Rubiás, in the Couto Mixto, where his family possessed various villages, agricultural stock, and estates. An orphan from a young age, he took vows as a Benedictine in the monastery of Celanova. After the compulsory secularization he embraced the Legitimist cause, following his brother Don Baldomero the Elder, who died from a spray of grapeshot in Luchana. Between 1835 and 1839, Don Xosé Benito became well known as "The Monk of Diabelle", being prominent as a Carlist guerrilla and an enthusiastic supporter of King Miguel of Portugal. He took part — more as a clandestine organizer than as a military leader — in the Second Carlist War, up until the death of the commanding officer Don Fernando Gómez, known as "The Cabinetmaker", on 3rd September 1847. It is known that in 1855 and 1856 he served as confidential agent to the Secretary of the Portuguese Section of the Spanish-Portuguese Boundary Commission, Engineer Guilherme António da Silva Couvreur, supporting him efficaciously in his disagreements with the President of the Spanish Section, Ambassador Don Fidencio Bourman y Carvajal, and in his tenacious opposition to the conduct of the President of the Portuguese Section, Brigadier Federico Leão Cabreira. A steadfast supporter of the incorporation of the Couto Mixto into Portugal, Don Xosé Benito seems to have taken great exception to the discharge and dismissal of Couvreur by the authorities in Lisbon and to the adjudication of the territory, until then a free one, to the Spanish Crown. In his rage the Monk of Diabelle raised in arms a band of former Carlists and Miguelists who, during 1857 and 1858, terrorised, with destruction, robbery and violence, the liberals on either side of the border, especially those who had opposed the integration of the Couto Mixto into the Portuguese nation. Captured by the Civil Guard—as a result of the denunciation of Don Celso Texada Burdeos, the scribe in Bande — he confessed and was tried in Ourense Court, and sentenced to death. Being a fidalgo, Don Xosé Benito Brandón e Elices claimed the privilege of being executed with the pomp and deference of the noble garrotte, as established in a Royal Warrant of 28 April 1828, although he was made to go to the scaffold dressed in a yellow cassock with red stains, since the Court had declared that the prisoner's crimes had been impelled by an animus of regicide, in accordance with the provisions of the statute of 1850.

Despite being an ecclesiastic, Don Xosé Benito refused the sacraments. Eye-witness accounts state that when the condemned man made his entrance into the Main Square on a horse draped in black felt, the crowd kept a religious silence while a small group of fanatics and reactionaries broke into brief applause before running away along Rúa da Gloria. It is said that the sound made by the heels of Don Xosé Benito's boots on the boards on which the paraphernalia of the garrotte were installed echoed and re-echoed on the walls of the Bishop's Palace as a demonstration of his firmness and serenity in that predicament. His body not having been claimed, it was buried in the cemetery of Santa María a Madre on the day of the execution, 14th April 1858.

Don Xosé Benito Brandón e Elices had had no vices that were known of. He had lived a chaste life, and those who had known him asserted that he could be kind, generous and beneficent with his friends and with the humble, but cruel, wrathful and vengeful with his enemies. The memory of the borderlands will never relinquish the figure of the Monk of Diabelle, the renowned horseman and famous dandy.

(From *Arraianos*, 1991)

Cold Hortensia

A Nosa Terra has been invaded five times, Cold Hortensia told us at the beginning of the most unforgettable of summers, in Vilanova dos Infantes. That year my cousin Maribel had been given good marks at the Carmelite School. What would you like as a present? her parents had asked. A tandem, she had replied without hesitation. A Nosa Terra was an island then. The sea surrounded it, at Maceda, Lovios, Corte-gada, A Merca. Cold Hortensia told us these things and we sat in silence by the fire, where vine cuttings burnt in a rapid, intense flame. There had been a flood in the world, and A Nosa Terra had been left isolated by the sea. Other countries were islands, too. Before the flood, A Nosa Terra had not been inhabited. After the flood, it was occupied by five races. Or maybe you thought that the same men and the same women have always been living here. At such moments I had no thoughts for the tandem, the ride to Pontafechas, Maribel's printed skirt, bathing in the dark lazy waters of the River Arnoia among cool willows, that summer of fire and of rabid dogs on the roads of A Nosa Terra. Cold Hortensia was tall and she smoked cigarettes she rolled herself. She had a pocket-watch, and wore a head-scarf in the style of mountain women, tying it tight around her head and setting it in position as country men do with their berets. Near Corbelle there was a channel separating A Nosa Terra from the land of Tagen Ata. Along that channel warships had often sailed. In Tagen Ata there was a man called Enmek Tofen who had been chosen to be king of all that country. He was taller, stronger and more handsome than any other man. One day Enmek Tofen was taking a stroll by the side of the sea, in the company of his brothers Malabron, Lodr and Kodraf, when they saw that a fleet of fifteen great ships was approaching the coast. Enmek Tofen immediately started to shout orders to his servants to prepare a great banquet to welcome the foreigners. The beach on which the brothers stood was four leagues from Enmek Tofen's palace. The king's voice was so powerful that it was heard both by his servants and by the foreigners, who must have been astonished as they dropped anchor and lowered the sails. That winter had been extraordinarily foggy in Ourense. Each morning it was torture to hear the alarm clock and trudge through an underwater city (the Main Square, Rúa de Colón) to school. What do you want a tandem for, if you've already got a bicycle, Maribel's parents had asked her, and they did not have to wait long for her reply. She wanted it to go for rides with me in Vilanova. Months earlier, during the winter, Maribel and I had spent long hours together, translating Caesar and Cicero, on the brazier-table in her study. My uncle and aunt and my cousin Maribel lived in Outeiro, next to Pelamios bridge. It was an area where the fog mingled with the steam from the Burga wash-house. My hand would often, with studied indifference, take Maribel's hand, perhaps in the pretence of emphasising a point in a discussion about some historical *cum*. A knee of mine would touch a knee of hers. Separating them, the cheviot of my knickerbockers and the tartan of her skirt under the cloth covering the brazier-table. I was becoming warmer, what with the brazier and brushing against Maribel, and in my eyes shone affirmations like plerosque Belgas esse ortos ab Germanis and so on, wanting to hug Maribel and give her a long kiss. Cold Hortensia lived in a rubblework shack right next to Vilanova Castle. Maribel, I, and other youngsters went to see her every night. We would sit on low stools and on the table-bench, watching the flames. We would talk among ourselves, sing or quarrel. We were tired of eating fruit, of cycling again and again to and from Celanova, of running errands for my parents, of bathing in the pools in the River Sorga, of reading Jules Verne during immense sestas; and Cold Hortensia's shady little house offered us something different. I bet you don't know what ships those were, approaching Tagen Ata. Well, they were ships from A Nosa Terra and they were carrying our king, called Dindadigoe. This man's idea was to marry Isebelt, Enmek Tofen's sister, and so forge links of friendship between A Nosa Terra and Tagen Ata. Enmek Tofen resolved to call an assembly to decide whether Isebelt was to be given to the king of A Nosa Terra. All those present, except his brother Kodraf, declared themselves delighted at the prospect of the marriage. There are men who hate butterflies and are only happy when contemplating strife. They are the wickedest men. I knew one such in Pontevedra who was worse than any other, worse than Kodraf. Enmek Tofen ordered a celebration to be held on the Isle of Amores, to the south of Tagen Ata, a delightful place, full of palm trees, apple trees and mimosas, ideal for eating and resting on summer days. On the third night of the banquet, Kodraf went armed with a knife to Enmek Tofen's palace stables and cut the testicles off all the horses belonging to Dindadigoe and his men. The handsome, long-haired mountain horses of A Nosa Terra neighed in terror and fled into the darkness leaving scarlet streams behind them. They all bled to death in the scrublands of Tagen Ata. How vile, Maribel said. Cold Hortensia was rolling a cigarette. She passed the tip of her tongue, as pointed as an awl, along the strip of glue. Don't forget that in every story there is a man who has to do all the evil, all the evil in the world. But Hortensia, castrating horses like that..., Maribel insisted, with a waving, up-and-down motion of her head. The flames were reddening my cousin's cheeks. On her broad face there were patches of light and patches of shadow, and her blond plait shone like a fairy's plait. The affront filled all Dindadigoe's men with fury. We shall sail back to A Nosa Terra and return with an army that will reduce Tagen Ata to ash, they said in their rage. Enmek Tofen realised that he had to placate the king of A Nosa Terra and, without a second thought, said to him: If you agree to forget about the offence you have received, I shall compensate you with two horses for each one that you have lost, and with my sword Derbfoll, forged by the gods of yesteryear, and capable of cutting marble and stone. Dindadigoe said that he would accept the compensation and forget the affront, he and his family too. But his promise of marriage to Isebelt was no longer valid. Enmek Tofen acquiesced and invited Dindadigoe to a festa of reconciliation. And what a festa that had been, cousin Maribel's birthday party, a fortnight earlier! After tea, my father had lit his pipe and had smilingly gone upstairs for his sesta with mother. We were left alone downstairs, we youngsters, with the gramophone. We all kept on drinking Marie Brizard anisette and coffee liqueur, and Maribel smiled at me while Lolo's arm pressed against her waist in a cruel slow fox-trot that was a dagger in my heart.

Maribel was a year older than me and this hurtful fact filled me with sadness, as it put me in a clearly inferior position to older lads like Lolo. At the end of the party Maribel asked me, with a splendid smile, if I would like to go for a ride with her on her tandem. The principal rule to be observed when on a tandem is that the one riding behind must pedal in time with the one riding in front, recognising in that person some kind of leadership. Maribel usually went in front. That night, surrounded by darkness the colour of wine, we reached A Roda. We stopped and sat on a rock, looking at the shadows in the valley. In that blackness the whole summer was redolent of dust, of dry earth, of manure. From the depths of the valley thousands of sounds of children, women, carts and dogs ascended to us. A sudden coolness came down from a rivulet on to our sweaty foreheads. I could not find the courage to take Maribel's arm or her hand. Little lights were filling the land. We went back to Vilanova for supper. I remember that as my mother was placing the soup tureen on the table, a stag-beetle came in through the open window and, after flying several times round the light, fell on to the plate in front of Maribel, who laughed with a forced, tense laugh, looking at my father and not at me. But Cold Hortensia had remained silent. The kitchen was cold, and with an imperious hand she gestured towards the board covering the kneading-trough, on which a tablecloth was spread and, on top of it, a heap of beans. Lolo, Maribel, Carrollas and I began to shell them, in silence. You might think — Cold Hortensia began to say — that Enmek Tofen had given up the idea of marrying his sister to the king of A Nosa Terra. Not at all. Halfway through the feast, when the wine was painting its colours on the apple-face of Dindadigoe, Enmek Tofen begged him for a full pardon. If you grant me it, and again agree to be my brother-in law, I shall compensate you with a marvellous gift. I shall give you a pot of gold, called the Pote de Gradel; if you boil a dead man in it he will emerge alive, although dumb and addle-eyed. With great pleasure Dindadigoe accepted the offering and promised to sail at dawn for A Nosa Terra, taking Isebelt and the pot with him. Maribel, much impressed, interrupted Cold Hortensia to ask her all about the marvellous pot. I don't know whether you want to be told about what happened to Isebelt in A Nosa Terra or whether you want me to tell you the story of that stupid bucket, Hortensia said, planting her hands, her enormous hands, down on top of the kneading-trough. She blew her nose into her fingers, and wiped them on the stone sink. Lolo, Maribel, Carrollas and I looked at each other in silence and went on shelling beans. Maribel said that we could perhaps be given the basic facts about the Pote de Gradel, and then Cold Hortensia could tell us the rest of the story of Isebelt. But — I protested — that means that when Hortensia continues the true story, our imaginations will still be bound up with the Pote de Gradel and we shall not be as attentive as we should. The Pote never darkens anything! The Pote gives out light! screamed Maribel in an outburst that filled me with fear. Her eyes were fixed on me and they gave out a flickering green light, like glow-worms. I looked at Cold Hortensia and I surprised on her lips a smile of satisfaction as she gazed at Maribel. The truth was that the Pote de Gradel was not only for resuscitating the dead, or at least returning to them some of the properties of the living; it was also for distilling in its depths certain liquors that could feed hundreds of men and keep them all well fed. Then Lolo asked if Enmek Tofen was a sorcerer, in view of the fact that he was the owner of this magical object. Not at all, Maribel replied with the same phosphorescent look that I had seen earlier. In the first place, Enmek Tofen accepted the Pote de Gradel as a gift; secondly, this pot is not a magical object but an object from the Other World. Maribel is right, Cold Hortensia interposed with a satisfied smile, adjusting the front of her headscarf. The ownership of the Pote de Gradel is always a matter of chance, and also a test for the person who owns it. So that you can see what's what, let me tell you that the Pote de Gradel, which at this stage in the story is a present made by Enmek Tofen to Dindadigoe, could have become Dindadi-goe's property many years before the events I'm relating to you during these sessions of ours. One day Dindadigoe was hunting in the lower regions of A Nosa Terra, beyond the hill we now call Furriolo. He halted his horsemen by the waters of Lake Beón, which is now called Lake Antela. Its surface was a resplendent green glass. Suddenly the waters shook and from them emerged an enormous black man, fol-lowed by a woman who was even more enormous and even blacker. The manes of Dindadigoe's horses stood on end and many of the horses reared up and threw their riders to the ground. That summer I had gone down with Carrollas and the older Vilanova boys to poach trout in the River Sorga. We had discovered a small meadow by the river. We all stripped. Bony white bodies darted about as the net was spread. Large penises swayed in the summer afternoon amid a smell of grass, maize, deep earth, slow waters. The older boys told me to keep watch from a hillock just in case the two civil guards came, which they wouldn't, and I lay face down on top of my towel. I let the sun warm my neck, my back, my thighs, my waist. Up on the road cars went past every so often, hooting. Chaffinches were singing in the branches and the water was singing, and so were other noisy birds, among the stones of the old dam. All of a sudden, at the top of the road, not the two civil guards but a glimpse of Maribel's red skirt, where the road turns. I shut my eyes in happiness, I opened them, and she wasn't there and maybe she hadn't been there and yet I had almost made out her rope-soled sandals with their long laces criss-crossed over her shins and tied under her knees. The boys' shouts, the beating of their sticks on the water, their laughter and their oaths filled the vault of the alders. I slumbered, thinking that A Nosa Terra was beautiful. That whole summer was beautiful, apart from a few clouds, pangs of jealousy and worries about my cousin. That summer, Maribel's parents had gone off on their travels and it was decided that she would stay with us for three months, which we would spend in Vilanova. My father spent the mornings reading upstairs, and my mother kept herself busy in the house. She received visitors and seldom went out. Maribel and I had the whole day together, and the tandem brought us even closer. Pedalling in time with her excited me and made me happy and complete, that unrepeatable summer, now so far away, so far away. Our mutual visits and chance meetings in Ourense, during that foggy school year, had been an island in a sea of desolation. She in the Carmelites' School in the Praza do Corrixidor, and me in the cold corridors of the Posío Institute — we had been living in different worlds that mingled now in Vilanova, under the sun and crowned by wasps and bunches of sherry grapes and mozafresca grapes. It seems that you two often go and see Cold Hortensia, my father said one day, slowly lighting his pipe as he looked towards the window as if he could see through the curtains. He smiled as though smiling to himself. I used to go to her kitchen, too, when I was a youngster, he said before he stood up to slowly climb the stairs for his sesta with mother, for his books, for his silence, for his late-afternoon Daiquiri. We did not say a thing, but both Maribel and I were wondering whether it could be true that Cold Hortensia was as old as all that. And what happened next was that the gigantic man who was appearing from the waters of Lake Antela, that is to say Lake Beón, had a pot of gold hanging from his neck. Captivated by the beauty of the pot more than by the ugliness of that horrendous couple, Dindadigoe started speaking to the presence that was emerging from the water. The truth is that he was coming from the Other World, said Maribel

63

with a snort, and Cold Hortensia, as if put out by the remark, kept a long silence as she calmly rolled a cigarette. She lit it with lowered gaze, like one who is wondering whether further speech is worth the effort. We all sat there in a heavy silence, and Cold Hortensia continued her story as if she was speaking only to the shelf on which rested the old wooden bucket with its bands of rusty metal. Dindadigoe invited the giant to live in A Nosa Terra, intending, no doubt, to wait for the chance to take possession of the golden pot. The creature that had emerged from the waters accepted the hospitality offered him, but he warned Dindadigoe that his wife was pregnant and that a fortnight later she would give birth to a son, armed with all the proper arms. Carrollas, Tripas, Xela all shouted together and then gave a great laugh in which I joined, too, not really knowing why. Hortensia, asked Xela, so the story of the son who is going to be born is the story of the redeemer of A Nosa Terra, the story you so often promised us last winter? I looked in perplexity towards Maribel. Last winter neither she nor I had heard Cold Hortensia's stories, neither she nor I had been in Vilanova. Maribel was smiling, with her eyes lowered, and she was waving her head in a gesture of peaceful negation. Look here Xela, said Cold Hortensia in a voice in which reproach mingled with patience, every story has its own trickery. This is just a digression in the margin of the story of Isebelt, which is the one that should concern us. Sorry, mumbled Xela, embarrassed and with an attractive smile on her little weasel mouth. The redemption of A Nosa Terra is a story that has not yet begun, Xela, insisted Cold Hortensia, pulling her headscarf down above her left eye. So Dindadigoe welcomed the two giants into his kingdom. He granted them countless favours, with the secret intention of being given the pot of gold in return. And what happened was that the giants, feeling protected, kept making mischief all over the country. Tired of putting up with them, the people of Vilanova, a town that then had a name I cannot yet reveal to you, decided to do away with such bothersome guests. They built an iron house in the place now known as San Vivián, in the Extramural Quarter. That is, as you all know, where there is a great underground chamber belonging to the family of Don Pepe Gómez, now used as a wine cellar. The people of that Vilanova of yore presented the house to the giants, telling them that it was a mud-and-straw house but that despite the humble materials of which it was constructed it was a gift that the townspeople made them with all their hearts. The giant and his wife, who in her pregnancy looked all the more deformed, locked themselves into the iron house and with joyful hearts began to drink the brandy and the coffee liqueur that the townspeople had given them in abundance. All the blacksmiths and charcoal-men of A Nosa Terra hurried to the spot and filled Don Pepe Gómez's underground chamber with charcoal, and buried the giants' house, also in charcoal, from the foundations to the roof. Then they set fire to it and, bringing hundreds of bellows into action, turned it into one great live coal. The house's iron walls went red and then white. The giant, choking, tried to hack his way out with his sword. He failed, and he escaped being burnt to death by smashing the roof with a blow of his fist and jumping out with his enormous wife on his shoulders and the Pote de Gradel on his head. He crossed the sea to Tagen Ata. Grateful for the welcome extended to him there by Enmek Tofen, he gave him the pot of gold before disappearing. As you have just seen, the Pote de Gradel could have become Dindadigoe's property long before Enmek Tofen presented it to him. This shows that we often have the greatest good right next to us and don't know how to acquire it. And where did the giant go? asked Carrollas, frowning and thrusting his chin up. Cold Hortensia rose from the table-bench, on which she had been sitting motionless, with her hands crossed over her apron as she spoke. That is something I cannot tell you, she said. And what about the son who was going to be born armed with all the proper arms? I asked for my part. Cold Hortensia scratched the back of her head with the ladle-handle, as she gave a faint smile. That boy, she replied with her eyes fixed on my eyes, is never to be mentioned here again, is that understood? That day Maribel had a cup of coffee after supper, something she never did. My parents went to bed and I suggested a trip to Celanova on the tandem. She placed her hand on my hand and her aquamarine eyes sought out my eyes. Today I'd rather go to bed and read a while, she said, gently imploring, in a velvet voice that melted my insides and fired my blood. I went outside alone to watch the moon rising. I climbed the echoing steps of the castle and I leant, chin in hands and filled with yearning, against the parapet, gazing at distant dark grey blotches over towards Allariz, Bobadela, Orga, sad sets of little villages called Einibó, Xixín, quivering belches puffed out along the entire Arnoia basin towards a leaden sky. It was warm and a light breeze brought me comforting smells of the country and of fruit. Among them all a pungent smell of smoke made me imagine an interior in which taciturn men and women sitting round the fire gulped down great bowls of broth with lumps of bread and thin red wine. The horizon began to distil a pink milk. Soon the moon began to show like the red back of some animal. It rose at a speed that seemed vertiginous, artificial, intimidating. It had turned into a globe of fire over the great valley of A Nosa Terra. I lit a Chesterfield that my father had given me after supper. My eyes were full of fine silver, of soft flour, of foam of frost. The moon was enormous and looked like a distant lamp of alabaster. I thought bitterly about Maribel, and the moon took possession of my inner being. But then I caught sight of two still figures at the foot of the tower. One of them was sitting on a scutching-stone and her head was iridescent, sprinkled with timid stars. She was looking upwards, towards the lank figure of Cold Hortensia, who was making a sign in the air with outstretched arms. Maribel was gazing at a pale statue that was Cold Hortensia and that, under the power of the full moon, was saying some unthinkable thing to her, without words. What a horrible presence of Maribel, far from me, receiving from Cold Hortensia the devil knows what clamours of dead beings and broken wisdom! The roofs of Vilanova, seen from the castle balcony, were blue now, and vaporous. I sat on the ground, hidden in the shadows of the door, and I wept because I felt alone and caressed by the moonlit hands of A Nosa Terra. Maribel had refused to go with me for a ride on the tandem that night I shall never forget. Well, now's the time to find out what happened to Isebelt with Dindadigoe, Cold Hortensia had said as soon as we trooped in through her kitchen door. I realised that my lips were shaping a bitter grimace. Unless you aren't interested in knowing the rest of the story, continued Cold Hortensia, looking at me with her eyes almost closed and a ripple of irony under her nose. I believe I blushed. Cold Hortensia, I'm very concerned to know everything you tell us, I replied in a tone that I tried to make distant and restrained, and that provoked a brief guffaw in Maribel. The fact is that, back in A Nosa Terra, Isebelt and Dindadigoe had a son whom they named En Dovel. But great discontent was spreading among the people of A Nosa Terra. They could not forget the affront that had been received in Tagen Ata. The memory of the horses mutilated by Kodraf, instead of dissolving in oblivion, was becoming more and more vivid. The episode was continually being sung by the poets and unrest was growing. Everyone thought that it had been very wrong of Dindadigoe to accept the reparation of fresh horses, the sword called Derbfoll and the Pote de Gradel. However spirited those animals might turn out to be, and whatever marvels those objects might do, Dindadigoe should never have taken Isebelt as his

66

wife, said the people of A Nosa Terra. And their resentment was so stubborn and so poisonous that they convened an assembly in which they decided to take full vengeance. And so they decided that Isebelt would go to live in a hut by the door of the king's palace; her employment would be to gut the animals that were to be eaten each day; and, at the end of each day's work, she would be given a thrashing by the master butcher as a reward for her labours. And finally that when Isebelt had no work to do she would rest by the palace door, and would carry all visitors and foreigners arriving there on her shoulders to Dindadigoe. Dindadigoe had no choice but to carry out everything that the assembly of A Nosa Terra had commanded, and Isebelt was reduced to that sad condition. Isebelt was sad, Isebelt yearned more and more for the Great Forest, for the hills, for the streams, for the houses with their blue slate roofs, for all Tagen Ata. But what happened next was that the unfortunate woman made friends with a starling that lived in a handsome hazel tree that spread its flower-bedecked branches by a secret spring where Isebelt used to sip water to assuage her thirst. Isebelt asked the starling to fly to Tagen Ata bearing news of her suffering to Enmek Tofen and her other brothers. How could Isebelt talk to the starling? asked Lolo all of a sudden. We all fixed our gaze on Cold Hortensia, as if to lend our support to Lolo's interruption and make his perplexity our own. Hortensia stopped stirring the cauldron of broth, which was left swaying on its chain. She came to her feet, made an imperceptible adjustment to her headscarf, placed her fists on her hips, put her body into an almost circular oscillation. What do you think? she asked, with that distant, stupid and self-sufficient air often assumed by schoolteachers. Perhaps Isebelt knew bird-language, ventured Xela. Or perhaps she didn't, said Maribel, perhaps the spring belonged to the Other World and, when close to it, people and animals could understand each other. Or it could have been a human being who, because of some spell, had been forced to take the shape of a starling, commented Carrollas, without much conviction. Cold Hortensia loosed a loud guffaw and lit a cigar. You'll soon get your answer, she said, blowing her nose on the edge of her apron. The fact is that the starling agreed to Isebelt's request and flew across the sea then separating A Nosa Terra from Tagen Ata. When the bird arrived there, it took itself off to the Great Forest which, as you all know, occupies the interior of that country. The starling of my story, young friends, was called Gelra, and it found itself in an awkward situation. It understood and spoke the languages of all beings, including plants and also stones, plots of land, buildings and winds. The only languages it could not speak were those of human beings, even though it had a perfect understanding of them. So it needed someone who could convey to Isebelt's brothers the news of the misfortunes of that unhappy daughter of Tagen Ata. Gelra flew into the depths of the Great Forest, where Vela the wolf lived in its den. I need, said Gelra, to take a message to Enmek Tofen on behalf of his sister Isebelt, but I cannot express myself in the language of human beings and I would like you to be the one who speaks to him as my interpreter. Vela the wolf slowly shook its head. What is this message? it asked at last. After listening, it sighed and said: It is true that I can make myself understood by human beings, but for fifty years now Enmek Tofen and his brothers Malabron, Lodr and Kodraf have been hunting me to try to wrest from me these silver scissors that I bear on my forehead. If I appeared before them they would put me to death and steal what is mine. But my advice to you is that you try to discuss the matter with the oldest being in the world, Cirus the eagle. I am sure that it will be able to convey Isebelt's message to Enmek Tofen and his brothers. Cirus was an enormous eagle that lived on the highest mountain in Tagen Ata, where this land borders on the dusty plains of Terra Ancha; from those heights it pecked the stars each night, continued Cold Hortensia after a brief pause in her narration. Once Gelra had taken its leave of Vela the wolf, it flew to the lower slopes of the mountain range where Cirus lived. Gelra called to Cirus, because the small wings of a starling could not carry it to the distant crags where lived the oldest animal in the world. As soon as Cirus the eagle heard its name, it flew down. At first it was scarcely as big as a wasp. It grew and grew and when it was above Gelra's head its wings covered the midday sun and plunged the countryside into black night for many leagues around. Gelra asked for its help to take woebegone Isebelt's message to her brothers. Cirus asked what this message was. It is true that I can speak the language of men, said the eagle after hearing Gelra. But there is just one man whom I would not dare approach, and that man is Enmek Tofen. He is the only human with the strength to carry me on his fist and make me practise falconry. I cannot, therefore, be your interpreter without grave risks to my freedom. Still, I do know who could do so: Sella the trout. This is the wisest creature in the world. And what happens next is that by now you must be growing a little tired of all this flitting from the oldest animal in the world to the wisest animal in the world, Cold Hortensia suddenly said, gazing open-mouthed at us. No, of course not, we all replied together. Indeed we were all burning to know how Enmek Tofen had responded to his maltreated sister's cry for help, and Cold Hortensia was deliberately interrupting her tale to keep us on tenterhooks. Her cigar had gone out, and she relit it with an ember from the fire. If you are so concerned, Cold Hortensia continued, I can tell you now that Sella the trout, an immense slimy being that had lived in the depths of the deepest lake in Tagen Ata ever since the beginning of the world, told Gelra the starling that it could not help, because it could not speak the language of humans. The starling was so disheartened that it began to shed bitter tears from an alder branch overhanging the pool in which Sella's enormous eyes were moving to and fro. The lake was one red sheet of metal. The sun was setting in the horizon of the western serras of Tagen Ata. Gelra's laments even affected the clumps of St. John's wort perfuming the banks of the lake. Don't you cry, said Sella with a merry laugh that made the water in the pool bubble and boil. Don't cry, because Isebelt's message has already reached its destination. How can that be? exclaimed the confused bird, letting loose a warble that was, in truth, a sob. Don't you forget, said Sella, that I am the wisest animal in the world. Look: Vela the wolf took your message to Enmek Tofen as soon as you left the Great Forest. Vela was hoping that Isebelt's brothers would, as a reward, stop hounding it to steal the silver scissors from its head. Cirus the eagle did exactly the same, hoping to squeeze out of Enmek Tofen, in return for the favour it was doing him, the promise that he would never capture it. The two of them, Vela and Cirus, were deceiving you when they said that they could not convey Isebelt's message. Neither of them wanted to take you with them, because they wanted all the credit to be theirs so that they could achieve their goals. Actually, once Enmek Tofen had received unhappy Isebelt's message, he — with the aid of his brothers — stripped the silver scissors from Vela the wolf, and enslaved Cirus the eagle. Gelra the starling felt happy because her mission had been accomplished, and she flew off in search of some hazel tree in which to rest and remember Isebelt's hair, as yellow and gentle as corn. Like Maribel's hair, I thought, closing my eyes for a moment so that all the golden light that my cousin was could flood the spaces of my wounded breast. I awoke from my daydream when Carrollas, with that comical air of concern that was characteristic of him, said in a loud voice: Can I ask you something? No, you can't, Maribel cut him off in a strangely resolute way. Only one little thing, insisted Carrollas. Maribel stood up. She had her back to the fire and her face was covered with shadow. There was a steely meekness in her manner. You know that certain utensils cannot be talked about in this house, Cold Hortensia finally said. I remember that time began to circulate sluggishly, the crackling of the fire became a roar, something like ice was chilling my neck. Cold Hortensia plunged her hand into the depths of her waist-pouch and for a while, which seemed to us like a century, a hard, long century, she rummaged around inside it. We were all looking at Hortensia because the silver scissors were inside each of us and they could not be talked about. Those were moments of horror. Finally Carrollas shrugged his shoulders and shook his head as Cold Hortensia took her watch out of her waist-pouch. It's time for you all to be going back home, she murmured in a hoarse and even rather tired voice. As the summer progressed, I was feeling more and more uncomfortable. It was clear that a secret spider's web was being spun between Maribel and Cold Hortensia. To tell the truth, it was not just a question of the cruel effect on me of seeing them, very close to each other, in an enigmatic attitude and bathed by moonlight, by the castle. It was that Maribel seemed to possess some strange previous knowledge of the story that Cold Hortensia was telling us. I realised, of course, that Maribel did not know the concrete facts, but she did seem to be able to interpret them in accordance with some deep meaning that was quite beyond me. How had she managed to gain control over such dark torrents of viscous liquids that had never existed? To tell the truth, distanced as I am by time and by the experiences I have undergone, I now think that what hurt me was a contact between Cold Hortensia and Maribel that left me out, excluded me. This sense of being an outsider was winding a hurtful ball of thread in my breast. I came to consider myself hounded by all those around me. And nothing could infuriate me more than those occasional references to stories told during the winter by Cold Hortensia to the youngsters of Vilanova, when neither Maribel nor I had been there. I even began to imagine that the stories Cold Hortensia narrated during the summer holidays were watered down for us, adapted to Lolo's and my (and perhaps also Maribel's) urban paltriness, while she reserved for the winter, for an audience of apprentice shoemakers, some smoking epic of cruelty and radical beauty. I also felt left out as I sat at table with father, mother and my cousin. There were days when I hardly spoke to Maribel and when, in spite of her insistent proposals of a ride on the tandem, I preferred a solitary walk to the top of Castromao Hill, to be eaten up by sadness there, and by sadness recreated. I don't know if it was just my imagination, but I thought I could observe, out of the corner of my eye, a glance of mutual understanding between my cousin and my father on a certain occasion when he asked her and not — as he always did — me to crush some ice for his mid-afternoon Daiquiri. And what happened next was that Cold Hortensia told us to meet her that evening in the Chaos wash-house. She had her sleeves rolled up and her big hands were red and wrinkled from washing clothes there all afternoon. The exercise had put colour into her sunken cheeks and sweat was dripping from her forehead beneath her headscarf. She placed the clothes in a great tub and we all sat down on the wall, next to the Brook, which was singing in an almost imperceptible voice. What a lovely time of the day that is, as dusk gathers, smelling of the soap, of the mud, of the green of the fields, of the coolness of birches and willows quivering in the gentle breeze in their profound, enamoured seclusion! Maribel was coming on roller skates along the upper road and her red skirt was clinging to her legs as she skated into the wind. I could feel my heart shattering inside me. When Enmek Tofen made the discovery, Cold Hortensia began, when he found out about the misfortune besetting Isebelt in A Nosa Terra, he summoned an assembly. At this assembly the Azerratas decided to invade A Nosa Terra. The Azerratas? What are Azerratas? I asked. I thought I could see looks of surprise on the faces of my Vilanova friends. Maribel smiled and shook her head, exactly as Cold Hortensia did. The inhabitants of Tagen Ata are called Azerratas, Hortensia explained in a matter-of-fact way. In the course of the assembly it was decided that Malabron should remain in the kingdom as its governor and that the army should be led by Enmek Tofen, with the assistence of his brothers Lodr and Kodraf. Our aim is to free Isebelt and recover our horses, the sword called Derbfoll and the Pote de Gradel, Enmek Tofen had said in a voice that echoed like a thunderclap throughout the Great Forest. The powerful voice of the lord of Tagen Ata soaked up humidity and fragrance as it passed through the Great Forest before soaring over the highest mountains and reaching A Nosa Terra. There's thunder at sea, said Dindadigoe's butcher as he pounded Isebelt's face. And she, smiling mysteriously, knew that the message taken by Gelra the starling had reached its destination. Enmek Tofen gathered together his company of human beings and his company of monkeys. He ordered them all to board a fleet of five hundred ships that immediately set sail and cut through the sea towards a certain port in A Nosa Terra in a town near what today is Gomesende. The blue sun of Tagen Ata shone on every prow and on the forehead of every warrior. The monkeys sang a monotonous and interminable barcarole. When Enmek Tofen calculated that his army must have reached A Nosa Terra and disembarked, he dressed himself for war in great garments of purple and ermine that reached his feet, he seized an assegai the shaft of which had been carved from the trunk of the tallest tree in the Great Forest, and he fastened to his hat the silver scissors of Vela the wolf. Then he called for Cirus the eagle, mounted it and flew off towards A Nosa Terra to place himself at the head of the army of Tagen Ata. In the interim, a boy who was scrambling over the rocks gathering mussels came panting before Dindadigoe. Sir, said the lad, at the entrance to the harbour there is a reedbed of enormous reeds that grow out of the sea. They aren't reeds, shouted Isebelt, who was sitting on a scutching-stone in the courtyard, they are the warships of Enmek Tofen, who is coming for me. A little later, a charcoal-maker came from the hills to the palace and informed Dindadigoe that something very strange was happening. On to a forest of walnut trees in the south of the country (in the place now known as Castro Laboreiro) a cloud of locusts had dropped, so enormous that they were like men, and they covered the branches of all the trees. That isn't a plague of locusts, shouted Isebelt as she swept the palace courtyard, that is Enmek Tofen's army of orang-utans, advancing on the branches of the trees so that his army of men can march over the ground. Not long after that the master of the hounds appeared before Dindadigoe, saying: In front of the forest of walnut trees a tower has appeared, as tall as the tower of your palace, with the sail of a boat on its highest part; on each side of the sail there is a flaming beacon; above the sail there is a star. A vast cloud hangs over the tower, and throws a black shadow for many miles around. You're wrong, shouted Isebelt, who was getting ready to tear the guts out of a stag, as was her duty, the tower is Enmek Tofen, the sail of a boat is his nose, and the beacons are his eyes, burning with rage and with his desire to free me. Dindadigoe climbed to the parapet walk of his palace. Curses, he said, looking to the south, it's true. That is Enmek Tofen, marching against me at the head of his armies of men and orang-utans. What shines on his forehead is not a star, but the silver scissors of Vela the wolf; and the black cloud is not a cloud, but the wings of Cirus the eagle, which are darkening the entire country. What was happening was that Enmek Tofen was making a display of his magnificence and was unfolding before Dindadigoe's startled gaze a fearful show of power and strength. Good for Enmek Tofen, shouted Lolo. Tripas and Carrollas kept silent, but they turned towards him with looks of displeasure and reproach. It's only a story, said Xela, with an obvious, although diffuse, intention to reprimand him. The fact of the matter, interposed Maribel with a disdainful look, the fact of the matter is that Enmek Tofen is an enemy of A Nosa Terra, and for myself I consider him to be a boastful, arrogant show-off. Well, insisted Lolo, I identify with Enmek Tofen. As far as I am concerned, A Nosa Terra is in the wrong; you have to be objective. Cold Hortensia was laughing away at us and looking at her watch. All that week Maribel was unusually nice to me, as if she wanted to show me clearly that she liked me. This, instead of cheering me up, made me feel a little uneasy. Something inside me was telling me that Maribel was feeling guilty and — this is the sad part — to blame for some kind of disloyalty towards me. And yet the ride to Allariz had been lovely. In Podentes, as the children came out of school they waved when they saw us go by on that strange bicycle. The heaviness of fields and mountain plots lightened as we approached the town. We walked through shy little squares, along charming streets. We compared Allariz to Santiago de Compostela, and Maribel, talking non-stop, displayed pieces of wisdom and erudition acquired, no doubt, from Otero Pedrayo's *Guide to Galicia*. She loved Romanesque art, and seeing her so happy made me happy too. As we walked along the bank of the River Arnoia, Maribel stayed silent before its dark, slow waters, and took my arm. Then she let me hold her hand. Her touch inflamed me, and I was the object of a rapid glance of amused reproach mixed with a smile. She gently freed her hand and I felt half happy and half dissatisfied. We returned home in the evening. As we arrived, we saw a pair of civil guards leaving my house. We were so tired that we hardly ate any supper and didn't ask any questions. Father (now, so long afterwards, I can picture it) had a serious look on his face and kept passing his hand over his shining bald head, which was nut-brown that year thanks to his morning constitutionals around the town wall. I didn't remember the visit of the civil guards until the following afternoon. I supposed that my father would be reading upstairs, and I went up to ask him about it and to chat for a while. I had an uncomfortable feeling, like a foreboding of something sad and harmful. When I walked into his study, without knocking at the door, I found Maribel sitting face to face with him. They were both silent, looking vaguely into space. They noticed my presence and they directed at me looks of great concentration which I interpreted as expressions of displeasure at being interrupted. Again I felt alone and betrayed. I was about to turn on my heel and retrace my steps. I bowed my head for a moment. When I looked up, I confirmed that Maribel was wearing, for my sake, the most resplendent of her smiles. Father was taking his automatic pistol from a drawer in his desk. It was a nine-bore short-barrelled Astra. I thought something horrible that I did not dare spell out, not even to myself. Look, he said, placing the pistol on the desk, the civil guard have been going round the houses warning everyone. There's a rabid dog wandering about and it could be dangerous for you two to go outside too often. I was discussing it with Maribel. If you ever want to go down to the river, tell me and I shall go with you, armed with my pistol. Just for safety's sake. A clucking of hens came up at this point from the street and filled my father's study with the sounds of the afternoon. Everything suddenly became normal and balanced. It was summer and we were in Vilanova. Its peace was threatening to crystallise everything, to stop the hours in their course. All was complete. Cold Hortensia had bought a red headscarf in Moreira's shop and we told her that it made her look really good. She laughed with satisfaction and scooped up water from the wooden bucket with a metal mug. We all drank of that cold heaviness and felt full up and longed for more. It was hot outside, the fire was out, all in the kitchen was coolness. Cold Hortensia was at work in the kneading trough and her naked arms displayed muscles tense from effort. She stopped to smoke and talk, sitting on a stool with her legs apart. So there you are, she said. Dindadigoe stood aghast in the terrible presence of Enmek Tofen. Isebelt was laughing and laughing. Isebelt in the courtyard of Dindadigoe's palace was like some mad woman. She was laughing and twirling around as if dancing. She was laughing and chanting the names of Enmek Tofen, Lodr and Kodraf as if they were the words of some absurd and monotonous canticle. Then she stopped her dancing and her singing and, with no pause in her laughing, she began to slit the throats of cows, pigs, hens, horses, smearing her face, her hands, her clothes with blood in an eternal, circular movement. The orang-utans howled while the human soldiers banged on their shields, on which the blue sun of Tagen Ata was depicted. Cirus the eagle flew back and forth over the houses of A Nosa Terra, and its cry was sonorous, felling maize-garners and weirs, tightening a noose around the hearts of the people. Then Dindadigoe sent heralds to Enmek Tofen. When they came before him they were received with severe courtesy. Isebelt has a son by Dindadigoe, they said. His name is En Dovel. If we come to an agreement, he will reign one day. He will unite the lands of A Nosa Terra and Tagen Ata. And so a balance will be maintained in the world for ever and ever. Very well, conceded Enmek Tofen, on the advice of his brother Lodr. The peacemaker, I commented. Maribel threw me a glance in which I noticed a clear warning-sign. That is true, Cold Hortensia agreed. That is true. His other brother, Kodraf, kept silence, a silence laden with displeasure, because he loved discord above all things. What happened next was that the men of A Nosa Terra and the men of Tagen Ata decided to make a feast to celebrate the peace agreement. The two armies came together around a great bonfire to eat and to drink. Cirus the eagle flew to Furriolo Hill and rested there with its head under a wing. The monkeys separated from the men and concentrated on a plain at the places we now call A Merca and A Manchica. There they began a series of lively dances to the rhythms of their drums and their horn-pipes. Since orang-utans don't drink beer or apple wine — which were the drinks of those olden times — they always prefer to separate from human beings on the occasion of assemblies and feasts, and to cel-ebrate their own peculiar ceremonies among themselves. Just when I was making up my mind to ask Cold Hortensia about the origins of Enmek Tofen's army of orang-utans, she, as if she had read my thoughts, turned her face towards me and, pulling her headscarf to one side, said: the war-monkeys were a present that Rama, a famous Indian prince, had made to Enmek Tofen one hundred years earlier, on the occasion of certain conflicts about which none of you will ever make me speak. You must know, though, that En Dovel, the son of Didadi-goe and Isebelt, was a handsome child, always smiling, who won everybody's heart. A crown of gold and precious jewels was placed upon his silky, jet-black locks. He was seated, naked except for his velvet belt studded with pearls, on a tall bench presiding over all the guests' chairs. En Dovel had his little hands crossed over his rosy breast. The heat of the great bonfire made his lips as red as two cherries. Everyone loved En Dovel. Both armies felt their hearts softening and weakening as they contemplated the boy who one day would unite the two lands and bring harmony to the whole world. But don't forget Kodraf. He is the traitor, the villain, the wretch who never rests and has to do evil without measure. I have already warned you about this poisonous presence. Blinded by fury in the face of so much happiness and so much beauty, Kodraf grasps his knife. He's going to kill the child, he's going to kill En Dovel, cried Xela, beside herself, covering her eyes with her apron. Course not, said Carrollas in dialect, he can't do that. The two armies and the two kings are there. Lodr is there; Cirus the eagle is on Furriolo Hill, and that's very near. Maribel took my hand and squeezed it hard. I do not remember whether Cold Hortensia continued speaking but we all saw clearly how Kodraf was leaping like a panther and seizing the child by the neck and slashing his breast open with one stroke of his knife. Kodraf, in front of everybody, was leaping up to the seat of honour occupied by En Dovel, taking hold of him and pulling his heart out. Silence fell on the feast. A metallic silence. The king of A Nosa Terra and the king of Tagen Ata were two statues. Kodraf, with an animal cry, was holding En Dovel by the legs and tossing him into the bonfire. He was holding En Dovel by the legs, as the huntsman holds the hare, and throwing him into the bonfire. And what happened next was that a blood-curdling clamour rose up from the army of A Nosa Terra, followed by the voice of Enmek Tofen who calls to Cirus, to the monkeys, who orders all his troops to withdraw, who seizes Isebelt and carries her on his back. Because the war is about to begin, my dears. A long, terrible war that will manure the valleys of A Nosa Terra with blood and carcasses. This was the situation, then, when we went to Celanova, to the festa of St. Roch. Maribel was wearing her patent-leather shoes, her white socks (with pompoms on the garters), her pink dress and a cardigan for the cold of the night. In the square the band was playing an interminable pasodoble. We walked side by side around the Cross. I could feel Maribel's chest on my arm. This dirty, hostile town, which we disliked so much, seemed at that moment like a piece of paradise. By the Galo bar, an argument erupts. The Vilanovans pull out their knives, and a lemonade bottle smashes against one of the pillars in the colonnade, a few inches from my head. There is a lot of shouting and the two gangs are going to meet again behind the houses, where it's dark and the maize grows. I joined the Vilanova gang, gritting my teeth and clenching my fists. There were as many in the Celanova gang as in ours. One of them brought out a revolver, with the stupid cackle of a peasant fool that turned my stomach and put a bitter taste into my mouth. I felt the lash of fear on my back and on the nape of my neck. I turned towards the lamp-post where I had left Maribel, as if to ask for her help. She was smiling calmly, looking in the direction of Calle Abaixo. Her hands were stretched out before her, as if she were asking someone's advice about what to do. Two stray punches connected with my cheeks and I fell flat on my face. As I lay on the ground I saw the lank figure of Cold Hortensia, who consulted her watch, looked at Maribel and made a brief, significant gesture (or at least I thought she made one) before she disappeared under the balcony of a mud and straw house. It was then that Maribel stopped the fight. After a silence in which the murmuring of the crowd in the square came across to us, the band attacked a Brazilian samba. As if she were obeying an order from Cold Hortensia, Maribel placed herself between the two rival gangs. People were emerging from the bars near the Cross, prudently gesturing towards us and arguing among themselves. Maribel gave a graceful little leap and told us all to go and dance. She pounced on the cretin with the revolver and threatened him with that enchanting little hand that I loved. In the light of the street-lamps, Maribel's head glittered like burnished metal. I suddenly realised that Cold Hortensia was watching over that scene from some dark dormer or attic. She was somehow encouraging and directing Maribel's movements, I was sure of it. Muttering among themselves, the braves of Celanova withdrew towards the tombolas and the merry-go-rounds in the Alameda. It had all been very quick, and I was already in heaven. We were dancing. Maribel's waist was yielding to my encircling arm. We were so close that I could smell the aroma of her face. But in the middle of a waltz she suddenly broke free and curtly asked if we could go back home. I'm very tired, she said. Maribel's eyes were searching for something or someone in the crowd. I felt sapped by sadness and solitude. Why was it always the same? Why? as I still ask myself, so many years after that unforgettable summer. Why did a sign of interest from that adored being always have to be followed by another one of indifference, or even a certain mute hostility? What feelings did I inspire in my beloved cousin? Oh, what a miserable ride back to Vilanova, the two of us pedalling away on the tandem like complete strangers, with me plunged into the blackest of moods and her humming under her breath snatches of stupid rumbas and sambas! At all events, when we said goodnight in the sitting room, Maribel took my cheeks into her hands, which I noticed were strangely damp and cold. She directed a deep look at me, with a faint, quivering smile in the corners of her mouth. I felt a mad desire to take possession of that mouth with my mouth of fire. She kissed my face and went to her room, as she pulled the rubber-band out of her pony tail and a starry cascade of hair flowed over her back. Cold Hortensia consulted her watch. When it was five o'clock in the afternoon of the day after the criminal sacrifice of the child En Dovel, she said, the king of A Nosa Terra drew his sword Derbfoll from its sheath and a blinding light made all his men cover their eyes with their shields. Facing him, Enmek Tofen placed his hat on his head, and from the scissors of Vela the wolf shot seven lightning flashes that wounded the eyes not only of the soldiers of Tagen Ata but also of those of A Nosa Terra. It was the sign for battle to commence. It was, you know, a hard, bloody battle that lasted four days and put an end to the second of the invasions suffered by A Nosa Terra, the invasion by Tagen Ata. The first day was dedicated by both armies to a review of their own troops and a scrutiny of the enemy troops, to deciding upon their strategies and celebrating their banquets. Tagen Ata had five thousand men, ten thousand orang-utans given by Rama, and one eagle, Cirus. A Nosa Terra only had five thousand men on a war footing. Tagen Ata's numerical superiority was, then, evident. And so, while Enmek Tofen's men spent the night in anticipated celebration of their victory and their monkeys danced in Sarreaus and Cirus pecked stars in the Serra de Silva Oscura, Dindadigoe's men drank beer and apple wine with the melancholy of those who already consider themselves dead and defeated. Nevertheless the king of A Nosa Terra just smiled and smiled, like someone who knows the most hidden secret of things; and, in some mysterious way, his men had a vague trust in their leader's legendary wisdom. On the second day, at dawn, the two kings decided on their battle plans on a plain near to what we now call Parderrubias. Enmek Tofen put his human beings in the rearguard and formed three divisions of orang-utans. The first of these was to attack the centre of A Nosa Terra's ranks, splitting its army in two. Each of the other two divisions was to attack one of these halves. And finally Enmek Tofen would order Cirus and his men into action to finish off A Nosa Terra's army. They're going to defeat A Nosa Terra, Carrollas said, jumping to his feet in alarm. We're done for, Hortensia, Xela exclaimed. Maribel let loose a splendid guffaw (how beautiful she was, my God), and just hearing it made me feel hot between my legs. Don't be afraid, you cowards, said Maribel with conviction and with the indifferent and disconcerting gesture of one who knows and understands the affairs of former times, just like Cold Hortensia who, disregarding us, stirred the pot of broth as she puffed away at a whiff that Lolo had brought her. But the next thing that happened was that the monkeys carried out their task to perfection. They divided Dindadigoe's ranks. They attacked the two separated halves. They howled and screeched like devils. Many men of A Nosa

Terra were killed. A lot of orang-utans died, too. But what happened was that Dindadigoe's men did not diminish in number. In the course of the battle, there were fewer and fewer orang-utans, yet the number of A Nosa Terra's human beings remained the same. The Pote de Gradel! Enmek Tofen's prudent brother Lodr exclaimed. The Pote de Gradel! Tripas, Lolo, Carrollas, Xela and I all exclaimed together. Cold Hortensia and Maribel were slyly smiling and looking at each other. The Pote de Gradel! Enmek Tofen finally exclaimed, and his voice carried to the furthest extremes of A Nosa Terra, as far as the sea and beyond the sea. Yes indeed, what had happened was that Dindadigoe had commanded a great fire to be lit. Upon it he had placed the pot of life and death, that is to say the Pote de Gradel. He ordered each man that was killed to be boiled in the pot and the man came out alive, giving off smoke and ready to continue fighting. Alive maybe, Maribel objected, but unable to speak. Actually, Cold Hortensia clarified after a silence, actually the dead men were turned into men of the Other World, and that was the reason why they didn't talk. But they were of use to Dindadigoe for fighting, and that was A Nosa Terra's main concern at the time. What is more, who can affirm that many people in this story, even entire nations, did not belong to the Other World? Isn't that so? And without giving any of us a chance to reply, Cold Hortensia went on with the story of the battle of Parderrubias. And so it was that, at midday, Enmek Tofen ordered his men, amassed in one corps, to deploy in a single line and to charge at the men of A Nosa Terra, so as to harry them with their strength of numbers and prevent them from boiling and resuscitating the dead in the Pote de Gradel. He also gave Cirus the eagle a precise order: to seize Dindadigoe in its beak and drop him in the middle of the sea that separated A Nosa Terra from Tagen Ata. Standards were hoisted aloft and A Nosa Terra was deafened by war-cries. Like a flood of turbulent waters, Enmek Tofen's men poured on to the plain of Parderrubias. You would have seen so many lances shattering on shields and breast-plates, so many spears plunging through men and out of their backs, the pennants red with enemy blood, so many riderless horses neighing in the scrublands. When all the lances had been broken, and their fragments littered the plain and protruded from the bodies of men and war-palfreys, the soldiers of both armies drew their swords and struck each other such well-aimed blows that they sliced men clean through the waist or split them down the middle, and their guts spilled out over their saddle-trees. For a moment Dindadigoe thought that he was not going to keep up with the work of retrieving and resuscitating dead men. But he ordered the fire to be built higher and the Pote de Gradel belched smoke like a volcano, boiled in a fury of bubbles and speeded up its magical work. Enmek Tofen's army, on the other hand, only dwindled. In the late afternoon a fearful shriek came down from the clouds and halted the battle awhile. It was Cirus the eagle carrying out its mission and swooping like a thunderbolt on to Dindadigoe. And this is what happened next, my children. In this desperate predicament, the king of A Nosa Terra seizes his sword Derbfoll backhanded and hurls it at Cirus like a dart. The sword cleaves the air, casting a divine splendour upon the battle, and buries itself in the eagle's breast. Mortally wounded, Cirus disappears into the horizon with heart-rending cries of farewell to Enmek Tofen and plunges into the sea, where to this very day the sword called Derbfoll awaits the one who it is said will rescue it from silence and defeat. At the uncertain hour of sundown, when the shadows were turning long and cold, Rama's host of orang-utans retreated from the battle and, after a short meeting, decided to desert to A Nosa Terra. Hostilities were interrupted at nightfall and each army withdrew to its encampment. Great bonfires were lit and the cries of the wounded pierced the stench-filled air hanging over the plain of Parderrubias. Both armies gave themselves over to drink. The full moon spilt frozen silver on to the carnage. The third day of the battle of Parderrubias dawned with a clouded sky. Isebelt, seeing the men of Tagen Ata on the brink of defeat, dreamed up one last trick. She disguised herself as one of the warriors of A Nosa Terra, and armed herself with all the appropriate weapons. Under the cover of the fog, she hastened to the part of the plain closest to A Nosa Terra's camp. And there she fell to the ground, and the men of A Nosa Terra thought that she was one of their dead. They carried her to the Pote de Gradel and began to boil her in it. And then Isebelt pushed with her back and with her feet against the sides of the pot. She pushed with immense strength, with superhuman strength. She thought of Tagen Ata, of the outrages that Dindadigoe had perpetrated against her and her people. She thought of Enmek Tofen. Her small strength became an immense strength. With the power of a giant, of an atrocious being like Enmek Tofen, Isebelt split asunder the Pote de Gradel, and perished in the effort. Isebelt split the pot. And then, deep dark voices of lament were heard. They came from the Lake of Antela, that is to say Lake Beón. They were the bitter voices of the people of the giant who had brought the Pote de Gradel out from the Other World. The battle ceased. It was cold. The mist had got into the bones of men and of monkeys. On the fourth day, Enmek Tofen convoked his brothers Lodr and Kodraf. All he had left was one hundred men willing to wage war. After mourning Isebelt, they agreed to fight the men of A Nosa Terra to the death. The enemy has an advantage of one hundred to one, Lodr the prudent had said, but it has to be borne in mind that they no longer possess the Pote de Gradel. And what happened next was that, drawing strength from where they had none, and bleeding from appalling wounds that left their entrails exposed, the men of Enmek Tofen entered the battle to the cry of Tagen Ata, Tagen Ata, Tagen Ata. The men of A Nosa Terra, saddened and unnerved by the loss of the Pote de Gradel, responded without enthusiasm to the attack. A clangour of blows and cries, a ringing of metal, a loathsome howling of monkeys, filled the plain of Parderrubias. The least valiant fought like wolves. The men of Tagen Ata knew that each corpse remained a corpse. The thought that the Pote de Gradel would no longer bring any enemy back to life increased their strength a hundredfold. Tagen Ata, Tagen Ata, shouted Lolo, burning with excitement. Shut up, you fool, we belong to A Nosa Terra, I interrupted in a firm voice. Cold Hortensia served all of us with bowls of that thick, redolent broth she made. However long I live I shall never forget the smell and the taste of the broth that Cold Hortensia made. By early evening, the forces of Enmek Tofen and Dindadigoe were even. In the twilight, the two leaders were confronting and killing each other. When the western sky of A Nosa Terra was turning into a kind of violet pottage, the battle of Parderrubias was ending with the annihilation of both armies. After making a pyre out of all his fallen, with Enmek Tofen and Isebelt on the top, Lodr put Kodraf to death. He had been the cause of all the ill that had befallen Tagen Ata. He had castrated Dindadigoe's horses and he had killed En Dovel. Kodraf's corpse was left unburied, upon the earth of Parderrubias, to be the food of beasts and birds of prey. The pyre burnt in a vigorous, intense flame. Soon the plain was filled with the stench of burnt flesh. The smoke rose straight towards the skies of A Nosa Terra. Weeping seas from his eyes, Lodr withdrew towards the sea. But before he embarked he decided that so much death and destruction must not be definitive, and he fervently wished for something that I shall not tell you by any manner of means, however much you ask me to. As far as wishing is concerned, what I had wished for time and again, that summer, was rain. And what happened next was that the rain was here. The summer was showing signs of coming to an end and, with it, our holidays in Vilanova. A new time stretched before me: the return to Ourense. The return to a tedium of fog and cold. From a certain day onwards, Cold Hortensia changed the way she wore her headscarf. As if the cold had got into her, she started going about in a hunched-up position and with her headscarf tied under her chin. In the morning we would see her walking with her arms crossed over her chest and a thick shawl over her shoulders. It was the end of the summer. One day, when I was coming back from buying a "Gran Chicos" comic (with those drawings by Ben Bolt that I liked so much) in Celanova, the grey afternoon suddenly became darker. The light went and an uncomfortable breeze presaged rain. Together with the shower, a cloth of sadness fell on to my soul. I entered Vilanova through Porto de Outeiro, leaving behind a window the face of Dona Sara, Luís Soto's mother, signalling to me to take shelter in her house from that deluge. When I reached the Square, I don't know why I took it into my head to look in the direction of Areal. From its depths, from the shadows and the dust, my father and Maribel were emerging under an umbrella. Maribel was hanging on to my father's arm and tripping happily along. The umbrella was covering their faces. They didn't see me until they were upon me. I thought I could detect that they were feigning naturalness and deliberately ignoring my harsh, sullen expression. I don't know if there will be room for the three of us under the umbrella, I had said. This was an unexpected shower, my father had commented. If the shower was so unexpected, I don't know why he left home armed with an umbrella and Maribel in a raincoat and fichu, I thought bitterly. As if everybody was conspiring to push me away into a corner, as if nobody wanted me, as if the whole world was isolating me cunningly and with meticulous care, I felt myself die as my father put an arm round my shoulder and Maribel took into her warm hand one of mine, stiff and wet. When we reached the porch, father went whistling upstairs to his books and his work. The tandem lay on its side in a dark corner of the porch, strangely forsaken (I thought): like a dead tandem. When I turned my gaze to Maribel I noticed that she, too, was looking at the tandem. The holidays are coming to an end, Maribel said with glassy, empty eyes. She came to my side and asked me why I was shivering, and ran her fingers through my wet hair. The holidays are coming to an end, Maribel, I said on the verge of tears. At this moment, with the hindsight of one who remembers events many years later, I am thinking that at that instant a certain sweet, magical sequence, the unrepeatable summer, drew to a close.

The tandem lying on the stone floor of the porch, the cold invading my bones, Maribel a statue, anxiety, anxiety. Even mother, at supper, deposited her absent look upon me and asked me if I felt ill. Cold Hortensia is going to miss your visits, my father said with a smile that seemed to me to be intended as some kind of suppression of my mother's solicitude, always so cryptic. Maribel was nibbling at a biscuit and vaguely humming a song that I had never heard before. I felt overwhelmed by an enormous, vacant jealousy of I knew not what or whom. We were all gazing at the window. Suddenly a kind of milky gleam passed backwards and forwards in white, broken lines against the shadows behind. It had stopped raining. It's the owl, my father announced. We did go to Cold Hortensia's a few more times. She gave us lots of broth, and even cake on her baking days. But she refused, with various excuses, to continue the story. The lads of Vilanova explained that Cold Hortensia was much less talkative in the winter, and that what little she did say was very hard to understand. Finally, when just one day remained before our return to Ourense, Cold Hortensia told us that what Lodr had so fervently wished for was Enmek Tofen's rebirth. Before laying his corpse on top of the pyre, he tore out his heart. Lodr was sailing towards Tagen Ata with the heart of Enmek Tofen. Of the fifty ships just one was left. The objects from the Other World, lost for ever. The orang-utans, the human beings and Cirus the eagle had all died. In Tagen Ata, Malabron was waiting to reconstruct the country with Lodr. In A Nosa Terra assemblies of peasants were going to be held, to start a new epoch that would do away for ever with the tyranny of the feudal lords. Kneeling on the bridge of his ship, Lodr held aloft the heart of Enmek Tofen in a silver goblet. A blinding light emanated from the heart and strange winds took control of the sails and the rudder. The sea was singing a manifold song of sadness on the gunwale and on the keel. With a stern face, Lodr drops Enmek Tofen's heart into the sea that separates A Nosa Terra from Tagen Ata. As the heart enters the waters, Lodr is blinded by a resplendent lightning flash. The day darkens, fearful thunderclaps resound, the whole world is covered by a cloak of cold. And what happens next, my children, is that the heart of Enmek Tofen is eaten by a ballan wrasse of the rocks. Days later, the fish is caught and sold at market in a small town in Tagen Ata, lost in the dark confines of the Great Forest. Bought by a girl called María, it is eaten by her with chestnuts and virgin olive oil. At this moment María conceives Enmek Tofen, by mouth. In her womb the powerful hero of Tagen Ata is formed again. And he will be born again, in accordance with Lodr's wishes, and maybe A Nosa Terra will be threatened again. But all this is the stuff of other tales, suitable to be told at another time that is not this time. Go away now, because I'm feeling very tired and I've told you the story. It was the story of one of the five invasions that A Nosa Terra has suffered. A story that, like all stories, is incomplete. On the following day we loaded our suitcases on to the old De Dion-Bouton coach of the Suárez Bus Company. We installed ourselves in the saloon compartment. The Campo do Cristal was damp and invaded by fog. Mother and I sat on one side; in front of us, Maribel and father. I could feel my heart shrinking with nostalgia and love for A Nosa Terra. We were going back to an Ourense of disillusionment and discomfort. I looked at my cousin and saw her smiling that enigmatic smile that I had hated throughout the summer. Her still eyes were fixed on a precise spot. And then she made a clear gesture of farewell with her beloved little hand. As quick as lightning I pressed my nose against the coach window and looked at where Maribel was looking. There was nobody on those roadside rocks. Maribel was still smiling in that direction, smiling at nothing, as she arranged her pony tail and even muttered some slightly dubious words. Suddenly it came to me. Suddenly the smell of Cold Hortensia's kitchen came to me. The coach was clattering into motion and I realised that father, as he lit his pipe, was winking at me as if something had amused him. I felt a concentrated rage and I put my arm round mother's shoulders and the De Dion-Bouton was already negotiating the Carfaxiño bends; the tandem was tied on to the luggage rack; and goodbye Vilanova, all of us on our way back to days of sorrow and certainties.

(From *Amor de Artur*, 1982)

Return to Tagen Ata

In memory of Francisco Cerviño and of those hours, dead now too, in
Pontevedra, when it all began and Tagen Ata was being born.

I

The forest was all aglow, a tiny star on every leaf. The atmosphere
was damp, still, warm. Seminal smells and dense pollen heralded
spring. My feet sank into a mass of rotting leaves, moss, tender shoots,
cytinus and bluebells. I was walking along, following the old king's
highway. The Great Forest of Tagen Ata[1] was like a huge bell which
echoed the proud beating of my heart. My horse, behind me, snorted
from time to time, and I could feel the pungent blast of its breath on
the back of my neck. How deep was the emotion I felt as I went into
the wood, in search of what was mine!

1. The central part of Tagen Ata is taken up by a huge stretch of forest which comprises
60 per cent of the total surface area of the country. The Great Forest is a national
symbol. It is formed mainly by boreal species (chestnuts, oaks, ferns) with a fauna of
weasels, squirrels and capercaillies. There is a notable Mediterranean influence which
adds scrub and evergreen trees to this base. In many of the clearings in the forest,
there are small towns and villages dedicated to the manufacture of charcoal and to
forestry. Some of the large factories in the city of T. use wood as a raw material.

II

My name is Rotbaf Luden, I'm a single woman, 23 years old, and I was born in a colony of Azerratas[2] on the island of Anatí, a steamy land crackling with flying ants, inhabited by poor, beautiful negroes who eat a fruit called mandinga or arahuaco, practise spiral magic, express themselves in physical contact and dance, and are barbarously exploited by a perfumed class of opulent half-castes. I close my eyes and pronounce the warm syllables of Anatí: my mouth fills with molasses or coffee, before me appears Nana Rigolade, the servant who brought me up, showing off her bright organdie turban, with her hands on her spare tyre, like a jolly, racist cocoa advertisement, and all the sulphurous matter of the Creole language convulses my ears and brings swarms of green and yellow flies before my eyes.

How far away Anatí and all my past life seem now I am here in Tagen Ata! The community of Azerratas was made up of merchants and political exiles. Those of us who had been born in Anatí learned the language and the customs of Tagen Ata from our elders and lived with the memory of our far-off land. Conquered seven hundred years earlier by the monotheistic green-skinned warriors of Terra Ancha, Tagen Ata had become a part of their dusty religious empire.[3] The mystique of a conquered people filled the evenings of the emigrants in Anatí, who dreamed of returning victorious and liberating their beautiful country, the centre of which was the Great Forest. Ever since I was a teenager, I had learned to hate Terra Ancha, to curse its oppression, and to abominate the treachery of those Azerratas who had sold out to the colonialists. At an early age, when I was fifteen, I joined the overseas branch of I.T.A.[4] At that time I had an image of myself as a round-faced girl with bright almond eyes, a huge, fresh

2. Azerratas is the name given to the natives of Tagen Ata. It is a word of learned origin. In the old language — now extinct — of the Len Empire, the provinces — seven at the time — which now make up Tagen Ata were known as the Azerraten. The word Azerratas (both masculine and feminine) in the modern language of Tagen Ata is a calque from this toponym, with the loss of the Len nominal flexion and plural formation.

3. In former times, a variant of the Muslim religion took root in Terra Ancha — a parched, infertile plain to the north-east — and this turned the good pastoral people into fanatics, and impelled them to conquer neighbouring kingdoms. This happened towards the end of the twelfth century. Since then, Tagen Ata has been under the control of Terra Ancha.

mouth, black tresses, rather quiet, shy and nostalgic, long legs. Because I.T.A. didn't have any specific women's sections, I joined a mixed "mutual".[5] This enabled me to have relationships, not of a very erotic nature, with boys of my own age, mainly during festas and patriotic excursions. We were unredeemed, frustrated, consumed by longing. But something inside us, the knowledge that we were racially pure, the chosen ones, helped us to keep our heads held high.

Terra Ancha was a country of grovelling Moorish fanatics. For us emigrants in Anatí, the technical and cultural inferiority of the blacks and the creoles only reinforced our comforting ethnic self-satisfaction. At that time, encouraged by refugees from the old country, the overseas branch maintained a strong belief in a short-term victory. Our brothers in the Resistance would soon launch the liberation struggle which would conclude with the end of Terra Ancha's rule. What we did was to lay on plenty of festas, with a profusion of bunting, children singing, lemonade, piqué skirts (and pleated ones), flashy white trousers, Panama hats, boaters, raffles for literary prizes, and classical poetry readings. There were also suppers for elders and heads of families, with stereotyped speeches and ritual allusions to our enslaved homeland. Cordial links, in general, with the distant Tagen Ata, and a certain languid aversion towards any analytical awareness of its social evolution. Our hearts were in control of us, and we lost ourselves in the pleasures and the passions of our ghetto, and we abandoned Tagen Ata imperceptibly, inexorably, to the cotton-wool paradise of familiar myths.

This, then, was the world in which, at the age of twenty-three, I became a member of the supreme council of the overseas branch. After a long, forty-eight hour session, pausing only to eat and sleep, the ruling body decided to send me to Tagen Ata, with the mission of making contact with the Resistance. I refused, secretly hoping that my refusal would not be accepted. It was not accepted. There was nothing suspicious about my appearance: I looked normal and even reassuring,

4. "Irmandade de Tagen Ata" Tagen Ata Brotherhood. This was a secret society formed in 1903 in order to fight against the oppression of Terra Ancha. In its first period called "the Ulm Roan period", it was feeble, racist and idealistic, with a cultural leaning. It later changed its orientation.

5. The name given to I.T.A. groups.

I could use my doctorate in classical Len[6] to justify my trip, and these facts made me the ideal person to carry out the task. That was how, a virgin, full of faith in our liberation and willing to make any sacrifice, I set sail for Tagen Ata.

It wasn't difficult for me to make the change from the land where I had been born to the country of my ancestors. It was really just a return to Tagen Ata, where I had always been. And my parents were not the centre of my world. They were cheerful, young and sceptical. They had always lived right on the edge of the ghetto, with one foot in the cosmopolitan neo-colonial society and the other in the inbred rituals of the Azerrata community, and they regarded my involvement in I.T.A. and my interest in comparative linguistics with a mixture of affectionate irony and proud respect.

Fortunately, both they and I had seen and read so many Azerrata plays in which the patriotic youngster, born in New York, leaves his mother and father to go and fight in Tagen Ata, that everything worked out magnificently from the start. I shall never forget Mum: pleated knee-length skirt, satin stockings, picture hat tipped to the right, lips of a baby painted in the shape of a heart, tall and slim. I felt proud of her elegance, in the latest Yankee fashion, and the studied indifference with which she fanned herself with her gloves. Dad, making great efforts to hide his feelings, lit his pipe and, hands behind his back, started pacing around the wicker chairs and tables on the roof terrace, rolling off pieces of advice for the journey. But Nana Rigolade, who had never seen an Azerrata play, made the group lose its bourgeois composure, hugging and kissing me and making me cry in her arms before the impatience and vague irritation of my parents, who ended up adding their tears to ours, just as if they knew nothing at all about Azerrata theatre. Finally we set off, somewhat calmer, towards the docks.

6. Some two thousand years ago, the country of Len imposed its language and its rule on hundreds of other countries throughout the world that were physically accessible to it. Invaded, centuries later, by neighbouring countries and torn apart by internal centrifugal forces, the Empire broke up, giving rise to new ethnic groupings whose languages were based on local corruptions of classical Len. Tagen Ata and Terra Ancha are among the nations that were built on the ruins of the Len Empire.

III

It was night. I wrote this page in my diary: "From the bridge of the ship which was slowly approaching the shore I could make out the lights of the never-before-seen dreamland of my heart eternal husband Tagen Ata wine that fills my mouth horse of my heartbeat gardenia in my breast oh oh and then like an indescribable wave the spiral of wails overflowing from the salt of the sea all the heart of this blue land Great Forest centre of my world arising towards me with all its vegetable aroma fleshless hand welcome of my unseen dead ancestors turned into earth repeated in ferns oh penetrating my nostrils making me oh quiver flooding my eyes." I wept.

IV

I disembarked. I went through customs. Unshaven men in uniforms, with gold teeth and the typical hard look of Terra Ancha in command of their faces, opened my luggage and questioned me. I spoke to them in the Azerrata language, and I noticed that they were containing their indignation. I rented a car — a powerful Bentley — which left me at an inn right on the edge of the Great Forest. Then I decided to go in search of my first contact, Ulm Roan, and took the necessary steps.

Ulm Roan was heir to the teaching of C. Roaç, who in turn had been heir to the teaching of Diugo Nokao. All three of them had been considered, each in his own time, to be princes of Azerrata poetry, restorers of the language, and definers of our oppressed nation. They had all sung the mysteries of the Great Forest and of autumn in the vineyards of the valleys of the south, and had sung the praises of various heroes living between the thirteenth and the seventeenth centuries. Ulm Roan's beautiful thoughts circulated, usually by word of mouth, in Anatí. "It is necessary to give priority to the *spirit*." "Let us put into practice the values of our own *personality*." "We need to give our language cultural prestige: let us give it a *metaphysical* dimension." "Lyricism and fantasy are the expression of the intimate *spiritual* freedom of our people." These slogans, muttered by those who were most initiated, were to be heard at the routine I.T.A. meetings and were respected like strange, half-understood Latin mottoes.

I received a phone call: I was to be met at the Bar Encantiño in the village of Ok. I must not lose sight of the secrecy of my mission (be careful, be very careful).

The bar was tiny, and the village, too, was very small. An oak door creaked as I pushed it open. At first I couldn't see anything. When my eyes had got used to the dark, I managed to make out a square room with a few scattered wooden tables. I sat down at one of them, already occupied by a hazy figure.

"Ulm Roan?"

"No."

I got up.

"Sit down, please."

I sat down again.

"Wine?"

"Thank you."

He poured me some red wine into a china bowl. I drank, and it was cool yet hot in my throat. I flushed. (In Anatí, wine is virtually unknown.)

"When can I visit Ulm Roan?"

I was gradually able to make out his features. He was a shrunken old man. He was wearing a celluloid collar and a bow tie. He had a broad-brimmed hat on his head.

"Is Ulm Roan expecting you?"

"The overseas branch of I.T.A..."

"Hold your tongue. Neither the name nor the initials of that society can be mentioned in Tagen Ata. Remember this: it does not exist."

"Is this a security measure?"

"Just abide by what I have told you. That organisation does not exist."

The man's voice was weak, it sounded weary. In a corner of the tavern, a young man was passionately reading a poem in the Azerrata language to the girl who was sitting beside him. It sounded monotonous. The youth had long hair and he chain-smoked, pausing, coughing. A broken thread of words reached my ears. They surely contained some new light, steel, muscle. I felt that something alive and dynamic was assailing heavy, ancestral garments I was wearing. I felt lost in Tagen Ata. I became impatient.

"You must take me to Ulm Roan!"

"No."

"What's the problem?"

"That's the point: there isn't any problem."

"What?"

"There isn't any problem. You can go alone. There's no need to take any precautions at all to go and see Ulm Roan nowadays!"

The darkness was becoming less dense; other customers were sitting with their elbows on the tables, drinking wine or tankards of beer. A skeletal priest was staring at a calendar which showed a soldier in a kepi, a cape gathered behind him, and bands swathing his shins, cheerfully blowing a bugle. A pink cloud was coming out of the bugle, and in the middle of the cloud was a notice inviting all brave young men to join the Terra Ancha foreign legion.

"I need Ulm Roam's address, of course."

The old man gave me the address and got to his feet. He was tall and round-shouldered. He walked slowly towards the door. Half-way across the room he stopped, turned round and came back to me. He did not speak; he fixed me with a gaze I shall never forget: a gaze of affection and concern. He had a deep furrow between his eyebrows, and a pointed red nose. He raised my chin and kissed me on the forehead. Then he hurried out. "Sois sage," recited the youth, now in French, "oh ma Douleur." I don't know why I found a strange relationship between the poem and the uneasy feeling that the stranger's kiss had left me with. I got up slowly. I went out into the street. It was evening, and a soft breeze made me light-headed. I felt as if I were laden with jasmine blossom.

V

Before going to see Ulm Roan, I decided to pay a visit to my Aunt Natalia. Of all my relatives I chose her as the one to get to know, perhaps because my mother had singled her out, among all her sisters, for a special affection, which she passed on to me by means of "emanation" — as my father would say, fond as he was of his elementary expressive discoveries — or perhaps because what I knew about her could only attract my curiosity and favourably incline me towards her. At that time, I was also enough of a little innocent to give too much importance to a person's youth, as if this were a positive quality, and my Aunt Natalia was on that uncertain border of the ages, between thirty and thirty-five, when a person is firmly installed in maturity and yet in her glances and the mechanism of her gestures, in her desires and her physical form, active remains of youth still simmer (those remains on to which a person clings, with varying degrees of anguish, accumulating all kinds of ballast to try to slow the indestructible passage of time). What also played a part in my decision to go and see her was the image of a sceptical, worldly-wise intellectual conveyed to me by my parents, an image that captivated me, but also inspired me with a kind of fear — though I wouldn't admit it even to myself — that her cynical Voltairianism would undermine the solidity of my ideological principles.

I boarded the tram, then, to T., where she lived, and great was my surprise when, shortly after we left the area where the inn was situated, the countryside began to change into a city. It even seemed as if the houses, or rather shacks, had been made to appear by the spell cast by the thousands of metallic sounds made by the tram ("fe, fe, ferrové, ferrovello," an emigrant poet had written in Anatí, admirably capturing the clattering and the pounding of the trams of T.). The first houses, surrounded by sizeable plots of land, each with its pile of straw and its lean-to shed; then others, in the middle of little cabbage patches; further on, yet more of them, each stuck behind its tiny garden (where the heliotropes, the arum lilies and the ox-eye daisies painted the square of the tram window in tones of yellow, red and white, all mixed together in my retina by the vehicle's speeding and turning, like some fiery impressionist painting); and finally other houses, all joined on to each other, forming narrow streets that led into tiny squares where the tram stopped; and, as new passengers got on, all with a distinctly proletarian aspect (that old man with fair hair and an absent look on his scarred face, stiffly smoking an ancient pipe, carrying under his arm a blue folder that perhaps contained his accounts or the trade union receipts, or the petition demanding running water for his street, or the manuscript of an article for a socialist or anarcho-syndicalist newspaper, or the forms, cards and X-rays with which the complicated bureaucracy of the national health service sends him to and fro), I was taking the opportunity to study the semi-rural construction of the little houses, all so clean, with their outside stairs leading up to stone balconies, and their wooden shutters painted in bright, uniform, solid greens, blues and yellows looking so proud against a gleaming background of whitewashed stone walls.

I soon recognised the structure, or lack of structure, characteristic of the Northern Quarter, which I had heard talked about so often in emigrant circles in Anatí, mainly because it was indeed so characteristic, but also because it had been used and abused as a setting by Azerrata literary portrayers of local customs who, sentimentally attached to the countryside and to rural life — because of the romantic identification between peasant life and the deep meaning of Tagen Ata — but conditioned to write about urban realities, rather childishly made use of this part of T., a loose collection of villages that had in recent times spontaneously grown to create the Northern Quarter: an utterly false intellectual position that had already been destroyed by studies in social anthropology, applied to T. in general and to the Quarter in particular, initiated by that excellent man Kleines, whom I was to meet at my Aunt Natalia's house, and later to be continued by a group of brilliant followers.

Aunt Natalia had the habit of holding get-togethers in her house every Wednesday, attended by two or three people invited in rotation and usually selected from the city's intellectual circles. My aunt was then in her prime (meaning that she wasn't yet the unsociable, lonely person given to erotic obsessions that she was to become years later, after her strange marriage to Colonel Olsen and her subsequent widowhood and emotional neglect), she was sought after by the petty-bourgeois literary and academic sectors of society, and she could afford to select her guests, reducing her gatherings to the minimum possible number of participants because, as she herself said, "When there are more than four guests, there's no possibility of any real dialogue, and in the efforts you make to create one without people's attention wandering you waste a lot of energy, and by the end of the evening you're worn out, and it just isn't worthwhile even if you do manage to put some sort of order into the ideas put across, because then things become so forced that you get the impression you're at a committee meeting or a faculty seminar instead of a get-together of friends."

I became aware of her conversational skills when I first met her and she gave a cry of delight on hearing my name, as her round, fleshy cheeks flushed bright scarlet, a tuft of her hair fell over one eye, her glasses slid down to the tip of her nose, and the thin, semi-circular lines of her eyebrows were accentuated as she raised them high. She took me by the hand into the lounge; she sat me down on a sofa, while she made herself comfortable above me on the piano stool; she took my face into her hands; she talked and made me talk in such a way and with such discretion that not a single conventional question about my family, not one inopportune inquiry into the purpose of my journey, came from her full, optimistic mouth. Half an hour after meeting Aunt Natalia any traces of tension in me had disappeared, and I was surprised to find myself with my head resting on the back of the sofa, my legs crossed, a cigarette in my hand, watching how the beautiful grand piano gave out reflections as it was wounded by the shaft of light that came in through the slit between the two heavy curtains, and asking my aunt, in a hoarse voice and gliding over the consonants — the sign of perfect relaxation — what she thought of the latest Goncourt prizewinner; and laughing when she rose up with all the fury of the Eumenides, seized her silver-handled walking stick, and made the floor shake with her body, comically unbalanced by her limp and by her rage — a limp and a rage that, in the dim light of the lounge, surrounded her figure with a great sphere and made her homogeneous, attractive and beautiful — while, between coughs and giggles, she poured upon Marcel Proust the harshest and most insulting epithets that could ever be used about a writer.

Everything was peaceful yet lively in Natalia's house, as if its owner's character attenuated the colours of carpets and wallpaper, regulated the antiquity of the furniture, sifted the light and determined its different angles of incidence, and radiated activity and palpitation into the air, which seemed at times to be inhabited by a dense, friendly colony of invisible protozoa. I could, for example, turn my back on the corner of the lounge where Natalia and Dr. Kleines were smoking, sunk in comfortable armchairs, without any fear of offending them, and go over to the window, as if weightless, floating on an amber cloud, to contemplate in ecstasy the sunset glowing red on the windows of the small houses around that little oval praza, that unique praza, cut off from the world; and my heart would be filled with longing by the green bench in a corner that suddenly brought before me another time when I saw myself in an earlier life which in a vertigo of astonishment I knew I had forgotten and was soon to forget again, and I could achingly surrender myself to that inexistent time when I had sat on that bench, while a sudden terror sent a shudder down my spine and made me step backwards, at the very moment when the sun stopped burning on the windows of the houses opposite; and on the pane of my own window, dark now, I could see the reflection of Dr. Kleines in his elegant dinner-jacket, a camellia on his lapel and, in his right hand, a Havana cigar whose opaque smell reached me together with the lively sounds of his conversation with Natalia.

At night, my aunt would come to my room to wish me good night and to give me a kiss which had the effect of making me feel happy and slightly dazed. Longingly I heard her come down the corridor with her unsteady step, tapping the parquet floor with her stick, and I choked with a wistful pleasure I had never felt before, not even in my mother's caresses or Nana Rigolade's pampering, because neither of them had that incredible ability to reach inside me, melt my heart, and soothe me as she did. What else could have given her the idea of hanging opposite my bed that picture representing — under spheroidal crimson clouds and between two tall slender pines at whose feet caverns and grottoes gaped like shadowy eyes, at the end of an elemental beach like a sickle-blade and of a procession of seagulls, rocks and crags afflicted by petroglyphs and runes — the ghostly city of Ys, lost in some pneumatic corner of time?

That strange picture, anticipating what years later was to be achieved by the inimitable art of Ulises Fingal, had the ability to keep me in suspense, cut off from the concrete reality of my viscera and from the tangible forms that I felt and saw and classified day by day, to such an extent that I had to make a conscious effort to listen to the firm and, I now believe, very carefully chosen words of my aunt: "Remember you're in T. The industrial workers who live in the Northern Quarter, and who perhaps constitute the most dynamic section of Azerrata society, will never give their support to classical nationalism." Even though I didn't understand the meaning of this sentence — the meaning, for example, of "classical nationalism" — and hadn't the slightest interest in finding out its meaning at such a buoyant time in my life (probably the most blissful and fortunate of all, in the sense that happiness can be found in a pipe of kef), I deposited these and other words of hers in a secret archive in my brain, waiting for the moment when everything would be made clear in the presence of Ulm Roan, the central figure in my life, discarded for the moment in some purple attic of my unconscious, who appeared at times before me, in the least expected places and contexts. Such as the evening when I went out alone to stretch my legs and got lost in the suburb's compli-cated streets, wandering from one tiny square to another until, tired and thirsty, I walked into a huge tavern full of groups of people who sat around tables drinking wine and shouting.

I was certain that someone would call out to me, and they did. It was Dr. Kleines, wearing a checked shirt and a cheviot jacket, and he asked me over to the table where he was drinking and engaged in lively conversation with two young men of about my own age (one was displaying a grey tie with a broad knot, and the other had a white silk scarf around his neck), who were introduced to me as workers' leaders, something which I could have guessed, I don't know why, probably because of the metallic yet friendly touch of their hands, or because of the fiery obstinacy of their gaze, which both regarded me with affection and occasionally established a haughty distance between us (according, I suppose, to the degree to which my words and gestures followed bourgeois and aristocratic patterns of expression, or avoided them).

I was observing with interest the white, wolf's teeth and the paper-thin lips of one of the young men when a phrase of ironical contempt about Ulm Roan, spoken by the other, hit my ears; I can't reproduce it here because I don't remember it, but it was also something about "the old way of understanding Tagen Ata", which left me somewhat intrigued, but was dispatched to my secret archive so that I could pretend I hadn't heard a thing, shake both their hands with sincere cordiality, and accept their invitation to go to the People's Athenaeum one day to attend a debate, a political meeting or a speech, something which I had a deep desire to do, but which was not to be, for reasons that will soon be revealed.

At about that time I realised that a longing to give up my mission and to stay in Natalia's magic circle was growing daily within me, yet at the same time I was becoming more aware of my duty to break out of that delightful crystal capsule in which, like certain figures painted by Hieronymus Bosch, I lay in a state of absolute beatitude and inertia.

I didn't have to give her any explanations. Natalia must have read my thoughts because, one warm, wet afternoon, when my nerves were suffering the contradictory impulses I have just mentioned, she suddenly raised her hands from the keys of the piano — where she had for some time been repeating, furiously, a piece by Chopin, ethnic, cordial and passionate — and, although I had not mentioned the subject, said that as I had decided to end my stay at her house, she for her part was going to pack her bags and go off to spend spring and summer at the sunny spa at Sul.

VI

Ulm Roan's house was at the end of a narrow, deserted street. Total silence poured on to it, annihilating everything else. It was one of those brick houses built at the end of last century, whose original ugliness has been accentuated by age. In Anatí I'd seen any number of them in photos: my grandparents' house, my godparents' house, all the same. They had been mass-produced by the Terra Ancha Ministry of Town Planning, taking no account whatsoever of the geographical location or the landscape of Tagen Ata, and had been sold — in a great scandal of speculation and corruption — to families of the bourgeoisie and petty aristocracy of our country. When I suddenly remembered the legend of the horrible crimes committed by Ano Jhosco, the teacher, in a red-brick house just like Ulm Roan's, under the dead gaze of the most incredible collection of spiders in the world, a cold shiver froze my legs, and what seemed like a swarm of little metallic insects crawled up and down my back in an unmistakable sign of alarm. There was no sound, not even a bird singing, a dog barking, or a baby crying. I was gasping for breath. And I was afraid, when I opened that garden gate.

But — I don't know why — the cold cloud that was enveloping me like an omen broke up when I saw before me the manservant who, with a splendid, twisted smile, opened the door, addressed me by my name with warm friendliness, and told me that Ulm Roan was expecting me. I responded with incomprehensible complicity to his open, courteous look. We went down a long, dark corridor with ancient weapons hanging on the walls. Ulm received me in his study. Just as I had expected, I was fascinated by his long, blond hair and his radiant face, about which I had dreamed ever since I was a child.

"My name is Rotbaf Luden."

"Ulm Roan."

He smiled. His mouth was shrivelled and beautiful. He pointed a long, enquiring nose towards me.

"Have you had a good journey?"

"Yes, thank you."

"Welcome to Tagen Ata."

"The smell has already welcomed me."

"I beg your pardon?"

"On the ship. The smell of this land reached me. It welcomed me."

He passed a bony hand over his cheek, with the same tired movement of the old man in the bar. He recited in a monotonous, affected voice:

"Oh, this land! I've dedicated twenty-five years, a quarter of a century, to this land, sounding out its very substance. Little remains of a country after such severe reflection. Not much more than a handful of vague ideas which, at the very best, might be used in a half-decent essay. That's why I haven't written anything for some time. Perhaps the psychology of peoples will be able to provide the great answer when it becomes a true science. Sociology can't provide us with the answer, of course, because of its methodological pedantry and its nineteenth-century scientism, blind to the vibrant flame of the spirit and the radical experience of the absolute. For the time being, a country is a fluttering in the heart, a cordial recognition in the word, a breeze that brings us presaged fragrances. Poets can still be leaders of lands. At the age of forty, I realised that I could do no more than write poems. And save the essences, the language. I can't save the country, that much I know. We can only salvage the hull from the great shipwreck. We've lost the rudder for ever, and the engine too. We'll be a barge: we're doomed by history. We are overshadowed, Rotbaf, by many centuries of shadows."

The walls were stacked high with books. His desk was covered in dust, papers, leaflets and file-cards. It gave the impression that his work had been interrupted there, many years earlier. From the shelves hung portraits of his forefathers and of Azerrata literary figures.

A discomforting sensation of having come in the wrong door grabbed me by an ear and scrambled my brain. I couldn't understand a thing, nothing at all. But I was sure that I hadn't come in search of words like these from Ulm Roan. Eventually I said:

"I have been sent, sir, by the central committee of the overseas branch of I.T.A."

"No."

"What?"

"There are things that are not known overseas. Forget the organisation."

"What do you mean?"

"You people overseas have lost contact with the vital essence of the country."

"I don't doubt that. My mission here is to connect with the realities of the situation."

He stood up. He paced about the room. The coat of arms of Tagen Ata was delicately embroidered on his dressing gown. He lit a cigarette. The room filled with the fragrant aroma of English tobacco.

"You will dine and sleep here. It will be a pleasure for me, and it is safer."

"Very well. I'd like you to clarify..."

"There is nothing to clarify."

"Why must I forget I.T.A.?"

He said nothing. I got up. I adopted the opaque tones of a motion of censure at a branch meeting. I pointed my finger at him.

"Speak up, please. However much effort it might take, I'm going to get all the information I need for the overseas branch. You are the unquestioned leader of the Resistance. Speak up."

"I.T.A. has been disbanded."

I went red. I was vibrating. I placed myself a few inches away from Ulm Roan. I yelled:

"What sort of a dirty trick is this? Who are the traitors? I want their names!"

He clenched both fists, and raised them towards the heavens, accompanying this operation with a frown. I realised that Ulm Roan was taking the utmost pains over a dramatic performance in order to win me over to his ground. I felt flattered, but did not drop my guard.

"What are their names, sir?"

"What names are you talking about?"

"Their names. The names of those who have liquidated the Azerrata vanguard by liquidating I.T.A. Their names. All their names. The responsibility for this action must be established."

"Nobody is responsible. Or rather yes, just one person is. I am. I accept total responsability for the disbandment."

"I understand. Now I have a name," I coldly concluded, turning my back on him.

He sat down, exhausted. He passed his tapering hand over his head. He slumped in his chair. I couldn't stop myself: I sat down on the edge of his chair, put my arm behind his neck, ran my hand through his hair and hugged his head. I wanted to make love to Ulm Roan, my love. He allowed me to do as I pleased, and continued in a quiet voice:

"I.T.A. no longer exists. It was a maximalist, utopian organisation. We're tired, very tired. Terra Ancha is preparing a Home Rule Bill for Tagen Ata. They're going to recognise our language. We'll administer public works and education. It's the end of the struggle."

"Is the Resistance over?"

"It's over."

I could hardly breathe.

"There's one last question."

"What is that, Rotbaf Luden?"

"Are all the other patriots following your collaborationist line?"

"They are! And it isn't collaboration, for God's sake. It's realism, or practical politics, if you prefer."

VII

We had supper in a large room upholstered in garnet velvet. In the centre hung a huge lamp with a yellow satin shade which lit the round table, meticulously laid with a dinner service from which not one piece was missing. Large and small coverings with heavy, encrusted embroidery swathed all the furniture, absorbed all sounds of voices and of metal, calmed and indeed smothered the atmosphere, even mollified me. We were served by a beautiful maid who was wearing the national costume of Tagen Ata. Her high head-dress forced her to keep her neck straight, like a dove when it's listening to something. I noticed the same disconcerting look of affection in her that I had seen in the manservant. The silver shone and the wines tapered in delicate crystal glasses. Ulm Roan handled his cutlery with skilful elegance and nonchalance, in the classical three stages of the American school of etiquette, revealing, with this slight affectation, his Harvard education as a young man. He seemed sad and worried.

"Is there anything wrong?" I asked.

"Yes, there is."

He gave me a long stare. Again I felt fascinated.

"Terra Ancha's benevolence towards our demands might come to naught."

"Why?"

We rose from the table. Each picked up a glass of brandy. Ulm Roan was silent. Through the open window, from the viscous spring, a stag beetle flew into the dining-room, humming like a solemn autogiro. A fragment of the night forest came in with the great insect, and it thrust something vast and ancestral into me.

"We cannot speak in the presence of the servants," said Ulm.

"Why not?"

"I have good reason to suspect they're spies."

"For the police? Or for the secret service?"

"Of course not. For the others."

"The others? What others? Who are the others?"

"The cimarróns. Let's go out on to the terrace."

Ulm Roan softly put an arm round my back, and held me close to him. We went out on to the terrace, on the upper floor of the house. The peaceful Tagen Ata night came to us, like gauze. And it enveloped us, smooth and rustling. A gentle rain began to fall and, in the distance, the Great Forest raised its lament like a river. I drew closer to Ulm Roan, who ran his hand through my hair. We didn't go indoors, we let the drizzle soak our shirts and stick them to our skin.

"The cimarróns could provoke the Terra Ancha government, and destroy our hopes for self-government. They could spoil everything."

I have to admit that the physical contact with Ulm Roan was taking me into a state of delicious self-abandon. With my eyes closed, I allowed myself to be lifted and spun in some pink space. But in the very nucleus of vertigo and love, there was something like a polyhedron there that forced me to continue asking questions.

"Tell me: who are the cimarróns?"

"You know that the mainstay of our economy is the grape monoculture in the valleys of the south. Tagen Ata's wine is the basis of its exports, famous as it is throughout the world, and it's an important source of foreign exchange for Terra Ancha. The most important source, apart from the money sent back by emigrants in countries with strong currencies. It can be said say that, thanks to emigrants and to wine, Terra Ancha is able to balance its budget."

"But who are the cimarróns?"

The rain had softly soaked us. Ulm Roan gave me a nervous embrace, and kissed my eyes.

"The cimarróns are country people — servants, tenant farmers, day labourers — who are rebelling against the authority of the landowners; after making impossible demands, they commit acts of violence on the estates, such as holding meetings and even setting fire to property, they hold conspiratorial fraternal gatherings with industrial workers who, as you know, are poisoned, etc., etc. Pursued by the law..."

"The law of Tagen Ata?"

"The law of Terra Ancha, of course. But following the principles of natural justice, which safeguard the rights of property."

"I'm sorry. Carry on."

"Pursued by the forces of law and order, the rebels are growing in numbers. They have taken refuge in the Great Forest. There are hordes of them there, with women and children too. Some enemy power is supplying them with weapons."[7]

"An enemy of Tagen Ata or of Terra Ancha?"

Ulm Roan moved away from me like lightning. He seized my neck with one hand. He raised the other, his index finger pointing up to the sky. His long nose shook, and he seemed to me as handsome as a god, with his straight wet hair, the drops of water running down his face, and the light at his back.

"Do you realise that our possibilities of obtaining self-government will be ruined if the cimarróns manage to annoy Terra Ancha seriously? And there's something else you don't know. These ragged criminals have adopted the national flag of Tagen Ata as their own, and are declaring themselves to be the I.T.A. militia, while their real aim is to dispossess the natural landlords of the south and the honest factory owners in and around T., and to create social anarchy everywhere! As true patriots, we have been forced to disband I.T.A. and present ourselves before Terra Ancha in a different guise. There was no alternative."

"Ever since I arrived in Tagen Ata, I've had nothing but doubts. Now everything is clear to me."

I went back into the room. I looked at myself in a mirror. I looked wet and different. I seemed older and stronger. Had a new Rotbaf Luden just been born? I don't think so.[8] I threw a conspiratorial glance at my reflection in the mirror. Ulm Roan held me by the waist and kissed me. I yielded to him. He took me gently in his arms to his bed. Ever since I was a young girl in Anatí, I had been planning for this to happen one day.

---

7. It has never been demonstrated that the so-called "cimarróns" received foreign aid. Historians of the insurrection seem to favour a different hypothesis: the "cimarróns" accumulated a sizeable fortune as a result of various operations of expropriation — raids on banks and large foreign companies — and bought weapons from various private dealers.

8. This reflection by Rotbaf Luden is possibly influenced by the large number of metamorphoses which, according to legend, took place in Tagen Ata a century earlier, the most famous of these being the transformation of Nhadrón into a crow. Ever since then, the people of Tagen Ata have had a strange mistrust in the permanence of their own physical conformation, and a fluid, ambivalent consciousness of their own being. Perhaps the fact that they feel themselves to be divided between a national identity of their own and a state structure that has been imposed on them has conditioned — or determined — this complex sense of personal coherence.

VIII

The next morning I felt tired, angry. I had the amazing feeling that I had penetrated more deeply into the essential meaning of my freedom. The physical pain had been bearable, thanks in large part to the gentleness, which had even perhaps been a little naive, of Ulm Roan. He lay asleep on his back on the huge mahogany bed, his hair spread over his naked thorax and swirling like a torrent of gold on to the pillow.

I showered in silence. I washed, I scrubbed my whole body meticulously, obsessively. I put on my trousers and boots. A red cloud came before my eyes.

I took my pistol out of my bag. With great care, so as not to awaken Ulm Roan, I loaded and cocked it. With no feelings whatsoever I aimed from point blank range at the nape of the neck of the traitor, Ulm Roan. One shot was enough: hardly a quiver, the position of his body did not change. It's strange, but the shot reverberated in me with a sudden, acute pain in the area of my hymen. I took one of the knives from Ulm Roan's collection of weapons and engraved the three initials, I.T.A., on his back.

When I opened my eyes, awaking from my horrible vision, they were full of burning tears. I went to the desk and wrote:

"Ulm Roan:
You are mistaken, which is the most academic way I can find of saying that you are a traitor. I know that you will not take the right road, because you belong to the company of the powerful, and you even add beauty and colour to their principles. You will be left behind, you will all be left behind. The wind of history is blowing from another direction. I'm deeply in love with you. I've always loved you, and I always shall. Goodbye for ever.
Rotbaf"

I left the letter on the bedside table and took one last glance at Ulm Roan, who was breathing deeply and peacefully.

In the corridor I met the maid who, no longer wearing the national costume she'd had on the night before, stood herself before me with an efficient, dynamic air. Without a moment's hesitation she came up to me, a clearly interrogative expression on her face.

"Are you with us?" she barked without any preamble.

I knew in a flash that I was talking to one of my own people. I was overcome with joy, and took her by the hands.

"You must join the Resistance without delay."

"Where is the Resistance?"

"In the Great Forest. Zabrate will tell you the passwords and give you instructions about how to get there."

"All right."

The girl went into one of the rooms. She came back out at once with the manservant, who wore a more serious and concerned look than when he had opened the door to me. He said:

"We have great expectations of you. We were sure you wouldn't let the traitors convince you. I am Zabrate, a member of the local committee, responsible together with Els Bri for keeping a watch on Ulm Roan."

Both Zabrate and Els Bri fixed me with a composed gaze. He continued:

"I've got a horse ready down below. You'd better get away before Ulm Roan wakes up. You must take the old king's highway and go very slowly through the forest. When they challenge you, you must answer: 'I'm going to the house of Perceval'.[9] That's all."

"I'm going to the house of Perceval."

"That's right."

Els Bri and I kissed each other on the cheeks.

Zabrate gave me a broad smile and shook me by the hand.

IX

I rode into the Great Forest with my heart in my mouth. Intoxicated by green light and by the panting of my horse, which made the air vibrate, I broke into a mad gallop, frightening crows and silencing the turtle dove. Then I drew rein, dismounted, and walked slowly along the edge of the old road. I walked through the soft grass, I destroyed little worlds of ferns with my feet, I felt the dampness of the dew on

9. Perceval is a mythical figure of Tagen Ata. There are many versions of his story, both in the oral tradition and in written elaborations. They all agree that he is the master of the Great Forest and that he is extraordinarily ubiquitous, humorous, intelligent, shy and just.

my boots. The whole forest was aglow, after the drizzle of the night, and there was a tiny star on every leaf. I filled my lungs with the warm, heavy air of the spring forest. My people were calling me. And I was going to them. Tiny coal tits were going crazy with love in the branches.

Corunna, August 1970 (pub. 1971)

Men and the Night

"Want to dance?"

"No."

"OK."

Mingos had spiky hair and he talked sideways, out of the corner of his mouth. She was full-breasted and stocky. He insisted:

"D'you want to dance or what?"

She felt afraid and went to dance with him. There was dust on blue suits, in throats, and on cretonne skirts. A dirty, crowded festa. A tall, dark lad called Aloi appeared. He said to Mingos:

"Pitutas is down there. Are you coming?"

"Yes."

And Mingos set about getting rid of the girl. She grabbed him by the lapels and said:

"You're leaving me in the middle of the dance?"

"So what?"

On a track some distance from the festa Aloi and Mingos met up with Pitutas, a spiv from Vigo. Pitutas had one eye, an effeminate air, and the voice of a broody hen.

"Evening."

"Evening."

Pitutas spat sideways and said:

"What kept you so long? Never mind. I've got a nice job for you two."

"What sort of job?"

"Don't get all het up: it's only blood. Stop pulling those faces. The bloke who needs it will pay for it, full stop. Besides, it's an act of charity, the poor devil's riddled with TB. A thousand pesetas for nothing. Come with me."

Aloi and Mingos looked at each other. They shook their heads.

"No."

"No," they said.

"But all you've got to do is start a fight and make all the people and the two civil guards go and see what's up... I'll do the rest... If anything goes wrong, I'm the one who'll end up in clink. Nothing will happen to either of you. Come with me."

They went into a drinks stall and ordered wine. Pitutas explained:

"Don't be such bloody peasants. Don't be so squeamish... Besides, there isn't anyone from your village at the festa. I can't see why you're so bleeding afraid. You see those kids playing over there? OK. Well now it's dark you two get a fight going in the middle of the festa. Once the fists are flying I'll scram with one of the kids. Got it?"

"Yes. It's a deal." said Aloi.

"Yes," said Mingos.

Pitutas gave them the thousand pesetas and shook their hands. They both drank three half-pints of wine. The orchestra was playing a slow foxtrot. They sought out the couple that held each other closest as they danced. "Now it's our turn, Mr. Dancer." As Aloi said this he thumped him on the back. The lad stepped away from the girl and got a punch in the eye that knocked him to the ground. She screamed and more youths came to the scene. Aloi and Mingos fought like wolves. The women screamed:

"Call the civil guard!"

"Go and get the civil guard!"

And the civil guard appeared, clearing a path with its rifles. Aloi and Mingos were fighting in two opposite corners of the square where people were dancing, but they managed to slip away, like hares, and went to meet in a secret spot. Aloi said:

"Where's the cash?"

"Don't worry," answered Mingos, "I haven't lost it. Here it is."

They fell silent. Aloi said:

"I saw Pitutas and I saw the boy he took, too. He was only little. About five. And very dark."

Mingos licked the black blood that was trickling from his nose.

Then he said:

"That Pitutas is a son of a bitch! Five years old... and dark."

"Just like your lad."

"No, it can't be."

"Don't start getting ideas into your head. Who would have brought your lad to a festa so far from home?"

"Which way did he go?"

"Who?"

"Pitutas, you bloody fool. Which way did he go? Which way did he go, Aloi?"

"Down that track over there. Heading for the Ourense road, I suppose."

"How long ago?"

"Since what?"

"How long is it since he ran away with the child, Aloi?"

"About ten minutes."

"Let's go. Let's go after him."

Mingos mopped his brow. Blood was still trickling from his nose. He started to run. After him ran Aloi, as long and supple as a wickerwork cane. Mingos was in no doubt: he was certain that the boy Pitutas had kidnapped was his son and as he ran he visualized, in the minutest detail, how Pitutas was bleeding the child's neck. And then a pale, gaunt character greedily, greedily gulping down the warm blood. The wind was swirling the tops of the pine trees and drawing a continuous roar from them. Turning a bend, Mingos could make out Pitutas with something on his back. Mingos said:

"Aloi, there he goes."

Aloi did not answer. Aloi was not there. The track dipped and led into a cleft with high walls. Mingos' voice echoed in the cleft:

"Pitutas. Pitutas. Let me have the boy. Let me have the boy."

Pitutas broke into a run with Mingos after him.

"Leave the lad alone or I'll kill you."

Pitutas saw Mingos, with his spiky hair, shouting incomprehensibly. He was going to ruin the job. There was the crack of a bullet which scorched Mingos' shoulder. Pitutas aimed again, in the clear light of the moon. But a long, supple figure dropped on to Pitutas from the top of the cleft. Oaths mingled with the incessant sound of punches. Mingos reached the scene and picked the boy up: he was dead from a blow on the nape of the neck.

"Now it's my turn, Aloi," said Mingos.

Aloi stood aside. Pitutas, his eyes open wide, black, as deep as rifle muzzles, stared at Mingos' wounded, blackened, sweaty face. And then he turned his attention to the strong hands that were seizing him by the hair, and then a searing pain in the head and then nothing. But Mingos did not tire of slamming Pitutas' head against a slab of rock on the ground until he realized that the back of it was crushed to a pulp. Then he said:

"You killed my son..."

Aloi lit a match and examined the dead child. And he said to Mingos:

"Just like I said. This isn't your lad."

Mingos turned his head. He replied:

"So what?"

(From O crepúsculo e as formigas, 1961)

Sibila

Now that, bent beneath the burden of the clouded years, I have found
the ring again, in front of the house with the triangle (Rúa dos
Loureiros, 5, Santiago de Compostela) and I know I am going to be
visited by Sibila, I recall the gangling figure of the unforgettable
Domingos Areal as it looms towards me out of oblivion. And it had
all begun when we left the cinema (we had gone to see *Metropolis*)
and later met up again for dinner in the Asesino Restaurant, on a cold,
frosty night in 1925. Concha had been embarrassed by the glances
thrown at her by Otero Espasandín, and by the bold, merry tomfoolery
of the revellers, aroused by glistening Ulla wine and enormous glasses
of anonymous brandy. I remember every detail of that day which was
to be rendered horrible and ever-present within me by the events that
followed. García-Sabell had an examination the next morning and he
strode off home to Rúa de Xelmírez; Maside, erect as a birch tree,
disappeared into the cold; Xesús Bal decided to go and see the
processions in the Praza da Quintana and, a solitary figure, he waved
goodbye and walked away whistling "The Firebird". We were left
alone, Domingos Areal and this man who is sitting here now writing
this account with his heart lodged in his throat. We walked in no
particular direction, swathed in our overcoats, our hats pulled down
over our heads, puffing proudly on our pipes: Rúa do Medio, castel-
lated around by important chimneys; Rúa de Bonaval, like a transit to

the grey ash and the dense wretchedness wafted out of each door and window; the fields of Belvís, taking on frost and an opaque, melancholy-laden silence; Rúa dos Lagartos, a street unrivalled for timidity. A dog barked on the outskirts of the slums of Compostela as we headed back towards the relief of the city, with its shields of stone and its streets of slate, talking about nationalism, Manoel Antonio, maybe about Huidobro. We were free, the city was ours; we were discovering secret alley-ways and lighted windows that fired our youthful imaginations, so irretrievable, now so irretrievable. As I write this account, hardly lifting my pen from the paper, I am burdened with anguish and foreboding, oppressed by the emotions of times gone by: that arrogant insurrection which we bore in our eyes. Anything could happen that night because the presence of those towers, rising in clear outline against a pitter-patter of stars that wounded our eyes, made our saliva seethe with the unformed awareness of something absolutely new lying in wait for us. "There's going to be a cosmic sign. We had better be prepared," Domingos Areal muttered, without removing his pipe from his mouth. He was in secret contact with Krishnamurti, with Roso de Luna, with Vicente Risco. Like Amado Carballo and other sad youths who flitted through this life, he could hear the ethereal call of oriental perfectionism and other celebrated, despicable chimeras which I shall not specify here because I am on the brink of disaster and of the definitive loss of my own being. And it is now that I wish to record, to make a clear statement of the initial fact which caused everything else, as well as my present despair. We were in Rúa dos Loureiros, we were looking at a beautiful house (number 5) the upper storey of which consisted of a triangular stone pediment that captured my cubist attention and appealed to Domingos Areal's theosophic curiosity. A flash of lightning — or else some ineffable presence — forced us both to look down at the ground. *And there was the ring, shining like the morning star.* We both pounced. Domingos beat me to it and, with one swift movement, he placed it on the little finger of his left hand: I remember it clearly. He extended his long, hard hand and we looked at the ring by the light of a street lamp. It displayed a symbol that resembled an ellipse: both of us felt that we were in the presence of mystery. "It has something to do with the triangle on the house," suggested Domingos. I replied: "The ellipse and the triangle do not merely imply contrasting visions of the world, but different conceptual dimensions. That is to say: different ideal spheres." He was not satisfied, and insisted: "It is precisely because of what you say that I assert that the ring and the triangle are related. Read Frazer." I became somewhat annoyed at this and, after disdainfully explaining to him that in the *Golden Bough* (which Fermín Bouza had lent me at the Seminar of Galician Studies) there is no reference to any such relationship, I withdrew into a prickly silence as I contemplated, with decided envy, the lovely ring on my friend's hand. What a magnificent prologue to such a vast, vertiginous tragedy of death and beauty! Now, before pausing in the writing of my account to contemplate, with infinite nostalgia and infinite grief, the portrait of Domingos Areal (drawn by Maside, that same year of 1925, on the check tablecloth on that same round table in the Asesino Restaurant where this story begins amidst an inaudible clattering of metal), I wish to manifest my belief that terror and violence, when they acquire the support of aesthetically valid formulae, multiply their infamy and their denial of basic human dignity. As I say this, the dark eyes of the difficult and dour poet and artist Domingos Areal appear before me, witnesses to the roots of wretchedness, and lost now for ever. Maside had given him lips with bitter lines, the lips he gave everyone, yet the form of the cravat softened the whole, otherwise rigid and full of foreboding. It is possible that those persons for whom this account is intended will not fully understand what follows — and the blame must lie with me — yet what is certain is that the private life of the man who is writing it was left divided in two that night, as when a pear is cut in half. And, on this side of the divide in my existence, I recall meetings with Domingos Areal: at a reserved table in the Café Suízo, each of us puffing away at a Havana cigar generously provided by Filgueira Valverde's father, while a horripilation of vile flamenco music echoed around us and cabaret-fumes assaulted our eyes in a fury of raging colours; in the churchyard in Rúa da Quinta Angustia, listening to a distant clock strike two in the morning, as fog silenced the city and even invaded our valiant avant-garde hearts; in a sordid cafe on Rúa Travesa, with the boundless background of the thousand voices of the market bringing us the voices of the peasant and the pedlar, invading the strip of traders that starts at San Fiz de Solovio Church and ends at the Porta do Camiño; in Rúa da Caramoniña, displaying its navelworts (or perhaps hemlock) lodged in those crevices in the wall that offered spongy, secret, romantic shelter. On each occasion the ring, with its ellipse, was shining on Domingos Areal's finger, and pallor was clouding his cheeks, violet was invading the rings under his eyes of trembling jet, the burden of something abominable was bowing his shoulders with a cruel diligence, intermittent earthquakes muddled his words, and his aching teeth clattered like a jazz band as his saliva spurted into my face, the long-suffering face of a faithful friend. He was in rapid decline; wasting away; he no longer frequented the cafe or the promenade; he sought me out as a confidant. How he was rushing towards his end! How he suffered until the very moment of his last death-rattle (the horror of which I can imagine) with a disdain worthy of a stoic hero! (Now that the death of the present writer is imminent, that other death, my friends, will finally be revealed, a warning and a threat to all of you who are reading this.) Because the fact is — take careful note of what follows — that from the moment Domingos Areal took possession of the ring with the ellipse, in front of the house with the triangle in Rúa dos Loureiros, *a bewitching person appeared before him in his dreams each night.* A woman without equal. I remember Domingos' voice precisely, muffled by the books in the University Library, when, tormented by anxiety, he seized a pencil and said: "Look at her." All the silence and the sweet smell of a dusty past were captured in the sketch that he drew on the notepad before me. Castelao had always been warm in his praise of the tormented lines of Domingos Areal's Mattissian sketches, a counterpoint to the excesses of Cándido Fernández Mazas and other audacious Francophiles of the past, who had been encouraged by the butterfly-words of that man Rafael Dieste. But this was different: from the squares on the paper there emanated a powerful woman's face, softly strong (like the baroque cylinders on the Convent of Santa Clara, seen against the light, at sunset on certain days), balmy, with sweet, frightened eyes like meadows, or like crystal streams running through beech groves that are never wounded by the sun; with fleshy lips that betrayed some childish, velvety fear, a look of universal perplexity. "It's the Delphic Sibyl!" I cried instantly. Because nothing could have been more like that figure immortalised by Michelangelo in the Sistine Chapel. Domingos looked at the paper with infinite surprise. "Maybe she came to Michelangelo in dreams as well," he practically shouted, and Bustamante the librarian, who was passing by, his innkeeper's overall sweeping the floor, demanded absolute silence, thrusting his Unamunian chin into our faces. Because every night Sibila came, came to him. And now I warn you, the addressees of this text, that there are no words with which to bring to my narration the confidences of my unfortunate friend. She had appeared in the centre of his dreams, preceded by an immense triangle and enclosed in an elliptic line, ever since the moment he discovered the ring in Rúa dos Loureiros and put it on his finger. What at first had been a happy, astonishing surprise (as he told me in the Café Suízo), turned, night by night, into a sackful of lead. I had not yet read Freud, perhaps due to certain suspicions expressed by the timid Rof Carballo (a great admirer of Claudel). All that I knew — about dreams — was Carlos Maside's bold, interpretive ramblings, frivolously combined with white coffee in the Café Español. She (we had called her Sibila ever since discovering the similarity in the University Library) would come wrapped in heavy clothing, motionless and dynamic, and from each triangular piece of her robe there would emerge a soft, musical ellipse that filled Domingos' dream with a palpitating aroma of a swallow or any other slight, fluttering creature. She would draw him to her breast and delirium would follow in sweet and extraordinarily destructive copulation. He felt drained, more and more defeated day by day. Domingos' language could not accommodate such a wealth of pleasure and beauty, of sound and clashing of colours and messages of light and the progressive loss of his own being, (he said this in Rúa da Quinta Angustia). Domingos had almost reached the point of neither eating nor smoking by the night that Sibila, resplendent, arrived clutching an automatic pistol, with a cruel look instead of lips. She had sat in a large metal chair (the Bauhaus type, you know the sort) and *the ellipses had disappeared,* or had been rubbed off, or had been extinguished, which horrified my friend perhaps because of some secret intuition related to his theosophic beliefs. Sibila had sat there and had stared at my friend with eyes of steel and with all the evil in the world, until dawn and the sound of bells came to rescue him for wakefulness and for light — if there was now any rescuing him. He told me all this in the little cafe on Rúa Travesa, and he added in horror: "She had a blue swastika tattooed on her forehead." It seems that this was when Domingos began his last race towards degradation and destruction, and everything that he told me, after our meeting in Rúa da Caramoniña, was charged with horrible vagueness. In each dream Domingos performed rites of humiliation before Sibila while irresolute flageolets and organs sounded, and an abominable, wet substance flowed like pus from her mouth as she sat there — as she sat there on a bamboo throne, naked, her whole body tattooed with triangles. The terrible swastika would now always preside on her forehead, as clear as a November moon, and the ellipses had disappeared. For the suppression of the ellipse-triangle coupling and its replacement by the swastika-triangle coupling

I can find no noble interpretation, because everything leads me to a deep belief in the fatal establishment of an *until then unsuspected order of cruelty and beauty*. As night fell over Compostela, I would think of my friend, and I felt for him. In the absolute solitude of his garret, as soon as he fell asleep, Sibila would enter his dreams. And because I knew how these sessions of torture were developing, I suffered for my suffering friend. Sibila subjected him to nefarious treatment: the insertion of stilettoes into unutterable places, the chewing of vermicular objects, practices with his own excrement and that of others. "Everything always culminates in perfect ecstasy. More and more perfect in proportion to the increasing size of Sibila's blue swastika. And the colours become more dynamic in certain sounds and the music infiltrates the shapes and surrounds the torture itself, configuring it as is required. All I want is for night to come so that I can suffer and dream." Words such as these were the last I heard from Domingos Areal, two months after the dinner in the Asesino Restaurant that I have described. You, the addressees of this account, know that he was found huddled up in his filthy garret, wrapped in a tattered blanket, white as paper, with a delirious laugh traced like rock crystal upon his slender lips. He was dead; Domingos had left us: the gentleman who did poems and sketches (always unfinished) for cultural reviews like *Alfar* and *Ronsel*. Only I knew the secret: he had died of violence and pleasure, in the dubious kingdom of his own dreams. And now (take careful note), eighteen years later, in this year of 1943 which harbours all the viscous horror of the world in its belly, I am writing this account, hardly lifting my pen from the paper, to record the fact that I have just found the ring with the ellipse, in front of the house with the triangle (Rúa dos Loureiros, 5) and that, as my narrative advances towards its final full stop, the decisive moment is approaching when I shall enter into the dream, and there I shall be visited by Sibila, violence and beauty will put paid to this narrator who is looking, with melancholy, at the static stars through a misty window, and at the magical city that I do not blame; meanwhile Stalingrad...

(From *Crónica de Nós*, 1980)

Grieih

It was a warm night. The wind did not stir a leaf in the chestnut grove. The tree-stumps, old and gnarled, looked like Titans. It was then that the moon appeared, huge, lightening the light patches with its pallor, and making the darkness blacker and more fearsome. There was a gentle slope that raised its little belly beside a brook and, because of the dampness, lush grass grew there among the young gorse. On that slope the crickets made their holes, and their cylindrical burrows appeared here and there, well rounded and indeed beautifully formed.

Grieih was at the bottom of his burrow. He was a big cricket, with a strong chitinous case, sensitive antennae, a large head, a fat abdomen, harmonious elytra..., a fine specimen. It was the mole-crickets or "scorpions", the breed which bores tunnels metres long in the earth, as moles do, that shook him out of his immobility by letting forth their monotonous, unpleasant droning. His long slender antennae trembled; his abdomen, soft and palpitating like a maiden's kiss, contracted with fear; and then it was his tibiae and his trochanters that pushed him out. He emerged halfway from the hole.

That nocturnal woodland world in which Grieih lived was mysterious and thrilling. The air hummed on his left with the beating wings of an errant stag beetle; then on his right with the coquettish fluttering of night butterflies, their wings folded in treacherous triangles; moths big and blue, tiny, pale yellow, russet — a ghostly hue that has never seen the light of day and is only a promise of red —, moths with great skulls on their thoraxes, white as milk, chestnut brown..., moths unknown to playful little boys with their hats poised to catch the big midday butterflies; and then brown beetles, as fat as oxen and with horns on their heads would come hurrying into the wood, or else beetles black as feet, with shining elytra and sexual organs always craving choice cowpats; the grasshoppers, too, would leap in the night, elegant as shrimps, green, with pointed ovipositors..., they were night grasshoppers, like the night spiders and other species, innumerable and in rows a thousand deep, each with his role to play in woodland life. Death lurked behind every thicket; fights broke out, within the species over a female, outside it over food. The eagle owls flew silently, as did the little owls and the bats. A constant and vital buzzing pursued the tormented eardrums of the tiny living things.

The moonbeams fell on Grieih. Driven by a cosmic yearning, he went "Cri". And then "cri, cri, cri".

II

Above the chestnut grove there was an oakwood; and between the two was the brook. The oakwood was the cyclopic and wild kingdom of the stag beetles. Grieih knew them, and their horns and their deformed heads scared him. They were feared and formidable foreigners. The lower wood could remember with horror how a stag beetle cut Booth, the most fierce, full-bellied and unruly of all the nasicorns, in half. The inhabitants of the chestnut grove called the oakwood "Grohtegunk, the land of huge beasts".

It was a hot evening. Grieih was eating juicy grass and green wild chard. An almost imperceptible breeze fanned the chestnut trees. A faint noise, rustling, constant, moved from branch to branch.

And it was then that in Grohtegunk, in one of those mysterious urges which sometimes take hold of insects, the huge male stag beetle Rasgulkje took off, solemn and deliberate, fiercely beating the air, his horns held high. He crossed the brook and flew into the lower wood, known to the stag beetles as Kornkolinn, or "the land of the small, soft, singing insects".

Grieih watched the monster fly overhead and looked at him with curiosity; his retracted antennae, small and stumpy, gave the impression of rough kindness and he felt no fear at all. But something occurred there that kept the timid singer in suspense. It was a huge, strong bird, a lazy and deceitful cuckoo, which swooped upon the beetle wounding him with its steely beak. But the insect was not frightened and clasped the attacking beak between his powerful pincers, tightly. The bird flapped its wings in desperation and helplessness, and when it found itself free, flew away with a ruptured gullet, while the arthropod plummeted to the ground. Grieih saw him fall nearby, and rushed over. The animal had a deep wound in his abdomen which exposed his soft insides. Grieih moved closer.

"Who are you?"

"Grieih, the cricket."

"Have you come to hurt me?"

"No."

At that moment, a green spider scurried up to take its fill of the animal's exposed insides. But after a short battle Grieih crushed its thorax and left it on its back, kicking the air.

"What's your name again? I can't remember."

"Grieih. And yours?"

"Mine's Rasgulkje."

Grieih felt sorry for the great wounded beetle.

A busy, solitary little ant, scrabbling about in the grass, silently spied Rasgulkje lying there helpless, and ran off as fast as lightning. A short while later the two insects could see the advance of a hungry column of ants in the distance.

"They'll empty my insides little by little, until only my chitin and my horns remain, and then I'll be left to dry in the sun."

"No."

And Grieih started to secrete a deep red liquid from between his palpi and smeared Rasgulkje's wound with it.

"That stuff you're putting on is burning me."

"It's the only thing I can think of."

The hordes of ants arrived in a furious torrent. There were thousands upon thousands of them. An unassailable force. Every living creature in the wood feared a hungry horde of ants on the march. They devour every ailing or injured creature they find lying in the forest, from an earwig to a goldfinch. They begin by tearing off one tiny piece of flesh, then hundreds and thousands more, devouring the entire animal. Grieih took fright and fled. Rasgulkje was left alone, motionless, still. The assailants spread out and, each from a different side, they tried to take bites out of the creature. But suddenly they drew back, touched themselves with their antennae, and there was disorder, chaos. Eventually they turned around, and retreated in a great hurry.

"My spit made them run away."

"Thank you, Grieih. They didn't eat me."

And so it was that the stag beetle spent ten or twenty days hardly moving. Every now and then, Grieih applied a mixture of earth and water to the wound, which slowly healed. One day it appeared covered with a new, fine layer of chitin.

"Now I feel strong enough to return to Grohtegunk."

"Stay in Kornkolinn."

"No, Grieih, I'm going because there isn't any oak blood for me to eat here."

III

That summer had passed and a winter had come that had almost blocked up Grieih's little burrow. Another summer had come, then the rains, and by the following summer Grieih was an old cricket, slow and half deaf. Long gone were the days when — like a wingless cicada — he had fought against tight phalanxes of ants and overpowered spiders and grasshoppers. Now he knew he did not have long to live. One of his sons had already challenged him, some time ago, for the belly of a female. Grieih was plodding along, his femurs stiff. He saw a small clump of vetch and began to eat it, unsuspecting and engrossed. But death, in the green suit of a praying mantis, was lurking behind him. He felt hard pincers seize him by the thorax, and struggled desperately not to die. The mantis had found easy prey in the frail old cricket. Even as it was strangling him it was greedily nibbling at him. But at that very moment the powerful buzzing of strong sinewy wings was heard: Rasgulkje was back in Kornkolinn! The cricket's ganglions, half devoured, vibrated with joy. It was then that the biggest stag beetle in Grohtegunk dropped on to the vicious praying mantis and seized it by the head with the tips of its powerful horns, crushing its cruel, tiny brain.

Grieih lay there, his body a wreck, kicking in spasms, but he still had the strength to turn to his old friend.

"Grieih, I couldn't come sooner...; I wish I could die instead of you!"

"It doesn't matter. I'm old... It doesn't matter. You stag beetles last a long time..., but we're weak."

"Grieih, don't die... I want you to live." And as long as Grieih shook with the shudder of life, Rasgulkje stayed by his side; when he died, his impetuous and barbarous flight flew him off towards the wood above.

(From *Percival e outras historias*, 1958)

Elastic Boots

"...?"

"Daddy'd decided to dig a cesspit in Auguela. He dug it himself, one summer. That cesspit was a flash of inspiration. Nobody in Auguela had ever seen anything like it."

Auguela is on the Chaira moors, on the hillside where clumps of bracken mark a damp patch that, further along, develops into a trickle of water, and then into a marsh and stream which, far away, become a river called the Tuño.

"...?"

"No sir, Daddy never dug the cesspit with that idea in mind."

"...?"

"We found out about it later. I was an eleven-year-old girl at the time. We were living in Vilar, in the parish of Lavadores. Daddy was a building-site foreman in Comesaña, near Vigo. I didn't know anything about it. I found out about it later."

The plainclothes police had wanted to lay hands on the girl's daddy because meetings had indeed been held in the site hut. And on several occasions he had been seen entering Xosé Velo's house, in Rúa das Travesas. Daddy was, beyond question, a member of the organization. The girl, at that time, did not know anything.

"...?"

"Mummy and me left our little house in Vilar, in Lavadores. And we came to the serra. We came to Auguela, our home village. We came back to where we belong, and where Daddy'd built a new house out of brick, and dug a cesspit, too."

Auguela is ten houses and a few cowsheds and maize-garners. All the roofs are thatched, apart from the roof on the house that the girl's daddy had built with his own hands. The girl's grandfather had been arrested by the Falangists in Verín and killed in a ditch on the Alto do Furriolo, along with five other men whom they had marched out of the monastery. The people of Auguela keep some sheep and a couple of cows that graze on the Chaira moors. Mount Penagache, not far away, is a reminder of the Portuguese border.

"...?"
"Only Mummy and me knew that Daddy had come to Auguela too, to lick his wounds."

The girl's daddy had built the house and dug the cesspit as an affirmation of faith in human decency. Moving from one safe house to another, in various disguises, the fugitive reached Celanova and, from there, following the mountain trails, he arrived at his home village. He hid in the cesspit.

"...?"
"The cesspit was in the yard. In the house there was a wooden lavatory which was connected with the cesspit by a drain made of cement. The cesspit was about four metres deep. Once we had done our business in the lavatory, we threw buckets of water in, to swill it all down into the cesspit."
"...?"
"When Daddy went into the cesspit he scraped away at one of the sandy sides and made himself a den, quite high up. He could hardly move, because if he stood up in the cesspit itself, he sank into the slime. All the same, he told Mummy and me to carry on using the lavatory in the normal way."
"...?"
"Inside the cesspit he had a ladder which he climbed at dead of night, to stretch his legs in the yard and to be with Mummy. I only saw him a few times. At night was when he washed, ate and changed his

122

clothes. That's how it was, sir. The cesspit was covered with a wooden grating and a pile of firewood on top. He crawled out through a hole the size of a rabbit's. Nothing happened during the first winter, but it was awful for Daddy."

In the spring two men arrived in Auguela. Each wore a suit and tie, but their clothes were of poor quality, worn and dirty. Each had a stern look and an insolent stare. They both wore black boots, held tight to their shins with elastic.

"...?"
"No sir. I didn't know that they were civil guards from the local squad. I just thought that they were strange because they both wore the same kinds of black boots with two pieces of U-shaped elastic to hold them tight to their shins. They must have been very warm boots in the winter."
"...?"
"Yes. One of them was taller, and younger, with a little blond moustache. He was always smiling. His blue eyes made me feel scared. He often came back by himself, to talk to me."

The sergeant from the local civil guard squad wanted the girl to tell him where her father was, where he was hiding. He asked her time and time again throughout the spring, as the days grew longer. The sergeant would appear before her in the most unexpected places: from behind a tree stump, even. Like a ghost he would appear, when the girl was on her way home, carrying her little jug of milk from Angoreus.

"...?"
"Yes, me, he only really talked to me. He never talked to my mother after the first time, when the two of them turned up in their elastic boots. In the shop he just asked once how much food my mother bought."

The amount of sugar and rice that the girl's mother bought was appropriate for two poor people. In a brief interrogation of the woman who kept the shop in Santa María de Vilar das Las, a league and a half from Auguela, the sergeant extracted the information he wanted, and seemed satisfied. But he knew that they had a vegetable garden and a she-goat.

"...?"

"The first time he came up to me I felt very scared. He gave me a packet of rich tea biscuits, made by Oliveira. I'll always remember that. I didn't want my mother to see his present so I ate them all before I got home."

A certain complicity had tied the girl to the sergeant that day.

"...?"

"No. I didn't dare tell my mother that I'd spoken to that man."

"...?"

"No. The second time I spoke to that man I stopped being afraid of him."

"...?"

"I felt a kind of trust. It might seem crazy, but I'd become..."

"...?"

"Yes, fond of him."

During the course of their encounters, always in remote places, a bond had become established. A complicity as slimy as the filth that was flushed down the pipe. The girl had grown to like the sergeant with his mild smile and his blue eyes. She felt sad whenever he was away from Auguela for long. Sometimes he brought her lollipops, sometimes biscuits. One day he came with a little square box, decorated with sea-shells. She wrapped it up in rags and hid it in the loft.

"...?"

"Whenever that man was with me, he asked where my father was hiding. Whenever he did this, something burnt inside my breast. And then I'd lower my eyes, and what my gaze always, always came to rest on was his feet in their elastic boots. Those boots made me feel sick. And then I'd think about my father. And I'd clench my lips together. 'I'll never tell him where Daddy's hiding,' I'd think with all my might. And I'd run home."

"...?"

"I'd be on my way home after catechism, sir, my religious instruction class, walking along the old track that goes to Santa María, picking flowers and making daisy chains with the other girls. He'd be watching me, I don't know, lying in wait for me until all my classmates had gone their own ways back home. And then he'd appear in front of me and..."

"...?"

"Yes. I was happy to see him but, I don't know why, I stopped feeling happy and I started feeling sick as soon as I looked at his black elastic boots."

"...?"

"I think the worst thing for Daddy was the winter."

Even the slime in the drain that connected the lavatory to the cesspit froze. In his burrow, the girl's daddy wrapped himself in blankets and his teeth chattered. Chilblains had turned the top of his ears, his hands and his toes into raw flesh. His lips had split. When the snow covered the pile of firewood, the cold below became a little more bearable. For the girl's daddy, his nightly outing was a trip to Heaven. Those two or three hours in bed with his wife returned him to life and to happiness. Then the cesspit's exit hole, with daddy inside again, had to be raked over with snow. Before sunrise the girl's mummy would walk over her husband's footprints, mixing them in with other tracks that went in different directions across the yard.

"...?"

"So in spring, that's right, the man in the elastic boots came back and one day he told me that if I didn't tell him where Daddy was other men of the Guardia Civil would come and they would take Mummy and beat her until she told them everything. I cried that night and I decided that when the man came again I'd lead him to the cesspit and tell him that my father was in there. I'd do it to stop them beating my mother. That was after the end of winter."

"...?"

"It was the worst day of my life."

"...?"

"It breaks my heart just to think of it. Please don't make me say any more."

"...?"

"First the sound of horses' hooves woke me up. I peeped out of the window and I saw eight civil guards each getting off his horse and pulling a rifle out of its wrapping, apart from one of them who was holding a pistol. My soul froze over, sir. At almost the same instant I heard a car engine and suddenly a man appeared wearing a red cap. At his side was the man in the elastic boots. The men in the three-cornered hats half-destroyed the house with their rifle-butts. They fired at the ceiling-boards and at the doors. They grabbed my mother by the hair and dragged her over to the pile of firewood where Daddy was hiding."

A civil guard lieutenant had arrived in Auguela with seven men. The case of the ANG cell in Vigo had to be concluded. That bastard was the only one left, and he must be in Auguela. If the local squad hadn't been capable of discovering anything, he'd do so himself. They had come on horseback from Celanova. The sergeant of the local squad soon joined them in a Baliglia limousine from headquarters. With shouts and curses they searched the entire house, the chest of drawers, the kneading trough, the two wardrobes, the loft. They fired their guns. They ravaged without cease and with pleasure. As agreed, they set about raping the fugitive's wife, yelling what they were going to do, what they were doing. They wanted the fugitive to hear them. To hear that four men were pulling at her hands and at her feet and that the corporal was lifting her skirt. The lieutenant roared with laughter, his hand on his belly.

"...?"

"I ran to the man who gave me biscuits and who appeared before me in the lanes. For me he was a saviour, a best friend. 'Tell me where he is, tell me where he is,' he said. 'Tell me, me only. If you don't tell me I can't make them stop. If they find him they'll kill him.' I was opening my mouth to tell him that father was in the cesspit when I lowered my eyes in shame and my gaze fell on his elastic boots. And I kept quiet."

"...?"

"One of the men in the three-cornered hats grabbed me by the ears and said: 'Look, look. Look what we're doing to your whore of a mother.' I looked round at the man in the elastic boots, who was watching, still as still, his arms folded and a snarl on his snout, his otter-snout, which I'd once thought was a nice mouth. I can remember silly little things: the way a tip of his collar was bent upwards, the Falangist yoke-and-arrows emblem on one of the lapels of his thread-bare suit. He nodded his head at me in a strange way, as though to say goodbye. The man in the cap like a plate in a red cloth cover was smiling, enjoying himself. That was when Daddy from inside the cesspit screamed to them to stop, screamed that he was giving himself up."

"...?"

"No sir. The civil guards were shouting so much that at first nobody heard my father."

"...?"

"My mother hadn't made a sound. I know that my mother stopped herself from screaming so as not to make my father give himself away. I'm certain of it. But soon something moved in the pile of firewood and my father appeared, knocking the grate and the branches into the air, with his hands up. As soon as they saw him they all went for him, even the man in the red cap, and they knocked him to the ground. I shut my eyes and put my hands over my ears."

When the lieutenant saw the girl's father standing there, in the spring sunshine, as white as sperm, with his hands in the air, he charged at him and smashed the long barrel of his nine-bore Astra pistol into his face. He knocked him to the ground. They all pounced upon the fallen man and began to kick him and to beat him with their rifle butts. All the while they bellowed like animals and cursed and insulted him. The horses took fright and tugged at their reins, tied to the hitching rings. The girl's mother tried to obstruct the blows and was knocked away with a rifle butt in the belly, which left her writhing on the ground in agony. Only the sergeant from the local squad stood still, staring at the girl, his arms folded and the corners of his mouth set in a grimace of indifference.

"...?"

"They took my father away, his face covered in blood, tied to the tail of the lieutenant's horse. My mother filled the air with her howls. I went up to the man in the elastic boots. He looked at me in fury and screwed up his mouth and his little blond moustache. For a moment I thought he was going to hit me. I hated him and I still hate him now with all my soul. 'Why didn't you tell me where he was, you little bitch?' he said, with a drop of spittle lodged in each corner of his mouth. And he got into the car, next to the man in the cap like a plate in a red cloth cover. 'Why didn't you tell me, you little bitch?'"

As he was getting into the Baliglia limousine, the girl looked at his elastic boots for the last time, and she understood. The sergeant of the local squad had known from the very beginning where her father was hiding. But he had wanted the girl to tell him, so that he could leave her wounded with remorse for the rest of her life. His failure, caused by the irruption of the lieutenant and his men, was a great disappointment for him.

And the girl ran up to the loft, unwrapped the shell-covered box from the Isle of A Toxa, and stood in frozen contemplation of it.

(From *Arraianos*, 1991)

Lobosandaus

September 15th

My dear Uncle,

In accordance with your instructions, I am writing to put you au fait with the details of my arrival in this district of Nigueiroá and, more precisely, in the small town of Lobosandaus, the seat not only of the district capital but also of the local school to which I have been appointed thanks to your paternal protection and munificence.

Situated on the lower slopes of the range known as the Serra Grande, Lobosandaus has a population of one hundred inhabitants and has made a strong impression on me. It lies silent here as the oblique sun of these last days of summer lends it a Mediterranean air, dry and clear. The market place is a field of oaks several centuries old: it forms a terrace and is surrounded by cast-iron railings with two rosettes by Malingre, in the style of those at the Esplanade in Ourense, making an excellent belvedere that overlooks the plains through which meanders the small river known locally as Das Gándaras although in maps it is called Lucenza, as at its highest point it passes through the parish of that name. On the far side of that expanse of broom and brushwood, amongst whose undulations dolmens are not uncommon, looms an immense dark wall crowned by crags in unexpected shapes, like strange sculptures resembling fantasy organ pipes. This is the Serra known as do Crasto, which stands facing the Serra Grande. The boundary stones of Portugal are planted on its highest peaks. Even now, as I write you this letter, moments before I present myself at the school to take up my post, I can see from my room this awe-inspiring expanse of wasteland, on which the cattle belonging to these herdsmen graze and the early blossoms produce the clear, heavy honey that has brought such deserved prestige to the district of Nigueiroá. For the fact of the matter is, Reverend Uncle, that no sooner had I arrived than I was invited to take up my lodgings here at Aparecida's, and found them highly satisfactory.

I have a spacious room, with a writing desk, leading into a glazed balcony with which other rooms also connect. From here, contemplating the distant border peaks, I shall keep you informed of the little things making up my life in Lobosandaus, which already feels, only an hour after dismounting from the mare that brought me from Bande, following an interminable stagecoach journey, like an end of the known world, a secluded yet sunny, pleasant and hospitable place. Aparecida the inn-keeper and her husband Luís could not have been more attentive, ceremonious and warm in the welcome they gave me. It is they with whom I shall have to dwell, God alone knows how long for, and it is they who will introduce me to the life and the world of the people of Lobosandaus, this town of which I am now a resident, although a privileged one because of the educational and public function that has brought me here.

Wish me, therefore, much good fortune, Reverend Uncle, whose hand I kiss in filial reverence.

II

September 20th

Reverend Uncle,

Following on from my previous one, and without waiting for your reply, I hasten to send you a second letter from Lobosandaus in order to recount an incident of a most unfortunate nature.

This morning the earliest risers in the town found, hanging from the branch of a cedar by means of a slip-knot made in thick rope, the body of a fifty-year-old man which turned out to be that of Señor

Nicasio Remuñán, a gelder by trade from the neighbouring parish of Lucenza. "He always wore Mexican silver spurs and was a man of great presence," the old servant at the inn, Hixinio by name, told me. The event has left its mark on me because just a couple of days ago, the day after I arrived in Lobosandaus, I had occasion to see this man Nicasio come to Aparecida's wearing a large hat with a turned-down brim and a thigh-length sheepskin jacket, unbuttoned so as to best display his watch-chain with three sovereigns dangling from it. He had an honest laugh in which shone an abundance of gold teeth and he spoke in a loud voice, as if to announce himself by bugle-call. Long brown whiskers adorned his upper lip as though he were wearing two brushes set opposite one another beneath his red, potato-shaped nose.

The truth is that I had taken a liking to the poor gelder. As he shook my hand, he fixed me with an intense gaze and welcomed me to the lands of Nigueiroá. "Through which Jesus Christ did not pass," he said with a wink which seemed mysterious and something like a warning of danger ahead.

I should also like to inform you that, as you instructed me, I betook myself to the presbytery to visit Don Plácido Mazaira. I handed him your letter of introduction and, to be frank, I did not like the reception he gave me. He seemed a cold and ungiving man. He will not look one in the eye and did not even ask me to sit down or offer me any hot chocolate and cake, his afternoon snack. Nor did he enquire after your health. And so, Reverend Uncle, if you will allow me, I shall make no further advances towards this unpleasant priest who, evidently, shuns all dealings with strangers even if they be nephews of the Canon Penitentiary of Ourense Cathedral. Furthermore, he gave me the impression that he isolates himself from the people of his parish.

With nothing else to report and awaiting your esteemed news, I send you my respectful regards.

III

October 5th

Dear Uncle,

The fact that you happened to be acquainted with Señor Remuñán came as a great surprise to me. I did, indeed, realize that he was a supporter of the agrarian cause but, given that in these parts the ancient institution of fiefdom does not even exist, abolicionismo almost completely lacks relevance here. I was also utterly unaware that Nicasio Remuñán was, as you now inform me, a leading propagandist for "Solidaridad Gallega" and a dearly beloved friend of the parish priest of Beiro. Naturally, the discovery that the unfortunate gelder had, with his jokey talk, brought joy to the delightful gastronomical and literary gatherings which I know you regularly attend in the company of Don Antonio Rey Soto, Don Miguel Ferrín and Don Basilio Álvarez at the Pousa de Vilaseco Inn, made available by Dona Angelita Varela for such innocent pleasures — all this made me react with a strange intensity to the sorrowful event, already recorded as suicide, it seems, by the judge in Bande.

What can I say, Reverend Uncle? Ever since the day that Nicasio Remuñán hanged himself from the branch of a cedar by the water-mills of the River Lucenza or Das Gándaras, all one ever hears in Lobosandaus is the gelder this, the gelder that, Nicasio was this, Nicasio was that, and there seems to be no other topic of conversation at Aparecida's, where I spend all my time outside school hours because for a week now I have been living in the middle of a second Flood. A dense, impenetrable rain, immobile like a veil of milky light hanging before one's eyes, envelops the days, and the nights are a downpour of water chattering on to the roads, a fitful yet constant clamour of slates and thatch weeping out all the solitude of this God-forsaken place on to the paving stones below. And with each new discovery I make — that old Nicasio was a childless widower, that Señor Remuñán came from the Pontevedra area, from Poio to be precise, as the assistant to the blacksmith of Celanova, and that he married in Lucenza — and as you inform me of his life beyond these harsh lands, a strange feeling of danger steals over me time and again whilst in my mind's eye I see, usually at the instant preceding sleep, the face of the deceased, winking at me the day I arrived here.

Aparecida's inn and shop boasts an iron kitchen range with a wide marble slab all around it, at which sit the travelling salesmen, when there are any, people coming to market and, on a daily basis, myself, of course, for lunch, supper, and, above all at night, for long conversations and endless talk. The centre of attention there is Clamoriñas, a young servant girl with a peach of a face, whose headscarf lies on her shoulders so that the blue light of the acetylene lamp catches her hair, as golden as ripe corn, and who, while she laps up the kale in her broth with a wooden spoon, laughs under her breath and, her half-closed little eyes glinting, gossips about how old Hixinio had a terrible argument with poor dead Nicasio. And this old servant, who brought up Aparecida and her brothers, all now dead or lost in Cuba or up north, starts to say and then unsay, malicious laughter escaping from his toothless mouth, full of large soft pieces of bread, that this happened, that happened, and the other happened. And I reach the conclusion that Nicasio Remuñán was indeed an unrepenting Don Juan who had no respect for either single or married women and who had once been obliged to spend some time in Portugal because of behaviour forbidden by the sixth commandment, and the priest was sick and tired of dropping hints against him at mass. Yet the young people liked him and, after all, he was a welcome daily visitor to the spinning-place, where he had a special gift for worming his way into singing duels and where he was the best dancer of the bolero and the lancers which, as, Reverend Uncle, you are doubtless aware, are the rhythms most enjoyed by the people of this remote place, to the accompaniment of tambourines, triangles and frying pans. I am unable, however, to refrain from telling you, Reverend Uncle, that a possibly absurd, if persistent, idea is obsessing me. What if Nicasio the gelder did not commit suicide and was murdered as a result of his bad behaviour with women?

Having no further news, your loving nephew bids you farewell.

IV

October 22nd

Reverend Uncle,

In answer to the question that you ask me with regard to the doctor, Luís Lorenzo, I must tell you that he spends much of his time in Bande, that he does not attend the gatherings at Aparecida's and that he seems to me a townsman and extremely unhappy with his lot in this outpost of civilization. Only once or twice have we exchanged greetings. But I should say that, when we were introduced by the mayor, who I do not remember whether I have told you is Luís, nicknamed the Sparrow, the good-for-nothing, sickly-pale husband of the diligent Aparecida,

Luís Lorenzo dismounted from a mare as black as coal, doffed his bowler hat, stood to attention most courteously and held out his hand as he offered me his house and his services. "I am the locum and I can barely survive on what I'm paid in kind," he told me, his petulant lips puckering in disgust. He looked around and then stared straight at the Sparrow, as if defying a strange and powerful force. I understood nothing. If I may make so bold, Reverend Uncle, I have to say that, in my opinion, the locum is a fop.

As for the details of my life, they are of the simplest. I go from the school — where, as you know, I enjoy my teaching duties as others find pleasure in the forbidden fruits — to the inn, where an amusing, chatty society takes shelter, while outside, in the world, the rain never stops pouring down in violent, ferocious swirls.

And little by little I am becoming acquainted with facts relating to the family that houses me, facts that had not been revealed to me earlier, probably due to extreme reticence. Namely, that the Sparrow and Aparecida have a son and a daughter. The son, who is older, is known as Turelo — although he was baptised Artur — and he is often in Portugal, engaged in the gold and silver trade; he is married to Dorinda, by whom he has no children — she is a splendid woman with a dark complexion and a generous figure who spends long hours at her parents-in-law's, being on good terms with them. The daughter, apparently younger, is confined to bed in a place that I vaguely locate in the southern part of the house. Despite the malady that keeps her bedridden, I have not heard that Luís Lorenzo ever visits her. Clamoriñas has confided to me, with her heavenly little eyes wide open and astonishment on her lips, that the daughter's body is covered in gaping ulcers. She is called Obdulia, the bedridden woman.

With no more news for today, your nephew begs to take his leave of you.

V

October 30th

My dear Uncle,

The rain has all gone and has left the sky clear, so very blue that it seems in its purity to wound one's eyes. The temperature has plunged and, with it, my soul is growing cold, Reverend Uncle. Lobosandaus is a burden on my shoulders. Do not worry, dear Uncle, about the current of concupiscence that you have doubtless detected in my mention, a little over-adorned, I like to think, of Turelo's wife Dorinda. Believe me, do, she emanates a harmonious power, as when we are overwhelmed by the sight of a massive crag, but nothing could be further from me than a sensual inclination towards this married woman or towards any other individual of the female sex living in this deadly solitude. The cold has frozen the wells of my desire, of all desires. I find that I am distant, absent; I could not say that I am sad. Just as every morning the sun dawns over the thick frost that turns to white crystal the naked branches of the birch trees, so with every day that passes it is as if a hateful, hard indifference were taking more and more control of my inner being. I feel that the flow of friendliness between me and my pupils has also frozen. I say little and restrict myself to listening to the chatter that is interminably ravelled and unravelled in Aparecida's kitchen. And what is even stranger, Reverend Uncle, I realise that the people I mix with and whom I most often see are going through the same process. I know, without their saying anything, what they are thinking and I find myself more and more distant from, and with an increasing dislike of, Luís Lorenzo and Don Plácido Mazaira. I believe that they repay me in the same coinage.

I shall not trouble you further with my sombre mood, and respectfully kiss your hand.

VI

November 12th

My respected Uncle,

The lands of Nigueiroá are beginning to show their sullen winter face. The snow came, swirling down in the greyness, burying everything beneath its massive layers. It fell, at first, in a storm, with a glacial wind that lashed men's faces, this morning. They arrived at Aparecida's with their eyebrows and moustaches whitened with snow. Later, in the afternoon, the wind abated and the sky, of a dirty hue, sent out a pale yellow glow above us. Everything was saturated with a pallid premonition of terrible things: the rooftops, the fields, the mountains all seemed to vibrate with a strange dead life inside. I had never known Lobosandaus so disturbed, and I was frightened.

Something happened to me, Reverend Uncle, just yesterday, immediately after the snowstorm. I should tell you that at Aparecida's there is a wooden lavatory for the use, principally, of the customers and the proprietors, for the servants relieve themselves, as I discovered, in the communal cesspit between the rocks behind the yard wall and, if caught short, in the pigsty.

I felt the need to relieve myself and so (forgive me, Uncle, these insistent scatological references) I made my way to the glazed-in loft balcony at the back of the house, at the far end of which is the aforementioned lavatory. It was mid-afternoon, the snow had suddenly stopped falling and the wind had died down at an hour of tranquillity and bearable temperatures.

It was then that I felt a shiver down my back. A tall, thin figure was opening the lavatory door and approaching me along the balcony. Beyond the windows, the needle-like peaks of the Serra do Crasto made my skin creep. I stood to one side, truly afraid, I might even say terrified, Reverend Uncle. I stepped aside to let a woman wearing a white ankle-length nightgown pass by, protecting herself from the cold with a striped blanket pulled tight around her head and shoulders. She looked at me as she passed and I saw her pale face, her dark shrunken eyes enclosed by furrows. A forced, tense smile was directed at me. It was Obdulia, the bedridden woman.

With nothing else to report, your nephew bids you farewell.

VII

November 15th

My dear Uncle,

I have just received your much appreciated letter in which you show your concern about the state of my spirits and very kindly try to comfort me with the advice that I should focus my attention on my pedagogical work.

In all truth it seems as though the grey-brown expanses of broom and wild laburnum, the steely severity of the roof-slates, the terrifying halo of humility and the mists of poverty that cover sheds, houses and maize-garners thatched with the dark, damp straw of winter, the wretched puniness of the dogs, the cattle and even the people — as though everything, everything here had absorbed me, all of me, into its infinite mediocrity. I see the people here as intensely wan and in every face I observe globular eyes, large and protruding, I would even say cow-like, which make them all seem to belong to the same family. Eyes that appear even larger set in the eye-sockets of the charcoal men and herdsmen from Fraga de Mundil, who come down on market-day from the Serra do Crasto with the disquieting look of enigmatic and malevolent gnomes. The same eyes that the inattentive children at my school roll in the void, their tiny hands lacerated by chilblains; incapable of abstract thought and stupefied by the shots of raw brandy that their mothers administer every morning.

Whenever I come across Don Plácido or Luís Lorenzo, they drop their gaze and, after furtively greeting me, they quicken their pace and I *know* that they shun my company with the same intensity that I shun theirs. They regard me as one more inhabitant of Lobosandaus.

There is, however, one person in whom I do not see these cow-eyes that seem to confer a family air on the inhabitants of this damned place. I should like to make it clear that this person is Dorinda, whose body exudes, for me, the glow of a salubrious and comforting simplicity.

Your nephew kisses your beneficent hand.

VIII

November 16th

Reverend Uncle,

In the last few days the weather has turned from freezing cold to moderate and mild, with a fine, continuous rain that is sometimes no more than drizzle or light mist. Everything is grey and damp. And it happened that Obdulia (the woman whose body is covered in gaping ulcers) suddenly arose from her bed and started coming and going throughout the house, laughing and speaking with an unfamiliar stridency. I encounter her on pathways and in passages, in the back corridor and on the balcony. She always gives me a forthright look.

She always greets me in a powerful voice that to me seems *manly*. She drinks wine in abundance, much to the consternation of her parents, who do not know what to make of such a sudden improvement in her health. Indeed, ever since she rose up from the malady that had kept her bedridden, she has often been seen in the company of her sister-in-law Dorinda, the pair of them arm in arm, engaged in endless whispered conversations. As a result I find myself deprived of Dorinda's company and it is as if she were rationing her smile, on that fresh, dark rose of a mouth. I spend the afternoons in the clutches of melancholy, staring at the bare oaks in the market place, and I stand there almost hypnotised in contemplation of the cast-iron rosettes. An eerie silence has overcome Lobosandaus of late. Many of my pupils are staying away from my school.

I shall keep you informed, Reverend Uncle.

IX

November 21st

Reverend Uncle,

I insist that you should not entertain suspicions about my feelings for Dorinda. As I have already told you, and as I shall now reiterate, these feelings are quite straightforward and pure. She seems to be one of the few normal people to be found in Lobosandaus. And, if you will allow me the sincerity due to a person who, like yourself, is so familiar with the failings and aberrations of mankind, as much through your long experience of administering the sacrament of confession as through your rigorous study of Ethics, I can inform you that there is at the present time no danger that I am, or shall become, the object of Dorinda's sinful desire. There is no doubt that the beautiful young wife is in the diabolical power of Obdulia who, ever since she emerged from her sickly seclusion, has been exercising resolute masculine control over her sister-in-law. She loves her, unquestionably, with a nefarious love, with the blind fury of inverted passion. Dorinda, feminine, timid, is drifting into a vice that is perhaps replacing the legitimate love of her spouse, absent in Portugal. She has no eyes for me any more, Dorinda. The scandal exploded throughout the district of Nigueiroá, the news even reaching Bande, when old Hixinio caught them, mounted one atop the other, like calves on heat, in a corner of the straw loft where they (or rather Obdulia, I imagine) had made their nest amongst the oats; and he drove them away, beating them with a broom and screaming like a madman, calling them brutes and swine.

I hope to allay, with the disgusting episode that I have just related to you, your fears for my conduct. And yet my intuition tells me that there is more to this matter than one can see or hear. The gossip soon subsided and an icy silence has taken shape in Lobosandaus, and everyone at Aparecida's seems indifferent, yet pensive and serious. I think they are worried about deeper, more mysterious issues than a simple if somewhat sordid lesbian outburst, if you will pardon the humanistic reference and the excess of sibilants.

Awaiting your esteemed news, your nephew sends you his respectful regards.

X

November 23rd

Dearest Uncle,

There has been a change in the weather and the laurel-toppling north wind has come, as cold and sharp as a knife, leaving all of us here in Lobosandaus with bursting, stinging lips. The going away of the rains has modified the oppressive situation which we had been suffering here, and the secret, harboured as I had suspected in everyone's breast, has been revealed. Yesterday, Sunday, some surprising things happened. When everyone returned from mass, the men gathered in groups in the town square — which is, as is well known, the custom here — to chat and discuss their affairs. Suddenly, as I was considering the bulging, bovine eyes of those people who seemed to be in the grip of some strange spell, I saw Obdulia appear, coughing loudly on the wooden balcony at the front of the house. We all noticed that she was wearing a pair of man's trousers, which hung loosely on her, and that she was sporting a hat that might have been Luís the Sparrow's. Suddenly, at the top of her voice, Obdulia demanded everyone's attention, and raised her fists and her eyes. She opened her mouth and began to deliver a brief yet comprehensive harangue on the agrarian cause, speaking on the fundamental principles of the abolition of fiefdom, which you yourself know a great deal about, and even hold in common with Don Basilio. She had the unmistakeable voice of a man, did Obdulia, standing there on the balcony. I felt the shivers down my back.

"It's Señor Remuñán," the old servant muttered, gripping my arm.

"It's him," answered another man standing next to us.

That was when Clamoriñas burst bareheaded out of the door of Aparecida's inn shrieking and pointing to the balcony as she shook her head and her blond plait lashed the cold air like a horsewhip.

"It's old Nicasio! It's the gelder!" she was crying.

There were those who made the sign of the cross. Women thrust their heads out of openings, emerged on to balconies and at doorways, and leant far out of windows, howling like animals. And Obdulia was soon overwhelmed by her family and locked into the loft.

It was from that moment onwards that the inhabitants of Lobosandaus began to speak clearly to me. Everyone agreed that the spirit of Nicasio Remuñán, the agrarian reformer and gelder, had entered Obdulia's body, making the most of the fact that it was covered in gaping ulcers, and had taken her over. Everyone supposed that he had done so in order to possess Dorinda, about whom he had been crazy when alive.

In the certainty that you will find this letter extraordinarily strange, your nephew bids you farewell.

XI

November 30th

My dear Uncle,

You inquire after Dorinda's husband, familiarly known as Turelo. Well, in my first days here in Lobosandaus I have hardly seen him a couple of times. Clamoriñas, the pretty serving wench, says that he never speaks. He is a short, pallid, weak individual. He is similar in build to the Sparrow. He always carries a wicker basket, the instrument of his trade as a trafficker in gold and silver. He never looks directly at one, yet I still noticed his bulging eyes, the stigma of the peasants up here. It seems that he comes and goes surreptitiously; he appears and disappears without anyone noticing. It is common knowledge that he always crosses the border at Guntumil, in the Serra do Crasto, and that, from Turei onwards, he travels along the main highways, roads and railways that lead to Braga, to Lisbon. I believe that, as yet, he knows nothing about his wife's misdoings and misfortunes.

Regarding what you tell me about vain observances and superstition, I have to say, with all due respect, that one has to live here throughout a winter such as this winter to be able to understand the gloomy burden of mystery and the presence, which feels almost physical, of things and events that one knows are just ignorance and barbarism, but in the face of which one cannot maintain an attitude of haughty aloofness — fear, really — such as the attitude that the priest and the doctor and, I suppose, the apothecary, to whom I have not yet had occasion to introduce myself, adopt towards the inhabitants of Nigueiroá and even towards me, here, in Lobosandaus.

With nothing further to report, your nephew dutifully kisses your hands.

XII

December 8th

Reverend Uncle,

Something horrible and unexpected has happened. Obdulia, unhappy Obdulia, was discovered yesterday morning hanging by the neck from a branch of one of the cedars that form a copse near the water mills of the River Lucenza, sometimes called Das Gándaras, hard by the wall that encloses the field where Lobosandaus market is held. The weather suddenly took a turn for the better, as it did on the day when Nicasio Remuñán hanged himself at that very same spot.

The Civil Guard went to arrest Turelo in Terrachán, where he was staying, engaged in his trafficking. They took him to their barracks at Lobios, and there they beat him for two days and two nights. Then the judge at Bande released him, without pressing a single charge. Turelo was suspected, it seems, of being the murderer of his sister Obdulia, and they had also wanted to lay upon him the blame for the gelder's death. It is said that the authorities had heard the rumours spreading through Lobosandaus, Lucenza, Fraga de Mundil, Riomau, Santa Marina de Freixo, Riquiás, in other words throughout all the parishes in the municipality of Nigueiroá as well as the neighbouring areas beyond the Portuguese border in the Couto Mixto, according to which rumours Turelo had hanged those two poor souls out of jealousy at the thought of their being with Dorinda, his radiant, enchanting wife. With his face the colour of a blackberry and his back dark and bloody from the flogging, Turelo returned to his home in Lobosandaus, but he did not stay there long, and he made his way to his parents' house, where he went to bed, to that same bed in that same room where his sister Obdulia had lain for so long with her body covered in gaping ulcers.

Reverend Uncle: much as it may disgust you, I must tell you what all of us here think, that is to say what all of the townsfolk think: that Turelo did in fact kill Nicasio Remuñán out of jealousy because he was making advances to his wife, and that the gelder's spirit did in fact enter into Obdulia's open body in order to satisfy his desires for Dorinda and, finally, that Turelo did in fact kill his persistent rival for a second time by taking the life of his own sister. The judge in Bande naturally inclined towards the suicide theory, and Don Plácido Mazaira made an attempt to refuse the deceased a burial in holy ground, but he immediately changed his mind fearful, it seems, of the popular reaction in Lobosandaus, and he pretended not to know anything about what had happened.

Please accept, Uncle, a fond farewell from your most loyal nephew.

XIII

December 20th

Dearly beloved Uncle and Protector,

Everyone in Lobosandaus and the villages for many leagues around is witnessing with astonishment what is happening here. The days are becoming clearer and colder. The children's attendance at school gets worse and worse. Those who do come seem to be deep in thought as they follow my lessons, but in reality they just sleep at their desks with their eyes open. Rounded, bulging, bovine eyes, the eyes of this community in which I live, and in which I suffer much anxiety, Reverend Uncle. There are no longer any evening gatherings in the kitchen at Aparecida's, and one only hears, on occasions, the childish, angelic voice of Clamoriñas who, as she makes the beds, sings with a cadency and a malignant sweetness that I find frightening. And fear was indeed what I felt this morning as I lathered my face prior to shaving. I thought I saw in my own eyes, for a moment, the same dead, cold bulge of the eyes of the people of Lobosandaus. Old Hixinio sits motionless for hours on end, nobody knows what he is looking at, and he has aged many years all at once. No longer does he laugh. The people here hardly stir from their houses because a new occurrence has made them all withdrawn and mistrustful.

After a few days confined to his bed, in his parents' house, Turelo decided to get up and everybody realised that a remarkable transformation had taken place in him. He began to walk with a firm step, to raise that head of his which had always been bowed. On that day, a Sunday, he appeared as people were leaving mass and, seizing Dorinda by the arm, he ordered her to go straight home. She meekly did so and husband and wife began to live together again. Turelo made no further plans to cross the border. Dorinda was submissive, humble and passive, like a hen shaking her feathers after the cockerel has mounted her. The two of them would take long winter sestas together, until the sun had set. Then they would have their dinner, and the people of Lobosandaus would hear laughter from behind the kitchen window, as at a festa. Turelo began to wear tight leggings, iron-capped boots made in Vilanova, and spurs, and told everyone that he intended to go down to A Merca and geld piglets when the time came.

I do not need to tell you, Uncle, that here in this God-forsaken land everyone is saying that Turelo has been possessed by the spirit of Nicasio Remuñán, who made the most of the moments when Turelo's body was open after the Civil Guards' beating, allowing that old goat to fornicate with his desired Dorinda in total freedom by taking over the body of her own husband.

But it is the case, Reverend Uncle, that, even if all this is true, the spirit of Turelo, who has twice found the courage to kill his enemy, seems unwilling to tolerate the gelder's invasion, and sometimes we all see Turelo strutting around in the manner of Nicasio, haughty and proud, as brave and smart as anyone, and at other times it seems to us that he returns to himself, with his lowered gaze and furtive walk close to the walls. One day Turelo mutters that he is preparing a trip to Amarante, only to contradict himself the next day by ordering his wife to make a pie with meat from a roebuck that he has killed in the Serra Grande, and take it to be cooked at the bakery, so that the two of them can eat alone, at home. One effect of the struggle taking place in Turelo's open body is that sometimes he scratches his face and rolls about on the ground as if he wanted to injure himself. Aparecida never stops crying, while Luís the Sparrow has lost his speech and wanders along the lanes like a ghost.

This is what is happening, and I am telling it to you as it is, Reverend Uncle, even though I risk your attributing my narration to such forces as the influence of the milieu or any of the other forces that I keep suggesting to myself as I attempt to put an end to this nightmare.

Hold ever present, Reverend Uncle, my affection and my respect.

XIV

December 25th

Uncle,

Without awaiting your reply, your nephew sends you this letter from the very brink of confusion. This morning I was awoken by Aparecida's screams of anguish, which were soon joined by the wails of many other women in the kitchen. Turelo had been found, at daybreak, hanging from a tree in the cedar copse by the river. The snow covers everything and muffles people's voices. The sun glares down, making us screw up our eyes, these bulging, bovine eyes common to all of us in Lobosandaus. All of us here know why this has happened. To free himself from having Nicasio the gelder inside his body, Turelo took his own life. He killed himself to escape from an existence with Dorinda's lover inside him. My head aches and I have a fever. I do not know why, but I have moved into poor Obdulia's room. I have just noticed that Dorinda, as she passed me on the balcony on her way back from the lavatory, is not weeping. And she smiled at me, Reverend Uncle. When I offered her my greeting she showed her teeth and her pale gums and she smiled at me in an inviting way that inflamed my blood and aroused my lower parts, Reverend Uncle. I am terrified, I sense that there is somebody else in this room and I crave for Dorinda and I think that misfortune is going to return to Lobosandaus and that more bodies are going to be opened.

Come for me, Reverend Uncle; for the love of God, come and fetch me and take me away from here to Ourense.

(From *Arraianos*, 1991)

Artur's Love

"Icelui Preux vers les Roches décrites
Alloit chantant les vertus et mérites
Du Prince Artus, des bons tant regretté,
Et récitoit sur son luth argenté..."

Jean-Baptiste Rousseau, *Roches de Salisburi* (1713)

"......................................
non quelli a cui fo rotto il petto e l'ombra
con esso un colpo per la man d'Artú."

Dante, *Comedia, Inferno,* canto 32, 61-62

I

King Artur had discovered, from the mouth of the mischief-maker Galván, that Guenebra was being unfaithful to him with Lanzarote.

Along the ferny pathway, bordered with dahlias, the monarch with a wounded heart was walking alone. All the pain in the world was tearing at his throat with the ferocity of a lynx. At the end of the park, the gloomy, scowling Tower of the Dolorous Gard thrust its battlements upwards towards a leaden sky in which an army of tiny devils or shrieking swifts was wheeling to and fro. His noble face distorted in despair, brown and blue globes under his eyes, King Artur wept tears of fire and his sobs turned his beard and moustache white with spittle. Guenebra, Lanzarote! She had been his beloved, his only beloved, the gull in the rainy dawn, the blinding skin of burning snow, the stone-like certainty of the nations of the world, the saffron of the ceremonial banquets, the Persian sendal on the burnt forehead of the

146

summers, the nights of the bellowing of the stags by the hunting lodge that drowned those other cries of love of stately bronze among canopies and otter skins, and her naked body renewing itself in the incessant, manifold movements of a waterfall. He, Lanzarote, the he-goat so full of grace in combat, a burning coal in each eye, the faithful armed presence repeated for as long as Artur could remember — forever, it seemed — on every threshold, at every door, at the foot of every flight of stairs, at every triumph in a tourney; the power of the age at which a knight receives the finest gifts the sun has to offer, at which martial prowess is a simple matter and victories come to the hero with the submissive mien of a white-footed doe, the symbol of the boundless love of the man who serves and is honourable.

Now that the betrayal has been consummated and discovered, and the pain drained to the last hollow where dark doubts and longed-for explanations drift, King Artur, devastated on this leaden afternoon, wants only to retrieve, retrieve Guenebra's skin, bring her back to him, rediscover the heat of hours past and clotted liquids of satisfied desires and daydreams shared during evenings of glory and flowered banquets, he only wants Guenebra, the heron, the crane, the perfection of grace, to come back to him, and Lanzarote never to return from Armorica unless it be to receive dishonour at the hands of King Artur, who is weeping once more on the ferny pathway as he shouts for Galván, because they are leaving for the old convent of Dodro where Guenebra is being held prisoner and where, perhaps, she has reached a state of repentance.

II

The summer sky of Dodro was studded with lights. The Greater Dog, the Seven Sisters and the Plough gave off a pale, burning vapour. The full moon had earlier been a ball of fire behind the Serra de Sangres. It was rising now, as round as a coin, giving out coldness and manifold desires.

A severe cell whose austerity does not prevent a silk head-dress, adorned with emeralds and formed with hoops of gold, from hanging upon a rough iron hook stuck into the back of the worn chestnut door: there lies Guenebra.

The light of the moon alights on the queen's temple. Artur asks her, with solemn, unadorned words, to return to his bed and to the governance of the royal household. In Guenebra's mind a runic "no!" takes shape, a stony refusal, an absolute rejection made of broken, cutting flint. Amidst white lights, irises lie in wait like long, dark seaweed, the voices of the black rocks of the winter cliffs. Dona Guenebra flatly refuses to return to the great, absolute king, to his frondent love of ancient oak. Dishevelled, the disgraced lady spits out hard insults, beads of venom, propositions armed with stings that sting King Artur. That force King Artur into a situation of withdrawal, retreat, and finally hurl him towards the door. The many-sided notion of total self-abandonment explodes on Guenebra's lips and shatters into a thousand lights of something like hatred or some sort of madness, and the lights beat against the breast of the terrified King Artur. Narrow mines of repulsion are dug at the back of the unfaithful queen's mind and it is not Lanzarote and it really has nothing to do with Lanzarote; Lanzarote is no part of this pool of heartrending pain, or rather King Artur does not understand, King Artur is so far away, administering the words and the wild boars of Britain, that he does not understand, and sharp stars break up into schemes of severe anger that scorn the present and leave King Artur in the remote distance. Then internal birds of envy and rage swoop down upon Guenebra. Tatters and rags startle the unkempt queen in the long shadows and the echoes of Dodro Vello, and drive her to the edge of a scream. The imprisoned queen's clothes are pulled asunder. She tears her garments with nails of sharpened graphite. Blood flows from furrows on her breasts of amber. Like a stone hurled with murderous intent, the royal head-dress flies towards Artur's head and he, at that moment, cannot recognise Guenebra, and sinks back into his wretchedness and rides away from her cell, withdrawn into his horror.

The convent of Dodro Vello — sarcophagi, canticles, encounters of silk and shadow — was an underground beast: bristling with volutes and dishonoured crenellations; lust and isolation inhabited it, and it all spoke in the voice of the imprisoned Queen Guenebra, as Artur spurred his horse on like one possessed, among the white cloths laid out by the great moon.

III

The company had pitched its tents and lit its fires, at Galván's command, in a clearing in the forest by the River Esmeralda, which runs along the foot of Mount Sangres, on whose lower slopes the convent of Dodro Vello stands.

By the bonfires, the soldiers play at torturers and savour slow draughts of mead. When the King appears in the fog, sticky mouths growl the order, emit howls, and make the arms' soundless metal sing. Galván lifts the tapestry on the King's tent. King Artur walks into it, dismissing his knight with a doubtful gesture.

Alone in the shadows, men's distant voices in hoarse, insistent song, King Artur does not understand the reason for his immense pain. Why, why, the incessant question hits him again and again. The soldiers' laughter exasperates and enervates him. Guenebra, even when imprisoned, disdains to return to him. Artur paces up and down the tent. He thinks that only Merlín will be able to comfort his battered heart with words laden with good sense and consolation.

It is the hour at which the morning star burns brightest and sleepless eyes itch, heralding the dawn. King Artur decides to travel in search of Merlín. He shouts for Galván, who appears in an instant, bowing. Galván rides in his armour throughout the camp, alerting the men in thunderous tones. Shouts pierce the dawn, and there is a tumultuous clanking of arms and neighing of horses. The tents are torn down, rather than taken down. Bleary, drunken eyes confuse reins, caparisons and horse-cloths; harnesses fall to the ground and cuirasses resound like cracked bells against shields, helmets, bascinets, roundels, before being picked up and thrown on over shirts and then covered with tabards from which the glory of the Grail shines forth. Galván calls out. King Artur, uneasy, strokes his beard in a repetitive gesture. An ass flees along the bank of the River Esmeralda, chased by a boy with fair hair and frightened eyes, beaten black and blue from his knees to his shoulders.

At last the host forms up. At its head, a restless King Artur, spittle dribbling from between his open lips. Behind him, Galván and Keu the Seneschal, each with one hand on the reins and the other on a hip. The troops ride on to the plain under a summer sun that warms their backs. On the way to Francastel, Merlín's home, King Artur gives himself up to hopefulness and remembers Guenebra gathering roses in the gardens at Camelot.

IV

King Artur, Galván and Keu gaze at each other in silence. They are
horrified at what they see from the hill. Time and time again they stare
back towards Francastel. What has become of that keep, as elegant as
an Arabian cabinet, said to have been built in one night by the black
elves for Merlín, the wizard of Britain? What of those spacious
dwellings of blue-veined marble, where Merlín led his secluded, secret
life, with their hidden doors that led into other worlds? And what of
those walls, crowned with walkways of dark wood and roofs of the
finest slate? In their place, a shapeless heap of rubble was all that
remained of the famous, free castle of Francastel.

"Magic has been at work here, my lord," Galván had observed.

King Artur, without replying, dismounted and ordered the tents to
be pitched, so as to spend the night in that place and wait to see what
happened — to see, in other words, what Merlín had decided must
happen.

V

From time to time the sentries' steps can be heard and the sound of
arms shatters the frozen silence. King Artur sleeps a restless sleep. In
the depths of his eyes dark liquids and flowing amber swirl. Circles
come before him, and grey elytra, and red whirlpools. Sometimes, a
wave or a spiral changes shape and in its place appears a dagger, a
child, a mother's flight into the distance, filling Artur with fear and
making him moan as he lies on his creaking camp bed, sweating
between skins of ermine. In the middle of his dream, in which there is
now a blue plain, the buildings of Francastel take shape, and King
Artur recognises them at once. As he glides up the stairs and along the
corridors of the castle, the dream fills him with joy because great
flames are burning in the open fireplace and there upon a splendid
bench, adorned with gold and silver, sits Merlín, who is coming to his
feet and fixing his eyes of jet upon those of his lord, before going down
on to his knees and kissing his hand. Artur's heart beats as softly as a
moth at the sight of the wisest of the Britons, the wisest of all the wise
in the world. In his dream, King Artur raises Merlín from the floor and
the two men kiss each other on the lips. King Artur sits by the fire and
allows Merlín to comb his hair. Before the King speaks, Merlín

explains to him that he has destroyed Francastel himself, to avoid having to receive Artur there and, in accordance with the laws of British hospitality, having to answer his questions concerning the reason for the love between Guenebra and Lanzarote do Lago.

"I preferred," says Merlín, "not to tell you the truth."

Saddened, King Artur asks the wizard to offer him, at least, some advice.

"I shall give you more than a piece of advice," he says. "I shall tell you that the one who can guide you is none other than the enchanter Roebek of Tagen Ata."

He then explains to Artur that the first thing he must do is travel to Conarán. Once in the main square of this city he must sit down and await a sign. This sign will be unequivocal and will serve to tell him that Merlín's brother in wisdom is ready to receive King Artur. And Artur must be very alert to any unusual events and peculiar occurrences that he may witness in the main square of Conarán. Once in Roebek's presence, the King will ask him directly why Guenebra abandoned him for Lanzarote and why she refuses to return to Camelot.

And with these words the dream shattered into a hundred shards of glass. King Artur let himself fall into a well of wool, at the bottom of which he snuggled down and rested until dawn.

VI

And now, in Ireland, on the road between Francastel and Conarán, King Artur's company was caught unawares by the first night of the year, the night on which the sepulchres of the ancients open and the dead gods can walk among us.

Before sunset, King Artur saw a flock of swans flying over Lake Espadanedo, and he took this to be a sign that the shadows wanted him to stop at this point in his journey. He ordered the tents to be pitched and he detached himself from the crowd. He wandered alone through the broom, sighing and sighing.

As he reached the top of a hill he saw the red sun iridescent upon the sheer mists of the lake. Great rocks were silhouetted against the glow before him, their shadows blending into those of the broom, the gorse and the young oaks.

As the last ray of sun dies upon the sheet of water, a choir of muffled voices arises from the earth. The King feels confused and senses the presence of innumerable people. He grips Escalibur, the divine sword, but draws it no more than four fingersbreadths from its scabbard. He plants both feet upon the road, which disappears around a bend before him. The voices seem to be coming from that direction, and they sound faint, harsh, distorted: the voices of the dead. Suddenly a vague host of small lights and whiteness blinds the King. In a lightning flash he sees through closed eyes a hazy pool of milk in which shadows sail. He opens his eyes and the lights are still there, and a figure erect upon a motionless horse, as though made of stone. The song fades away, dies out. Artur recognises Dagda, an Irishman from the depths of the earth: the powerful lost god, the great champion of eating and loving. Driven by terror, King Artur tries to lift his hand to his forehead to make the sign of the cross, but an acute, crystalline pain stills it. Thus released, Escalibur falls back into position and the clash of the hand-guard against the golden mouth of the scabbard is an explosion that echoes like metallic thunder in the oak trees, in the great rocks. Dagda's voice is as graceful as linen sheets, as slender as a tapering cobra in the summer wetlands, as deep as the song of the waterfalls and the wind in the caves and the forests.

"Chan eil càil ceàrr air Arthur!" Dagda cries in Gaelic.

King Artur greets the ancient god, who tells him that in the Dead Kingdoms his grief for Guenebra has been the object of compassion and discussion, in the long hours with neither sunrise nor sunset that the Tuatha Dé Danann have to bear, with only the promise of the first day of the year to sustain them. Dagda has come to help King Artur. To do so he has had, in the presence of the Assembly, to defeat Lug of the Enormous Hand, who hates King Artur and the Britons. Throughout spring the two gods stared into each other's eyes, as each remembered the banquet a thousand years earlier at which they had held an eating contest. Dagda had won on that occasion, having not only eaten a greater amount of chestnuts and venison, but also, in his combative fervour, seized all the stones and clods of earth at the bottom of the cooking pit and dispatched them in the same way. With the simple act of meeting his gaze Dagda had again established his superiority over Lug. And so here he is, with his host. He says three things to Artur. One: that he should beware of Galván, who is Lug's protegé, and should not heed what he says because his only motivation is his envy of Lanzarote. Two: that he should follow the advice of Roebek of Tagen Ata to the letter. Three: that birds always return to their master's fist.

These words having been spoken, the lights begin to go back to where they came from and Dagda disappears among the songs that fill the thick fog, barely brightened by the moon, of Lake Espadanedo.

King Artur returns to the camp. He picks over the ancient god's pieces of advice, without understanding the meaning of the third.

VII

The Main Square of Conarán, beyond the borders of the kingdoms of Britain. Strange voices, squawks even. Earth-coloured faces and lowered gazes in which something is burning. King Artur, Galván, Keu the Seneschal, and their soldiers, disguised as merchants, all watch the festa. Dancing, shouting, booming music, laughter that pierces the dusty air. Girls lifting their skirts and the mouths of toothless old men screeching a wretched, pallid desire. Mummers, masqueraders, revels.

King Artur, afflicted by tedium, sits himself on the bench outside an inn. Galván orders food. Facing them, a knight sits down; in the midst of the merrymaking he appears serious and full of beauty and dignity. King Artur watches him and casually observes how he pulls a rabbit from his belt and instructs the innkeeper to cook it whole for dinner. The knight immediately begins to talk with Artur's men, and he sings them beautiful songs of love and sadness, to the accompaniment of the cittern that he carries with him.

And now King Artur remembers Guenebra, vividly. The music of the cittern and the sweet words of the songs fall into his breast like molten lead. He loves Guenebra with fury, with savagery: yes, with the very belches of his belly.

And behold, when the unknown knight's rabbit is placed upon the table, he opens his mouth, remains silent, drops the cittern to the ground. And, with his eyes fixed upon the rabbit, he turns white. The knight breaks into tears. His sobs move everyone at the table. King Artur feels the desire to weep with him.

Suddenly Galván stops a page dressed in green who is heading towards King Artur. But King Artur assents and allows the youth to kiss his hand. Galván jumps to his feet in wrath and knocks the long bench over. Drunkards tumble to the ground with jumbled oaths and mutters. The unknown knight picks up his cittern and runs away with leaping strides, leaving the roasted rabbit intact. The page, without releasing Artur's hand, requests that he grant him the favour of following him. Galván cries out. He tells the King, in harsh tones, that he should not follow the page, that it might be a trap set by Lanzarote to bring about his downfall. He reminds him that they are in a strange land. The page in green has the face of a little girl, and blue eyes. He smiles at King Artur, and waits. King Artur remembers Dagda's first piece of advice. Do not trust Galván. Galván never defeated Lanzarote in any joust or tourney. Artur recalls, as if he could see it, the pale figure upon the stone horse, in the land of rocks and mists. Beware of Galván, do not follow his advice. The youth squeezes the King's hand, gently, insistently. The King pushes Galván away, and Galván trips over the fallen bench and crashes to the ground. Galván lies among the drunkards. His wild voice merges with theirs.

In the middle of the square in Conarán, King Artur pensively follows the green-clothed page. He knows that he is being led to the house of Roebek of Tagen Ata.

VIII

King Artur followed the page and, as they passed through the doorway of a fine house with green walls, the youth seemed to be taller and treading with more firmness and assurance; as the doors opened on to a huge room hung with green standards, the green page seemed to be bearing an invisible burden of old age and wisdom upon his shoulders; as the youth placed his green coat into the hands of two servants with green tunics and long beards and turned towards Artur, the King saw upon him the wrinkles of far distant days, and what had once been bright, tender eyes, and a pomegranate smile, and lips of smooth stone, was turning into lights in a dark pool, a severe fissure in a face of rock, upon which there was not a single flutter of movement. King Artur understood.

"I am, I believe, in the presence of Roebek," he said.

The enchanter nodded. He bowed before King Artur. He showed him to an ornate chair upholstered in green velvet.

"I was born, Sire, in Tagen Ata, a land which lies on a dark confine," he finally said, in a powerful, metallic voice, "and there I was taught to practice the wisdom hidden in letters and numbers. I understand, from my lord Merlín, that you wish to know the reason why Dona

Guenebra was unfaithful to you with Lanzarote, and why she refuses to return to the governance of your household, and to share your bed."

"I also want to win Guenebra back; win Guenebra back. Not just to know; to have her again."

"I know all this," interrupted Roebek with a slight gesture of impatience.

"A few moments ago," said Artur as though talking to himself, "I saw a nobleman weeping in the square at the sight of a rabbit. I do not know why I cannot put it from my mind. I am beginning to think that this episode has something to do with the root and cause of all my misfortunes."

"You are not mistaken," replied Roebek of Tagen Ata, his voice sounding as if he were speaking into a vat, "because the knight's story is a compendium of your own."

Roebek lifted his head and, with his eyes staring into space, he spoke as follows:

"The knight you saw at the inn used to live very happily in his own land. With him lived his young son, whom he loved above all things. The knight greatly enjoyed falconry and owned a trained eagle that was the fastest and bravest bird of prey that ever there was. One day, the eagle snatched the knight's son from him and flew away, with the boy in its talons, towards the mountains. The knight wept at length for the loss of the being he loved above all others and, one day, out for a stroll with his crossbowman, he saw what had once been his eagle hunting down a rabbit. Wanting to avenge himself on the animal that had stolen his son, he ordered the crossbowman to kill the rabbit and deprive the eagle of its prey. The crossbowman did so and the eagle vanished into the heavens. The knight picked up the rabbit and headed towards the celebrations in Conarán. It was there that you saw him hand the rabbit to the innkeeper and ask him to cook it. When the innkeeper brought it back to him ready to eat, the knight looked at it and *he saw that the rabbit had the eyes of his son*, the son who had been stolen by the eagle. That was when he began to weep so bitterly."

King Artur, after a pause, asked him what the story meant.

"It is not a story," Roebek of Tagen Ata replied to him.

"What is it then, this that you have told me?"

"It is an enigma, my lord. I am the one who has been entrusted to tell it to you. But it is Liliana who will solve the enigma, and in doing so bring you peace once more, by explaining the loss of Guenebra and Lanzarote's betrayal."

"Liliana?" Artur asked, puzzled.

"Liliana, the secret wife of Lanzarote do Lago. Get Liliana, get Liliana de Escalot."

A sudden storm lashes down upon Conarán. A terrible wind blows into Roebek's room. The green standards of the land of Tagen Ata flap as though they were alive. Artur's heart shrinks before the mystery. A long silence settles between the King and the Wizard.

"Get Liliana?" King Artur finally says.

"Yes," shouts Roebek above the wind. "Get Liliana, make her yours. By doing this you will return to yourself. The shadows in your heart will be dispersed. Liliana and not I, nor Merlín, nor Dagda, will give light to your spirit, my lord Artur."

King Artur stands up and goes out into the rain. He locks himself away, as never before, in his deepest solitude.

IX

Kaer Vydr, the fortress where Artur dreams, has a round window of glass that floods the main hall with a strange light. Artur, King of Wales, Logres, Gaul, Armorica, Alba, and sometimes even Rome, rests his head in one hand, and the folds of his coif outline a pale, gaunt face. Upon his knees, Escalibur: his sword, his companion that, in the darkness of his dreams, is a youth called Kaledfwlch who spits death from his eyes of aquamarine, of clear winter sky. Birds are flying in the darkness inside Artur. Galván's black crows twisting and turning in their martial flight. Beasts heavy with shadow move about in there, like the Wild Boar that Artur had hunted throughout its life and which, when it was killed, he had devoured in order to take its hard, constant courage for himself. The hart that Merlín used to ride in the forests of his retreat. Artur recalls a modest, bloody King who, in his sadness, is wandering along the banks of lakes and rivers in search of light. Beautiful, smiling ladies offering his brave knights sunlight and sweet mead. A procession, now, of silence and brightness. The light in Kaer Vydr becomes even redder and, from the corners of the hall, dense shadows advance, like animals, like Cabal: the monarch's immortal dog. Now the King kneels upon the wrinkled rugs. A powerful sun is spinning inside his forehead, and the dream becomes almost unbearable. The procession in the house of the Fisher King. Silence, silence. It is the Grail. Why did Guenebra fuck Lanzarote do Lago? Why is

Artur the most wretched of lovers, a king unhappier than the Fisher King? Upon Artur's hand, the invisible hand of Morgana the fairy imparts a warmth that stiffens his lower parts. The procession, so often seen, and now craved by the King, who feels the touch of Cabal's invisible tongue upon his naked feet. At the head of the procession a lance, its iron shining with blood that, as it runs, drips upon the elbow of the pale man carrying it. Behind, two girls in blue gowns bear a silver platter upon which lies the severed head of an unknown man. Artur weeps and calls out, looking back. He begs the shadow of the Fisher King, he begs Peredur to recover the Sign, and for Perceval to appear, to find the emblem replete with multiple, liberating senses. Why the Grail, the Grail? Because it is denied us, we remain in ignorance of everything, and the fruits of the Fisher King are rotting, wild animals are taking countries over, the world's harmony is shattered: Guenebra, Gwenhwyfar, Guenièvre, my love who cast me to the ground. King Artur tears his linen shirt with his nails, scratches furrows into the flesh of his breast, tears out clumps of hair. His tears are silent and end at the moment when the windows of the Glass Castle stop spilling their scarlet liquid. Bloody cloths, Viviana's hated laugh in the depths of the Lake, the putrescent voices of the Tuatha Dé Danann, a child of gold who will save the Britons, innumerable hordes of southern assassins, a desert plain, voices in the fountains that summon us to a silence of roses and silver, the scythe that beheads the child of gold, hunger and powerful darkness filling Artur's eyes with cloudy desiring and joyful swarming. In search of peace, King Artur drinks ale and calls for Keu the Seneschal, who has replaced the traitor Galván in the search for the cause of his unhappiness.

X

The ruddy light of the torches is flickering on Liliana's back; Artur remembers the Wild Boar; muffled voices, smothered by the night, move about in the courtyard. Liliana is resting face down and her naked body dazzles King Artur. Remembering when he was young and when he hunted the Wild Boar that ravaged the world, Artur enters Liliana's body and the Wild Boar's strength comes to him once more and once more he feels the vertigo of the furtive thrust as Liliana screams and bares her powerful teeth and rips the crimson pillow with her curved fingernails. And she turns over and rolls her eyes backwards, lights, inside her eye-hole explosions and pink clouds and grooved candles, inside the eyes and belly of the secret wife of Lanzarote, lights of love in a craving confusion, lights. Perhaps Artur wants revenge. King Artur feels some sort of cutting liquid fire well up inside him and he contains himself in his arousal and he sees the shadow of the Wild Boar filling the darkness and he curbs the flames and fires invading his infernal lower parts like summer suns and now he rips everything apart, all the carbuncles and rubies, the bristling stars, like the knife that wounded him in a glory of wild dark roads because Artur is done and now she is the one who is bursting into tears and scratching the King's back with the fury that is the clarion of fulfilled desire. Later, sitting up in bed, King Artur watches how the ruddy light undulates on Liliana's back as she breathes calmly with her face against the pillow. The King remembers the death of the Wild Boar, the fierce beast's loss of strength, the collapse of its front legs and the infinite sadness of its powerful snout against the British earth. As he remembers, his hand runs over Liliana's back, covered with soft golden velvet, like Guenebra's back. Like Guenebra's back, thinks Artur, and he brushes Liliana's dark hair aside, like Guenebra's hair, and he kisses Liliana's forehead, Liliana's full, warm lips, just as Guenebra's lips used to feel after they had made love. The Wild Boar disappears into the distance of the dream and the torches seem to take on a different light that contains the spasms of Merlín's laughter. In the centre of the room in Liliana's castle, King Artur leaps up and seems to be trying to listen to the light's equivocal message and interpret it, and in his ear he can just sense the beating of a sentry's stupid voice singing of the love that is keeping the unfaithful wife awake. Artur, in his nightshirt, leans over Liliana, the secret wife of Lanzarote do Lago, and her hand rises slowly towards the King's beard and she fondles and plays doubtfully with the golden ribbons that thread through it, with the regal curls that nobody has ever pulled, just like Guenebra. And then Artur sees that Guenebra is opening her eyes and smiling up at him and that she is no longer entirely Liliana and that Liliana had made love with the same little tricks that Guenebra used and even her own words in the darkness of the search for the ultimate heights of deferral and desire, with everything between the legs overflowing with sulphur and slaughter, they were, they had been Guenebra's, lost Guenebra's words and movements of love. And in that instant Artur realises that he has reached the end of his pilgrimage in search of the root and cause: loss of losses that no king in love ever

158

suffered. Merlín's terrible smile takes on the face of Roebek in the depths of Artur's closed eyes. When he opens them, Liliana's eyes reveal to him a well of immense love from which Artur drinks the cloudy waters of wisdom. Because Liliana's eyes tell him everything. Liliana's eyes are Guenebra's eyes and Liliana was like Guenebra because they both loved Lanzarote and Lanzarote loved them both and through Lanzarote lymphs of dark, radiant identity flowed between them. And, in their ecstasy, they all loved Artur. And King Artur wept, like the knight at the inn when he saw the eyes of his lost son in the rabbit. Because the rabbit was Liliana; the stolen son was Guenebra; the thieving eagle was Lanzarote; and King Artur was the knight in Roebek of Tagen Ata's enigma. At that moment, Liliana's voice caressed the King's ear like softest velvet as she hummed a song. With the slightest flickers of her gaze, she providing the song with words of incomplete sweetness that were like the pink cotton-wool clouds of Cornish twilights. Without untangling her fingers from Artur's beard, she burst into tropes, verses, bitter stramonium, and the hook of the refrain that came again and again stretched out to infinity the eternal return of the secret song. And so the King heard that horns and battle cries and the Wild Boar's snout and the metal of Escalibur were not as strong as Lanzarote's love for Artur, were nothing when compared with it. That King Artur was a fire that consumed Lanzarote's eyes. That Lanzarote had only conquered Guenebra in order to possess in her, in her flesh of scented Camoese apples, the mysterious flesh of his lord Artur. That Guenebra had loved Lanzarote only because she loved Artur more than anything else, more than everything else and, when possessed by Lanzarote, she was being possessed by the man who loved Artur most blindly and he transmitted his blindness to her, the two of them drunk on Artur. That there had been certain couplings was only because in opening up tunnels of betrayal and shadows in forbidden bodies and imaginations, they were quenching the thirst for Artur that parched them all, that they all professed in limitless ardour. That Genifer or Gwenhwyfar or Guenièvre, or whoever the hell Guenebra was, had screamed in Dodro Vello that Artur did not understand and now he was beginning to do so, and realising that she felt covered by a body which, in that same act, was covering the man she loved more than anything, and in this way she herself was also covering that body, as a man, and they had a tender shoot in Liliana, who was Guenebra for Lanzarote, and who was both women in their fever for Artur. It was all like a fire in a thicket where three beautiful beech trees are burning together and cannot manage to make the fire spread to the sturdy oak that, at a good distance from them, remains untouched. Dagda's three pieces of advice had been true. At the end of his reign, Artur discovered the ultimate reason for his being. Lost birds always return to their master's fist: the last piece of advice. And that night, Liliana conceived Galaad, Artur's son and not Lanzarote's, out of very love for Lanzarote. Galaad, who was to achieve the quest of the Holy Grail. And, under Liliana's sweet, silent song, Artur remained in a deep sleep, because the castle was Avallon and Liliana was the fairy who would watch over his dreams for a thousand years until the days of joy return once more to the western lands of the world, these lands where stones and silences afflict our enslaved hearts, our enslaved hearts.

(From *Amor de Artur*, 1981)

Labyrinth

When I was a little boy I was taken away from my family community, with the ruling matriarch's consent, to be brought up by the "Circuits of Negation". I was painfully transplanted from my happy valley — rich in apples, mirabelles and plums, with terraces of quivering maize in long, slow, sugared nights — to the world, far from this world, of conspiracy. Every member of my community had been secretly taking part in the "Circuits of Negation", each to his own degree. Throughout the ages, my people had foxily feigned an absolute adherence to the system, while patiently preparing the rebellion, intertwining, like threads in cross-stitch embroidery, the yes with the no, participation in the authorized assemblies — which never varied — of the "State of the Six Books" with occasional absences in the Old City where, in dusty, deserted, metallic halls, they shared their hopes and their confusion. Hopes and confusion that they anxiously opposed to certainty in the full realization of the present, and rigid affirmation of the self (like an image which is confirmed in the quicksilver of a mirror and plants itself in the consciousness), which were the dominant characteristics of the "State of the Six Books". And so the old matriarch, holding my hand, took me through the community's territory, when I was about twelve years old. I could feel the hard fingers and the rough skin of the woman who ruled over us all, and a little shiver that came down every so often from her wrist. She invited me to say goodbye — in an orthodox, martial, mechanical way as laid down in the precepts in the Books — to loving mothers (my own mother, no doubt, among them), young and tense with the emotion of the parting and the fulfilment of my unique destiny, and to fathers who were stiff and humble as required by the norms of behaviour in force throughout the State, secretly opposed and cursed in their brave, ardent hearts. Fathers who, as I learnt later, looked at me in faith and in despair, incapable of fulfilling my mission because of the quadrangular imperative of the times in which they had been born, yet proud to belong to the generation that had procreated me, knowing that from my predestined brood I would emerge, the one who would be the Leader of the "Circuits of Negation".

And now the matriarch was taking me, through the twilight, in her craft. We cut through the air, in an instant which will remain in me for ever, indestructible, and we hovered over my home village. I saw the red buildings that gleamed in the fading sunlight, clustered together, making an irregular cross upon the fields, the grass dividing-strips intensely dark, their green dissolving into leaden blues, crowned by the evening mists. Something inside me was telling me that the natural order in which I had lived, the system of habits within which I had grown up, had to be broken. And this was exactly what the matriarch wanted to say when she operated the control panel to fix our route and came to kneel before me, in the central capsule of the craft. She asked me to look at her and I did so at length, lingering over the furrows, ditches and roots that ran across her noble face, her leathery thinness, the beautiful blue and yellow tattoos that extended down from her slender heron-like neck, intertwining all over her withered skin, around her long breasts hanging down like shrivelled grapes, all of her, in the green light of the craft, as if in a soft and unreal exhalation. I felt a deep love for her, placed my head upon her bony knees, caressed them and noticed, as I touched her skin, that unmistakable smell of age, repugnant and moving at the same time. She told me, calmly, that I had to forget the past, forget mothers, fathers, brothers, the old, all the generations, our entire family community including her. Forget everything I had accepted as truths, as fundamentals, as norms. Question the absolute, strip myself of myself, enter the "Circuits" in which I would become another man, a man with an immortal destiny.

"A task awaits you," the matriarch said, "which, if you carry it through, will liberate everyone."

I remember that I was frightened and wept. I covered the matriarch's knees in tears and she, in a sweet, hoarse voice, intoned a song that I had never heard before, as she caressed my curls. A song intoned and spoken in divergent yet at the same time coherent registers, unlike any music that had ever reached my ears, drawing itself up like a great bird spreading a warm and showy plumage of changing liquid colours; a song with powerful and strange meanings that were sometimes omitted, leaving round holes, and sometimes represented, as evident and hard as tree-bark, and the absolute was unutterable, and the song hovered over the world and, in sudden, rough outbursts, it would break off, scrape, screech, grate in sounds as cutting as scalpels. I knew then, as if a little window had opened and shed light on my confusion, that the song came from a different cultural dimension, until then closed to me. This was, I learnt later, the dimension of the "Circuits of Negation", zealously kept from children, the initiation into which was just beginning for me, at that moment, with the matriarch's song, in the central capsule of the craft that was slipping through the wind towards the Old City.

A few minutes later, the craft was descending vertically over the empty spaces of the Old City. Long avenues edged with pinpoints of inextinguishable light that no longer shone upon the dense bustle of people that had filled them in eras prior to the "State of the Six Books"; metallic buildings, uniformly blue. It all greeted me in silence, I was infected by its coldness, its desolation. We left the craft and penetrated the spherical constructions to places that were indistinguishable from each other, and that the matriarch recognized by making calculations on a portable machine covered in figures and lights, as she went back, again and again, to her song. The song, now gliding as if on its own rails over the curved roofs and walls, echoing on the metal with an echo of silk, letting the light pass through it and itself radiating light, like the walls.

When we eventually reached the right place, the matriarch left me in the care of a group of fifteen men and women who, dressed in heavy, old-fashioned clothes, lived in a vast domed space, and she returned, singing, to the lost valley, to the valley that had once been paradise.

I remained with the group until I was twenty years old. They initiated me into the principles of the "Circuits of Negation", of which they were the Supreme Council. I learnt in the course of long, exhausting days. In the course of long, exhausting days I learnt the thousands and thousands of wiles of resistance, of dissimulation, of secrecy, of violent struggle. They taught me the use of arms, the control of the great energetic forces, the techniques of propaganda by destruction and demolition. Little by little I acquired and assimilated the basic elements of wisdom, summarized in the "Principles of Doctrine", as follows:

I. The lie is static. Truth is movement.

II. Men can attain knowledge by themselves, independent of the "Six Books".

III. At present, Principle II is impossible, but in the times previous to the "State of the Six Books":
    a) Men could attain knowledge with no need of the "Six Books".
    b) A man could even write his own book.

IV. When men destroy the "State of the Six Books", they will be free, they will recover their natural disposition and their capacity for learning, within a society in movement (truth).

V. If truth is movement, then movement is in some way related to freedom.

VI. The state of the soul of the true man (the member of the "Circuits of Negation") should be *confusion*, for he does not know anything and rejects the static (dead) knowledge of the "Six Books", and *hope*, for his hope rests in the destruction of the "State of the Six Books".

The great revelation came unexpectedly on the day I was twenty. The immense dome was shooting out its convergent blue cylinders of lightning, in which the dust was dancing merry sarabands. My fifteen teachers appeared together. They explained the need for me to be emasculated, leaving my testicles intact, to render my manly spirit fierce, constant and never satisfied. For the simple fact was that I was destined, by calculations made long before, to become the Leader of the Rebellion, the day, time and duration of which had been determined by the machines, and the conclusion of which would inevitably be favourable to the Resistance, favourable at last to the "Circuits of Negation". I allowed them to prune my green branch and, once I had recovered, I was driven through dusty older galleries, which became narrower and narrower: fearsome ancestral galleries, made of a green metal unknown to me, in which, to the right and to the left, hairless backs of abominable viscous animals scuttled away leaving behind in their flight, perhaps, great blinking eyes or sinuous proboscises that writhed and died under the impact of the light and energy proceeding from our vehicle. From the galleries of green metal we moved on into the stone passages and from them to the stairs. Creaking wooden stairs that led us to the most secret and secluded retreat in the Old City, where I met the Three Grand Masters of the "Circuits", who rule over the Supreme Council. My fifteen educators kissed the Grand Masters on the cheeks and mouth, and they all laughed and laughed together, intermingling like comrades. Then we sat around a fire of oak logs and I discovered, from the three Grand Masters, that it was necessary to find the "Seventh Book", because in it, according to tradition, are contained the original truths, which were established before the "State of the Six Books", and which will facilitate the restitution of our personal unity; that, so long as the "Circuits" did not find the Seventh Book, it would be necessary to continue resisting in confusion and in hope, comforted by the Principles of Doctrine; and that, when the moment came, it would be necessary to fight tooth and nail until the "State of the Six Books" was destroyed.

"But this is no more than a general declaration," I retorted, looking one by one at those noble faces that had never seen the sun, the faces of the Grand Masters, sons of Grand Masters who had been born in the stone concavities of the Old City and had dwelt in them throughout their lives governing the "Circuits", grandsons of Grand Masters dedicated from birth to rebellion and knowledge, only communicating with the oppressive outside world through the Supreme Council, whose members, in turn, had been born and brought up in the metallic buildings of the Old City and who only kept in touch with the outside world through dissidents in the last circuits of the "Circuits of Negation", who deposited in them their boundless confidence and their news about the resistance, the confusion and the hope.

"From now on you are our Leader. But before you consider yourself empowered, you should know what awaits you. It is something that you must carry through, for it is so determined by the calculations and because nobody but you can do it. It is just a question of destroying the 'State of the Six Books'. Because, you see, the time is nigh."

They carried on talking, with nervous passion, as if they were adolescents planning some fun and games, or pranksters making ready to dupe somebody. I obtained knowledge, then, of many things that I had not known or of which I retained a vague notion acquired before I was twelve years old, when I lived in the outside world. In this way

I discovered that in the "State of the Six Books" time is divided into ten-year periods, each being ruled by the truths revealed in one Book. Every six periods the Books run out, for there are only six of them. But the Sixth Book contains information about what has to be done when the cycle comes to an end, which is as if the world came to an end and had to be restarted, recreated. When the cycle comes to an end, the Ceremony that commemorates the invention of death has to be performed. This Ceremony lasts eight years and is performed, therefore, sixty years after the beginning of the cycle. During these eight years the Keepers of the Books are between seventy-eight and eighty-six years old, because sixty-eight years earlier, when they were ten, they had been chosen from among all the children of that age by the Keepers of the Books, and during the eight years of the Ceremony all the knowledge of the State had been transmitted to them and they had been invested as Keepers of the Books, with the obligation to keep order, the wisdom of the State, and the Six Books for sixty years, until the time came to choose more children to be initiated in their turn as Keepers of the Books for six ten-year periods, and so on. During the Ceremony, nation mingles with nation, people flagellate themselves, murder is permitted, men have to wear old-fashioned women's dresses, and it is the appropriate time for tattooing. The Ceremony is a horrible and lucid time when every crime and every aberration is decreed in the last part of the Sixth Book. A pale young Grand Master, with eyes like burning coals and rapid, elusive speech, said to me:

"So we cannot hope for a better chance to bring down the 'State of the Six Books'. The heart of the beast must be attacked, in the Ceremony. The weakest link in the cauldron-chain, when the old Keepers transmit the secrets to the ten-year-old children. The attack must be launched before they turn eighteen at the end of the Ceremony, by when it would be too late. You must attack at the beginning. You know everything you need to know to be a Leader. You were selected by infallible calculation. Now, on the eve of the Ceremony, you are of the right age, you have all the right wisdom, and you have all the underground power of the 'Circuits of Negation' behind you. You must lead us to victory, fighting against the 'State of the Six Books' and discovering the Seventh Book."

I descended the wooden stairs, I walked down the paths and the halls of stone, of metal, I emerged into the empty avenues of the Old City where the only movement is the whirling of dust, guided by the relentless hand of the wind. I flew to the communities that secretly participated in the "Circuits", recruiting combatants, spreading slogans, conspiring, giving instructions and encouragement. And so, as the Ceremony commenced, a series of demolitions of State monuments made the action of the "Circuits" public and evident throughout the world. Following this, all those persons included in the lists of ritual expiation and extermination were arrested by the soldiers and executed by firing squad in the farmyards of the communities, or by the side of demolished temples. Or martyrized in the processions of drunken flagellators weaving their way like little vipers from village to village, as craft carefully misdirected by their crews flew into each other. Craft, crews, flagellators, drunken soldiers, pilgrims trudging through the State to proclaim thousands of times, in the same tone, in an incessant chant, the news of the invention of death and the origin of time! We, for our part, were killing many soldiers, but these deaths were not noticed in the general disorder, and we found it impossible to get near the Keepers of the Books, the main enemy, the head of the tapeworm. And so, without consulting the Supreme Council or the Grand Masters, I took my own steps to set in motion the mechanism for obtaining the Seventh Book. I descended into myself, I sank into deep concentration for many days and nights, I programmed the machines, I absorbed the data they provided, I descended to even more painful, terrible depths. I reached the last area of resistance, the combustion limit of my mental dimension. The result: I found the Seventh Book. I saw it clearly, in a rapture that convulsed the roots, the founts, the springs of my being. The Seventh Book was in the stone cavities, exactly where the thinking heads of the "Circuits of Negation" had been languishing since the dawn of time in search of liberation.

I immediately went, alone, to the immense hall, forgotten and dust-laden, in the centre of which, on its baroque lectern eaten up by woodworm, lay the Seventh Book. I opened it, I immersed myself in it as I read about the ritual. And a wave of terror left me petrified, for the Seventh Book established in detail how in the course of the eight years of the Ceremony the devils of former times were to become incarnate in the shape of rebels of the "Circuits of Negation", and indicated the vital role of the "Circuits of Negation" in the "State of the Seven Books" (usually called, among the uninitiated sectors of the population, the "State of the *Six* Books"). I felt that my body was losing weight, levitating, as I continued reading and realized that the death of the Leader of the "Circuits of Negation" was described in detail, together with every torture that he must suffer in commemoration and remembrance of the invention of death.

I closed the Seventh Book as I was surrounded by soldiers emerging from every corner of the hall, from the shadows and from the dust, heavily armed and wearing helmets, with the blue labyrinth of fear tattooed on their naked chests.

I know that from the moment I was torn away from my family community everything that had been done to me had been a preparation for taking part in the Ceremony, a participation that will culminate tomorrow at dawn when I shall be meticulously tortured and killed before the fearful eyes of the twelve-year-old children who in the next cycle will meticulously torture and kill another Leader prepared for such an end with precision and exactitude by the "Circuits of Negation".

For the time being I am not suffering. I am resigning myself to what is to be, but I fervently trust that some day a stone will fall into the cog wheels, a star will gleam, true rebellion will break out through different channels, the little lights in the matriarch's song will become a volcano, liberation. I do think, with yearning, of a happy valley, rich in apples, mirabelles and plums, with terraces of quivering maize in long, slow, sugared nights.

(From *Elipsis e outras sombras*, 1974)

The Castle on the Moors

I

"The Lieutenant looked down from the top of the Watch Tower. The barracks and the other buildings in the castle were buried in shadow. A murmuring of water mills mingled with the murmuring of the hundred thousand frogs of Lama Maior. The Lieutenant lifted his gaze towards the hills separating the Lucenza valley from the Limia plains. The mass of Mount Penagache could almost be made out. The skyline was turning blue and bright, to announce that the great harvest moon would soon appear there, and it did. At first it was a half a red coin on those crests. The Lieutenant could almost see it rising, that moon. Then it was like a ball of fire, until it detached itself from the horizon and began its ascent toward the firmament. As it entered the starry vault it shedded its light. Clear now, like a great tray it scattered silver flour over the valley, and the Lieutenant could pick out in detail the parapet walk and the sentry boxes in each barbican and turret. Moon and stars illuminated the valley, in which, all of a sudden, the country dogs began a concerto of howls, provoking instant pandemonium in the castle kennels. At almost the same time, one of the sentries gave the alert and his companions answered him at regular intervals, one by one, all around the wall, the focal point of which was the tower where the Lieutenant was looking at his watch.

It was twelve midnight.

Lieutenant Kleist loved being the Guard Officer on summer nights.

Standing in the middle of a vast moor, San Rosendo Castle was an outpost that Lieutenant Kleist adored, that Lieutenant Kleist valued more than he had ever valued any garrison to which he had been posted before.

The Lieutenant strolled from the Watch Tower over the creaking wooden drawbridge to the parapet walk.

He hung his sabre on his belt clasp, and removed his gloves to forage for his cigarettes in the top pockets of his greatcoat; he found them. Then, with his kepi tipped slightly to one side, his hands clasped behind his back, and his cigarette gripped in the corner of his mouth, he set off on a round of inspection of the sentry posts, with an informal, friendly grumble at the soldiers once each had made his report and presented arms. The moonlight drew sparks from Lieutenant Kleist's boots, sabre, buttons and clasps, while the glow of the cigarette lit up his meagre moustache. It was a warm night. The moors of broom and laburnum could only summon up the slightest of breezes.

Lieutenant Kleist entered the guardhouse, next to the main gate, and went straight to the officer's desk, declining to take a look at the room in which privates and corporals, their belts and straps slackened in defiance of all the regulations, were dozing as they awaited their turn for sentry duty. The unmistakeable smell of soldiers reached the Lieutenant's nose, and he screwed up his mouth in annoyance as he unbuttoned his coat and placed his sabre and pistol upon the desk.

Lieutenant Kleist had brown hair and lifeless, blue eyes that bulged like those of a fish. He smiled to himself, his pale mouth forming the expression of a man who is remembering the spiciest amorous fantasies of the summers. He tumbled into the armchair, crossing his legs as, with extraordinary precision, he sent his kepi spinning through the air to land upon one of the pegs on the coatstand. It was only then that he noticed another cap already hanging there, one that bore the badge of a Colonel."

II

"The Lieutenant leapt up like a spring and clicked his heels.

'Stand at ease, my son,' said a muffled voice, coming from the shadowy corner of the guardhouse office.

'Nothing to report, Colonel.'

The Lieutenant was soon able to make out the figure of Colonel

Junquera. As always, the Lieutenant's gaze was drawn towards his superior's short, knock-kneed legs, which provided him with so much secret amusement, and he stared at the loose-fitting trousers the man wore in an attempt to disguise this defect.

'I'm going to inspect the kennels,' said the Colonel, his shaven head sunk between his shoulders, casting a wary glance at the Lieutenant through tiny oval spectacles.

By lifting a hand to his mouth to remove his cigarette, the Lieutenant concealed the disgust that Colonel Junquera's words aroused in him.

Between the barracks and the old Gavieira manor house, where the officers in command of the regiment lived, was the old prison of San Rosendo Castle: a sombre building whose dungeons had been fitted out as kennels for twelve mastiffs of the Castro Laboreiro breed. The Colonel lived above the kennels.

'I hope that Your Excellency's experiments with the dogs have made progress since our last conversation,' the Lieutenant managed to say, with a slight stammer.

'Kleist,' said the Colonel, adjusting the belt around his small but prominent paunch, 'you are the only one of my officers with sufficient education to be able to comprehend the strategic importance that the training of brute creatures could have, yet you do not offer to assist me in my research in the kennels...'

This time, the Lieutenant did not even try to hide a grimace of displeasure.

'I hate dogs, Colonel.'

'The feeling is probably mutual,' said Colonel Junquera with a distant smile.

For a second, the dialogue between the isolated howls of the dogs in all the villages on the moors as far as the foothills of Mount Penagache, and the strident disagreement of the regimental dogs, was interrupted.

'A cloud must have covered the moon,' the Colonel commented as he took his kepi, signalled goodbye to his fellow officer with a brief nod of his red beard, and stepped outside, where the moon was indeed hidden, while at his back Lieutenant Kleist's heels snapped together.

By Colonel Junquera's watch it was a quarter to one in the morning."

III

"The moon was again allowing the central avenue of the castle, a road paved with irregularly shaped slates, to be seen. Colonel Junquera, grunting and gasping, trotted along it. Some kind of asthmatic attack soon forced him to stop. He could hear his chest wheezing as he breathed. Damn him, thought the Colonel. Damn Kleist. The sinister wall of what had once been a prison loomed before the Colonel, emanating ancient terrors and darkness. The sentries were again beginning to give another round of alerts, and their voices were lost in the vast expanses of the moors. The echoes dissolved into the small, distant farms where sleepless dogs were barking, close to border mountains such as Penagache. At the prison entrance, the Colonel lit an acetylene lamp. Everything was bathed in its metallic blue light, and a penetrating smell filled his nose and mouth.

He went into the kennels. Dogs, some regularly beaten, others well cared for, some satiated, others starving, some at the point of death, others trained to fetch, attack, destroy, tear to pieces. That was all his own work. The Colonel breathed down into his lungs the breath of the twelve animals that crouched in submission as they sensed that their master was there, talking to them. That he was deafening them with insults, in the night. Colonel Junquera, his face pale and distorted, blew a peremptory order upon his whistle. The Castro Laboreiro mastiffs fell silent.

Then the Colonel opened the door of an old punishment cell, and a great hound placed its paws upon his shoulders and licked his face. A sharp command made the animal sit, its ears pricked and its fangs bared. The Colonel hung the lamp from the ceiling and turned towards a small marble table upon which there was a gramophone. He wound it up and placed a record on the turntable. He unscrewed the top of a bottle of perfume. Mozart's *Turkish March* quickened the beating of his heart. The dog launched itself at a dummy dressed in a red dolman and a patent-leather full-dress lancer cap. The dummy's chest displayed an intricate system of gold braid with pendants, as worn by field adjutants, fastened to the top button of the dolman. The dog sank its fangs into the dummy's neck, knocking it to the ground. The Colonel blew two blasts upon his whistle and the dog obediently returned to its corner. The dummy's face was a reproduction, in rubber and celluloid, of the features of Lieutenant Kleist. Colonel Junquera removed the record from the gramophone. He replaced the lid on the bottle of perfume."

IV

"It was just before daybreak when Colonel Junquera went up to the top floor of the old prison. His little knock-kneed legs trotted up the stairs two at a time, until he reached the room where the orderly was snoring beneath a striped blanket. He crossed the orderly's room and reached his own. The walls of the Colonel's spacious bedroom were stuccoed in a shade of ochre, which spoke of the splendour of the days when San Rosendo Castle had first been adapted to meet the needs of a modern outpost in this land of hills, plains and moors that stretch away to the region's furthest mountains. With Mount Penagache on the border, and the River Lucenza like a cobra in the midst of this solitude.

In the Colonel's bedroom there was an electric light and an enormous bed beneath a faded cretonne canopy. At the foot of the bed, on a sackcloth on the floor, a dark-skinned woman was sleeping, wrapped in a blanket identical to the one covering the orderly.

The woman awoke with a jump and ran to close the window, through which flowed a moonlight that was still strong and a moorland breeze that was becoming cooler and cooler as the night neared its end. She was almost wholly naked, this woman, and her feet were bare. She wore a rough woollen robe and a pair of off-white gaiters. She was limping slightly, this woman. Colonel Junquera lay face upwards on the bed. His bald skull gleamed in the soft light of the chandelier hanging from the centre of the pink plaster ceiling. His jowl rolled over his high collar, where the insignia of the corps of infantry were glittering.

The Colonel's red beard trembled when the solemn, dark-skinned, cold-eyed woman came up to him, unfastened his belt and unbuttoned his trousers, and loosened the laces of his spats.

'I've been talking to Lieutenant Kleist,' the Colonel murmured.

The swarthy woman remained silent.

'I've been talking to your friend Lieutenant Kleist,' he insisted."

V

"The Colonel gets out of bed and, after switching on the light, he throws a campaign-coat over his shoulders. As he walks along the corridor, the long, loose garment makes him even smaller. His little legs emerge naked from his espadrilles, on either side of the central sag, almost to the floor, of the garment's hem. His bald head looks like a perfect sphere. He walks to an old iron-encrusted door that creaks as it opens and awakens, in the depths of what was once a prison, echoing howls of the dogs held in the vaults and passageways below. The Colonel thinks he hears the wails of prisoners of former times. He enters the small room and, without removing his campaign-coat, descends on to the wooden lavatory. He feels the cold wind whistling up from the depths; his buttocks nestling upon the round wooden seat; his penis snug up against the crevice carved out for this purpose. Colonel Junquera lets loose through his aching anus vexatious liquid excrement. The diarrhoea-afflicted Colonel starts imagining what will happen at the parade tomorrow, Sunday, stage by stage.

As is customary, our National Day is to be celebrated. As the occupying authority, the San Rosendo garrison will be inviting the village elders and councillors of the parishes under the jurisdiction of this outpost, placing them in the best seats on the platform — thinks Junquera.

The Colonel, stricken by acute belly-ache, sees in his mind's eye the grand hats and black corduroy suits of the notables who will come from the most distant places on the moors, even from the environs of Mount Penagache. And from the border, too. He sees their odious earthy faces from which pale eyes ceaselessly spy, full of hatred. Their powerful hands — accustomed to handling scythes, axes, and wagon-poles — crossed over their bellies in a sign of formal respect. The castle's parade ground will be decorated with imperial flags, with streamers representing the colours of the different protectorates, and with joyous strips of crinkled paper — simple indications that a patriotic celebration is being held, and that respect is due. The shadow of the Ladies' Tower will fall across the podium on which he, Colonel Junquera, will stand to attention, in his golden helmet, his blue gold-braided trousers (long ones, because they suit his shortness), and his red greatcoat. His medals, a spangling statement of what the Colonel thinks of himself, for they cover his noble martial chest with honour. His hand open and raised to the level of his visor, with his palm turned outwards. His chin jutting. Admirable, admirable. And he will not move a muscle as long as the regimental parade lasts.

Colonel Junquera is going to place Lieutenant Kleist four paces behind him. Yes, tomorrow. When the man awakes from his watch and goes off duty. Tomorrow, at dawn, when he is relieved at the main gate. Kleist will find in his room written instructions to assist His Excellency the Colonel of the Regiment, on the day of the Grand Parade, in his capacity as Field Adjutant, his uniform on the said day being: dolman and full-dress trousers; gold belt and gold braid — the insignia of that position of trust; on his head a patent-leather lancer cap with rear ribbons tied, in the regulation manner, under the chin. Lieutenant Kleist will be there, in a resentful position. One hand will be spread upon a thigh; the other will be holding his sabre up against the other thigh. With his stupid moustache and bulging eyes, ready to burst out of their sockets, bovine eyes. Perfumed Kleist.

To the right of Colonel Junquera will be the regimental band and also the band of trumpets and drums, and the two together will play the National Anthem and the Salute to the Flag, ending with a triple 'Hurrah!' from the whole regiment. The enthusiasm of these military throats will echo around the battlements, cellars and barricades of the fortress, around the blockhouses and casemates of the surrounding strategic positions, beyond the villages thinly scattered over the moors, perhaps reaching the distant mountains along the border, in an acoustic affirmation of our imperial grandeur.

Then the Major, sabre held aloft, will request Colonel Junquera's permission to proceed, and Colonel Junquera will grant it. The bugler will warble a call to attention in the burning summer air. The executive whistle, garde à vous!, provoking a clatter of boots and rifle butts on the parade-ground slates. Then on shoulders. Finally forward march, the Drum Major with his baton swirling above his head. Governed by the thundering hubbub of the military marches, the firm tread of the companies behind pot-bellied Captains with their tired legs and their feigned diligence, filing past the podium upon which rises, like a somewhat ridiculous statue, tiny Colonel Junquera, frozen in the first phase of the salute.

After the parade, there will be a reception, with a glass of champagne, in the quiet of the Renaissance loggia. The Colonel would like to make a sublime speech when he proposes the toast, and the wild peasant elders will have the chance to reply with infinite reserve, leaning their heads to one side, in their warm, humble tongue.

The morning is going to conclude with a display of training and obedience by wolfhounds. 'Performances', it will be called, in English. The band will tackle various pieces, not necessarily military in character, taken from their broad repertoire. 'Colonel Bogey' no doubt, and stuff by Sousa. Adaptations of Scottish regimental salutes, with lots of percussion. That splendid Galician march 'Ponteareas'. This acoustic climate will cheer dogs and spectators alike during the display: disarming a man, flooring a tramp, following trails, circus-like obedience.

The fact that Colonel Junquera is again feeling stabbing pains in his lower parts is put down by him to the cold and to the loosening effect of the approaching dawn; so without getting up from the lavatory, he gathers up the hem of his campaign-coat and wraps himself up in it as he vigorously rubs his belly. A little torrent of faecal slime slits the hide of his anus like knives while he imagines the applause of the audience and, when he hears the band launching itself into the march called the *Turkish March*, by Mozart, as a finishing touch to the celebrations, he sees how the biggest dog in the pack breaks away from its handler and, with nobody able to stop it, leaps at Lieutenant Kleist's throat, rips it out and leaves him lying there on the ground.

Someone — the Colonel himself — will shoot the killer dog, whose behaviour is totally inexplicable, and the cancellation of the official banquet and opening of an enquiry will be immediately ordained. Once he has finished on the lavatory, Colonel Junquera makes his way, with a smile of hopeful anticipation, towards his bedroom, where the dark-skinned woman awaits him with open eyes.

The sentries were beginning to give the round of alerts that greets the sun each morning in San Rosendo Castle."

On the 6th of August I got up very early to go to the festa of Nosa Señora da Peneda, walking across moors, grasslands and wastelands; through the hills where black-faced cows graze free. I went with my parents and a few others from my village of Casardeita, including the parish priest, and we were soon joined by people going the same way. We were all very happy. I was enjoying those school holidays more than any others I had ever had. When we reached the shrine, after long hours of hard walking, we installed ourselves in a nearby field to spend the day there and listen to the thin voices of the borderland people, which seem to pierce your very soul, singing their dance-songs. Mother had gone to hear the masses and father introduced me to two gentlemen. One was short, with a red beard, bald, wearing a uniform, and he turned out to be Captain Costa Beirão, of the Fiscal Guard Squadron at Melgaço. The other man, younger, with pale bulging eyes, tall and with a meagre moustache, was called João de Sousa Mendes; we got on very well from the outset, and struck up a spontaneous conversation about the Portuguese poets of the sau-dosista *movement. He was a primary school teacher in Castro Laboreiro. Well, as Sousa Mendes was bending down to put a piece of salt cod in the stream to soak ready for lunch, happily whistling Mozart's* Turkish March, *he was attacked by an enormous animal. A hound as black as the devil that sank its teeth in his throat and left him dead on the spot before anybody could prise its jaws apart. The brute, of a breed native to those mountains, only let go when the Captain shot it dead with his regulation firearm. Shortly before the attack and his terrible death, the unfortunate teacher, pleasantly surprised by my literary interests, so exceptional and rare in the borderlands, had given me, with a timid smile that underlined his meagre moustache, a narrative manuscript entitled* The Castle on the Moors, *which he pulled from one of his coat pockets. I noticed, as he did so, that he smelt strongly of perfume. It is those papers that I have just transcribed, word for word, although slightly modified on being put into Galician. All the same, I still retain, melancholically, the Portuguese original, in case some curious soul may wish to compare the two versions. Needless to say, the tragic event gave rise to a great deal of talk in the strange triangle whose corners are Celanova, Montalegre and Arcos de Valdevez.*

(From *Arraianos*, 1991)

A Family of Surveyors

It had been a great stroke of good fortune for Sabina to have landed that job; and if she had attended the interview with a certain repugnance, given the nature of the duties that she was being asked to perform, when she left it, elegantly stepping along the pavement of Rúa do Progreso in her worn wedge-heeled shoes, her feeling was one of surprise and curiosity. Señora Mamnek Kleines's faint smile had presided over the entire conversation, as if placing suspension points at the end of each sentence; and it had opened up meanings parallel to the concepts expressed, even the most trivial ones. Sabina had looked timidly at that bulbous white mass, swathed in rustling pink crepe.

A mug of malted milk restored the confidence that Sabina had lost that afternoon with Mamnek. She thought in words, almost aloud, of the señora's beautiful white hat, which had toned the light on her pink cheeks and on her sightless eyes. They had talked at length, until the September evening drew intense lightning flashes from the silver in the dining room opposite, and a ruddy dusk could be divined on the mountains that cut Ourense off to the west. Yet something had been left unsaid, thought Sabina, gazing sadly at the ladder running up her stocking to her knee. Something dark, which she could not even shape into the beginnings of thought, and which perhaps had something to do with the cobra, with its enormous hood and bat's wings, that she had seen engraved on a heavy gold ring displayed on the index finger of Mamnek Kleines's right hand.

In Sabina's situation, getting a job was important, even if it did have as little to do with her profession and her style of life as did the position of housekeeper for an old lady of foreign extraction. And so Sabina did not feel any nostalgia as she stared at the planks that formed the walls of the garret where she had been suffocating for twelve anguished months and, with her valise in her hand, closed the door and set out, full of optimism, for the cavernous flat where Mamnek Kleines was waiting for her.

From then on her days had been monotonous and quiet. Sabina would go out to do the shopping every morning and, with her basket on her arm, she would stroll down the aisles of the covered market, breathing in a thousand different smells and filling her eyes with the flurry of the fishwives in their clogs, amidst a thunderous murmuring; she would exchange pleasantries with the stallholders from Seixalbo and reach the Burga wash-house, teeming with women, and stand there in silence contemplating their ceaseless toil. It was the only outing of her day, and with the slightest excuse she would weave her way through the rings of people who stood listening to the hawkers, the fortune-tellers, the blind fiddlers, and reach the "El Encanto" haberdashery on the Promenade, "El Derroche", "Bazar Nieto", or any other shop on Rúa do Instituto, or Rúa do Progreso, where she would buy knitting needles, maybe a lampshade, crochet thread, and various other odds and ends that might come in handy, even aspirins from the "Pilarita" chemist's shop or a calendar from one of the bookstalls in the Main Square. It was during these outings that Sabina came across acquaintances who would look the other way, scrutinise their watches to avoid greeting her, or briefly acknowledge her existence and then hurry off. Sometimes she would be stopped by fellow students from the Training College, who were now teachers in remote mountain villages, and who were sincerely sorry about Sabina's dismissal and asked her how she was managing, and she would be happily telling them how she had taken up a position with Mamnek Kleines, until she noticed the nervousness in their eyes (she had even seen it in the eyes of the liberal schools-inspector who had been briefly investigated and then reinstated after pressure from Bugallo Pita), and the image of the Kleineses would appear, right there in the street, like a sinful ghost, and then the farewell kisses on alternate cheeks amidst the fumes of a car fuelled by gasogene, knowing that the next conversation with that person would be even more difficult.

Yet Sabina would resolutely look down at her new shoes, and out of the corner of her eye she would catch in a shop window a glimpse of her head crowned by the magnificent perm that Linares had styled for her, and she would remember the spectre of hunger banished by the adorable smile of Mamnek Kleines. Her father a railwayman who had been shot, her brother a schoolteacher who had gone into exile, Sabina had been abandoned in a horrible world that had collapsed on top of everybody and left her beset by terror, sick from it. Sabina liked the comfort of Mamnek's home, but she had a vague sense of a needle lodged in her heart, a needle of anguish and prejudice.

Mamnek Kleines lived on the second floor of an old building of mud and straw held together with bond-stones, access to which was through a filthy porch with a marble floor and tiled walls and up dark, creaking stairs, riddled with woodworm. Few of the objects in the flat suggested the exotic origins of the Kleineses, who had arrived in Ourense at the end of the nineteenth century and established themselves there as land surveyors of technical excellence and proven honesty. In an entrance hall with a waxed parquet floor, in constant shadow, it was possible to make out the set of gutta-percha chairs, the bureau, the console table, the mirror with its carved frame and the cabinet inlaid with ivory and mother-of-pearl. There was a large dining room with a dresser and a sideboard upon whose veined marble stood Sargadelos ceramics, Czech tea services, fruit bowls, blue-tinted carafes and an enormous, iridescent Murano glass bowl. At the far end of the dining room, the ante-chamber sheltered a snug boudoir, with its velvet-upholstered sofa, its Maristany piano of dark wood, with silver candelabras and pink candles, its sociable with two threadbare seats, and its onyx occasional table, upon which there were ashtrays, bowls and a violet-vase at which Sabina looked and looked again with apprehension, because it had the form of a winged serpent. The boudoir led on to a balcony overlooking Rúa do Progreso, from which ascended the rattling of the trolleybuses, the hooting of the lorries, the monotonous thundering of the military parades, the bawling of the demonstrations in front of the government buildings, the droning of the dawn rosaries.

Passing through the brocade curtains, heavy and charged with a perfume that vaguely reminded Sabina of church incense, one gained access to the other part of the flat where, it seemed, everyday life had been lived in the days when it had been home to a numerous and active family of surveyors. There was a broad corridor from which many

minority was unenthusiastic in its support of incipient Azerrata nationalism, lies and calumnies circulated, insults and jealousies took on ideological form, myths of racial purity were established and, finally, a fierce pogrom broke out, initiated by the patriots and completed by the occupying forces of Terra Ancha. Lacking any support in Tagen Ata, the survivors of the massacre decided that the best thing to do in their situation would be to go into exile. Carrying just the bare essentials, the Kleineses settled in Paris, where they spent a few years of nostalgia during which Mamnek's mother died. For a reason unknown to Sabina, the family came to Ourense in 1892 or 1893, and Señor Kleines established himself here as a land surveyor. He immediately forged links with the liberal sector of the local legal establishment, made relations with the radical surveyors who kept alive memories of the intense professional activity that had followed the expropriation of church lands, and gained the respect of the principal farming families of the province and of the lands of Lemos and Chantada. His two eldest sons, Alberte and Carlos, thus recorded in the registry office in memory of St Albertus Magnus and Charles Darwin, soon became qualified surveyors and began their labours in their father's office as they played with the idea of buying the Casardomato estate from the Novoa family and setting up tobacco plantations there. Señor Kleines died in 1935 and his burial in the unconsecrated part of the San Francisco cemetery brought together businessmen, wealthy farmers, country gentry, professional men and socialist artisans. In August 1936, Alberte and Carlos were eliminated in the clearing at Oira by a Falangist squad led by Fernando Salgueiro from Verín. In the course of a business meeting at local army headquarters, Police Officer Carril had given confused information about the Kleines's Jewishness, their masonic affiliations, and their Russian origins, which had led to Colonel Soto decreeing the lads' death, in a batch including another pair of brothers, the Fuentes Canals of the Fuentes Bank, their close friends and dedicated Galician nationalists. Mamnek was left alone, refusing to flee to Portugal with her daughters-in-law, both of whom were members of Tagen Ata minority families that, after the 1893 pogrom, had settled in Venice (where they became the joint owners of the Malibrán theatre and picture house), and so she lost contact with the world, isolating herself in her flat in Ourense, without relinquishing either her sweetness of character or her habitual generosity.

Sabina, a student teacher in 1934, cast down in a brutal world that was not her world, gave herself over to the special warmth of Mamnek's flat, but, from the very first moment she met the old señora, nameless worries nested in her heart and never stayed still, like a strange, ever-changing kaleidoscope of anxiety. The presence of the winged cobra in the most unexpected places perturbed Sabina, no matter how she tried to explain the image with hypothetical references to the sect's special religious rituals; a gratuitous explanation that was not supported by anything said by Mamnek, who kept absolute silence on the subject of the religion professed by her family.

But Sabina's growing unease had other causes, too. The two of them were sitting there in the glazed-in balcony at the rear of the flat, and Mamnek was instructively enumerating anecdotes from the past while Sabina crocheted a mat for the centre of the marble pedestal table in the entrance hall, which seemed so cold to her, and the grey autumn light was coming in through the balcony windows, slivers of cloud speeding over the Salto do Can Mountains, and Sabina thinking about how cold the cottages in Regueiro Fozado, for example, or Vila Valencia, must be by now, the vines quivering with loneliness and nostalgia for the burning suns of Ourense, and she does not know how, Sabina does not know how, in a sudden sharp shift this is not Ourense and Mamnek's mumbling tones are making her see slate roofs, little streets that are not there lined by low houses each with stone stairs up to the front door and a window on either side, and a tilbury passing by with the coachman sitting bolt upright and wearing a grey top hat because this is Tagen Ata for Sabina and Mamnek smiles and Sabina knows that she is not smiling at her and she is not at all afraid even though she thinks that she should be afraid, because the portrait of Mamnek's mother and the sightless eyes of Mamnek herself are definitely looking at something, they are seeing someone who is sitting in the wicker-work armchair which Sabina herself can hear creaking, unless it is the sound of the sudden shower on the balcony's hundred panes of glass; and there it is, Mamnek's smile, far away, a smile that is not for Sabina; then the end of the long narrative in an almost imperceptible voice, delivered in a language that Sabina does not understand and that must be the obscure language of Tagen Ata and Sabina jumps to her feet startling Mamnek who asks her, her now, and Sabina was going to the kitchen to boil a pan of water to make the tea, as the old lady takes her cane and strokes its silver knob on which, in worn relief, there is a winged cobra.

But it could also be the case that Mamnek did wish to have her bath alone. And it is certainly true that Sabina loved Mamnek's small, white, bulbous body, which she was only allowed to brush her hand over when she rubbed it with the big blue towels after the bath made ready by Virxinia, who heated water in great pans in the kitchen and carefully carried it in a pitcher to the old tin tub where Mamnek's little body lay, her face wreathed in the smile of a little girl. And she did not want Sabina to bathe her, out of bashfulness, and Sabina would then wonder why she did not mind being dried by her, until one day she felt the pangs of jealousy and, with her ear pressed against the door, she heard Mamnek talking very quietly in the bath, and laughing as if she were happy, with a laughter like tinkling bells and window panes, and splashing, and that was when Sabina heard the Azerrata words "agrova an" in the middle of a canticle chanted in a voice that, because of something that gave her goose-pimples without frightening her in the least, Sabina thought was not Mamnek's.

"Why don't you go and visit your cousin Merceditas?" Mamnek asked her in mid-November, as they stepped along the corridor towards the boudoir in the front part of the flat. "The life you lead is too secluded, my dear," she continued with a sweet smile and, as they passed the study door, Sabina noticed the lady's face turn towards the shadowy interior of the room and light up with a broad smile, she thought she saw something like a flash of life in the sightless eyes, just for an instant, and hanging on the far wall was the portrait of her mother, with the winged serpent on her breast; and then Sabina did feel frightened because it seemed as if something was trembling, and something like white frost and metallic screeching and spines in her throat. "No doubt the chestnut harvest in Entrimo will be very enjoyable, Sabina." And, as they passed through the curtains that led into the front of the flat, Mamnek's touch on Sabina's arm became a strong grip, and the brush of the brocade excited her like an evil gloved hand caressing her cheek in an obscene gesture, the first of others that never materialised; and now they were in the ante-chamber, with the standard lamp lit and everything as it should be, and Sabina's heart beating normally again because Mamnek was talking to her about Vienna and about Bruckner's angular music and was refusing to play on the piano the dances of Tagen Ata that had filled the evenings of her youth with joy, when she was still Señorita Olsen and had nimble fingers. An abrupt question from Sabina was followed by an uneasy silence and Mamnek answered "love". Yes, the word "an" meant "love" in the Azerrata tongue but she did not remember the word "agrova". "It comes from the dialect of Terra Ancha; at least, it has that air about it; but I couldn't tell you its meaning," Mamnek concluded sternly, treating the matter as closed. And Sabina felt uncomfortable and hurt.

Enlightenment came to her in the bathroom, bringing with it a miserable, infinite sense of abandon.

Sabina had known from the beginning, but had not dared allow herself to admit the ominous truth. From a corner of the enormous mirror with the nickel-plated frame, the tiny transfer of a winged serpent seemed to be smiling at her, mockingly. She spat at it in fury, and immediately felt ashamed. There were things that had changed places without either Virxinia or herself touching them. There was a new air of menace in the flat. All around, a cold presence that froze Sabina. It was no longer the flat that it had been months earlier, when, at the end of the summer, she had entered this haven of wellbeing harboured in warmth and cosseted in old, garnet-red comfort. What presence was this?

Sabina strokes the edges of her lips with the tip of a finger. She frowns in resignation. Outside lies Ourense, poverty again, maybe Merceditas's house in the lush valley of Entrimo, with chestnuts, a dog of the Castro Laboreiro breed, apple trees. Indignation squeezes Sabina's heart, for she knows that she has been banished from this little world that, in her delusion, she has come to love as her own.

More desperate than she has ever felt before, Sabina buttons up her cardigan. She checks that the seams of her stockings run straight up the backs of her legs, changes her pompomed slippers for low-heeled shoes, carefully covers her head with the Portuguese scarf that Merceditas (her next refuge, hardly guessed at, hardly confessed) gave her on her Saint's day, and now she is walking down the corridor, past the half-open door of Mamnek's bedroom, from which emanates a stench of feet that has never been there before, past the closed doors of the bedrooms of Alberte and Carlos, whom she has grown to love without ever having known them, past the door of Señor Kleines's study, where she shuts her eyes because she does not what to see what is not there, what at this moment is horribly missing from there; she continues on her way, caressing with her gaze the chestnut-wood bureau, the English clock with its metal face and motionless hands standing on top of it, Señor Kleines's diplomas in the language of Terra Ancha, the other diplomas, headed by the King of Spain, belonging to the sons of the beloved Señor and Señora Kleines; she passes through the kingdom that in her madness she had imagined was also hers, and she is left feeling like an abandoned lamb, wretched Sabina thrown out of Paradise. And now she is getting there and she does not want to see what she already knows to be terrifyingly true, she barely stifles a sob by placing her linen handkerchief over her nose as she leans her head around the front dining room door. Mamnek, sitting on the sociable, is wearing an English lace bonnet, and is stammering short phrases in a language that Sabina does not understand and, in the midday half light of the bright young winter, a dark shadow strikes terror into Sabina because on the seat next to Mamnek and maybe replies or maybe not or pockets of echoing silence, and Sabina would always remember how she ran out into the street, an army truck was rumbling by, she closed the door behind her (Merceditas could doubtless come and collect the valise) never to return because she knew that she had been replaced in her task of caring for Mamnek Kleines by someone else, by someone agrova an.

(From *Amor de Artur*, 1982)

Partisan 4

With precise movements, they alighted from their vehicles in the zone of the Reserve of Unproductives, surrounded the hostels and arrested the Old Woman. They proceeded without hatred, without any personalisation of their action, strictly and rapidly. As is laid down in the Security Ritual. From the blue holes that shone in her earthen face, as brown as summer, she watched the police alight from their vehicles and come to her rooms. They were wearing dark boots, gold helmets (with plumes of peacock and bird of paradise), long cloaks of dark serge that revealed a triangle of bare flesh on their chests where the Sacred Interlinkage was tattooed in thick blue lines. With a strangely graceful step they approached, distant and impersonal beings. They were so sure of their own power that their walk did not reflect any aggressiveness but rather took on the character of a majestic and stylised imitation of a contre-dance. They carried their guns elegantly, as if they were willow-wands or cigars. She meekly let them shackle her hands and put her into the vehicle, and the mask of leathery serenity that she had adopted from the first moment of her arrest was not modified by any crease, line or nervous tic. She noticed the pressure of the metal on her wrists, squeezing her through and through. Even squeezing her throat, her ovaries. She sensed shameful circles around each eye, on every sensitive millimetre of her skin, in her guts and muscles. She felt that those shackles were there to degrade her, to dispossess her of herself and of her spirit and of her dignity. To turn her into dust, demolish her, change her into another, more submissive and reverent person, deprived of movement and vitality. They led her into an enormous marble corridor, with volutes heavy with allegories, golden fruits, mottoes alluding to the Interminable Order. They went through a huge iron-encrusted door. Then another door, a small one, painted white. They came face to face with a young man who looked at the Old Woman with friendly fondness.

"You can remove her shackles," he said to the policemen.

Then, enveloping the Old Woman in a warm, filial look, he added: "The Guardian of the Security Ritual is awaiting your visit."

He pressed a button and a reinforced door swung open. The young man went through first, and the Old Woman was tranfixed by the aura of power and severity which emanated from his long robes — covered with slips of metal and hanging in vertical folds in which the Sacred Interlinkage twined endlessly — in sharp contrast with the smooth, soft tones of his voice. She was left alone, in front of the Guardian, in a chamber with panelled walls on which hung ancient and modern weapons combined in unbelievable panoplies, flags, emblems, slogans and ordinances sewn in gold thread on velvet banners. She placed her hands together and bowed her head before the Guardian, whose bulbous mass rested on a throne of polychrome stone.

"You must know that you have been arrested," the Guardian began, while she gazed in amazement at the beautiful embroidery on his yellow hood, the three rows of medals, the system of sashes, bows and colours, the helmet with jet-black plumes that rested on his knees, the hands with fists clenched and protected by iron gauntlets because she belonged to the Retarded Caste, although that was not the main reason.

The Old Woman followed the nasal hum of the Guardian's words very attentively. Words that poured from his small lamprey-like mouth, monotonous yet charged with a manifold inner life, like the buzzing undulation of a swarm of bees.

"The main reason for your arrest," continued the Guardian, "is that you know Partisan 4. We want you to tell us where he can be found. You are the only person who knows. As soon as we have this information, we shall set you free to return to the Reserve of Unproductives. And there you will be able to fritter away what remains of your life in peace. Because peace is our supreme objective. That unique peace which is born from the crossing, which occurs ceaselessly, of things in an eternal return to the centre and far from themselves, in expansion and periodical concentration, like breath itself. That is what we are taught by the image of the Sacred Interlinkage."

As he uttered these words, the Old Woman knelt down and beat her forehead on the floor in a gesture of absolute submission, as laid down in the Behaviour Ritual of the Retarded Caste. Then, in accordance with the same texts, she curled up on the floorboards in the foetal position, while the Guardian rose to his feet, clicked his heels, placed his helmet on his bald, spherical head, and hailed the Sacred Interlinkage, the symbol and the embodiment of the Interminable Order, with an endless howl, as undulating as an eel.

"Sir, I cannot tell you where Partisan 4 is because I do not know," the Old Woman said at last after a long silence during which her eyes gazed blue and unflinching at the Guardian's eyes.

She was put into one metal lift after another, which took her down at great speed to some lost underground place. She was led along a damp stone corridor as far as walkways lined with countless cell doors. One of them was opened and she was put inside. It was a square space, quite large, with granite walls oozing slime. Protruding from one wall there was a stone bed; in a corner, a pot to defecate and urinate in, and another to drink from. The bolts resounded in an extraordinary clangour, on the other side of the iron door. She was left in silence and solitude for thirty days, as decreed by the Security Ritual for first-stage treatment. Every day she had to empty the pot of faeces into a large vessel carried by two prisoners under the watch of the guards, and collect water in the other pot. That was the only time she saw or heard anyone. The rest of the time the walls caved in on her, crushed her. All the memories accumulated throughout her seventy years of poverty, humiliation and, in short, membership of the Retarded Caste, fell on to her cell like clouds, vapours, salty colours impregnating everything. And what this did was to sadden the Old Woman, and to confirm her in her courage and her resistance to the Guardian's question.

Moving on to the second stage of treatment was like entering another world, different from anything she had seen before. She had never imagined that a place like this could exist, a room like this upholstered in green velvet, soothing, softening, to which she was taken after having been given a warm bath. She was left alone, she felt clean, relaxed, almost happy. But her face retained its impenetrability. She lay down on a sofa, she slept, curled up like a child. She was awoken by a man's voice calling her by her name. She looked around but she could not see anyone in the warm, comfortable room. She stretched her legs and studied her toes, blackened like grains of barley after so much work, and she was astonished that a young, affectionate voice was asking for her, begging her to rest her head on the cushions, to close her eyes, to breathe deeply, to listen. To listen, to let the words into her ears without offering any resistance, to open up, to yield, to let herself be informed. Without any bitterness, without any remembrance of the days of horror, days gone by now. Days gone by, not here, not now. Dead, dead, if they had ever existed. And now a happy aroma fills, filled this world of green velvet: a pleasant plain of dawn lights, an undulating somersaulting plain crowned with wheat and poppies, memories of being pampered, of good health, the return to the springs of youth, to unforgettable afternoons, to joyful battles of love in those tranquil moments of the past. Imperceptibly the Old Woman opened her legs and her mouth, and closed her eyes. She surrendered to the hoarse, caressing magic of that voice, which affirmed that: a responsibility fell upon her, the Old Woman. The perfect world, the Interminable Order, was based on the principles of collective ownership and eternal return, symbolised in the Sacred Interlinkage. A collective ownership concentrated in the Pure Class, which condescends to support and educate at its own expense the members of the Retarded Caste, constitutionally incapable of ruling themselves and with an exclusively passive function in the Interminable Order. It is the Pure Class in itself that directs and controls power, culture and history, conceived as interminable and recurrent successions of a present that does not cease. And harmony triumphs in the world, it rules and will continue to rule. But ever since ancient times, unharmonious elements called Partisans have appeared on the glorious scene of the Interlinkage, and the most recent of these is Partisan 4.

The voice makes a pause; its breath can be heard, amplified, as if expressing contrition.

"Partisan 4," the voice repeats, "has gone further than anyone. He has even gone as far as to deny the recurring movement of history and to propose to young people another schema to replace the Interlinkage: a moving arrow. With this image, he intends that humanity should surpass itself and progress in a forward direction. You yourself will understand, you already understand, that this is absurd, because if it were true we would have to contemplate an unthinkable destruction of the Interminable Order, which would be chaos. Because of the threat Partisan 4 poses, then, and because of the obedience to which you are obliged by your membership of the Retarded Caste, you must, you must inform us about his whereabouts."

"That's impossible, I can't. I don't know the whereabouts of Partisan 4."

The Guardian of the Interminable Order knelt down in the company of his superior officers, and they offered up songs of praise to the Sacred Interlinkage. While he was praying, something in his brain kept sending forth green images of danger and abnormality that did not conform with the cultural standards and therefore took the shape of horrendous giant rats, otters, lizards, slimy toads with an indescribable gaze, abominable images, ghosts on horseback, fires, shadows, fear. Guardian and superior officers rose to their feet, tidied their vestments, their robes, the arrangement of the lines on their faces, imbecilic from rapture and prayer. They had a rapid discussion about the Old Woman's resistance, which was quite abnormal, and decided to move her on to the third stage.

So the Old Woman was taken to a smooth, metal chamber. She watched the police surrounding her, sinisterly forming a tight ritual circle. This did not surprise her, since it was what she had been expecting from the start. Not offering any resistance, she was chained to the rack. Then a team of five people came, men and women in white coats and the look of university graduates who, with sharp instruments, began to make small incisions and lacerations, interrupting their operations, from time to time, to ask the Old Woman, amiably, in voices that were impersonal yet laden with affection, whether she had anything to say about Partisan. She endured the pain and felt her consciousness disintegrating. Then she lost consciousness, it was swept away. When they revived her with the aid of stimulants, she saw before her a horrible figure covered in plumes, lace, and gold buttons, and with an infernal mask over its face. On its bare chest the Interlinkage glowed in muted tones of gold. The masked figure performed a vile gesticulating dance with allusions to the female genitalia, whose significance the Old Woman knew precisely. She was equally certain of the monstrosity that would come next, with the aim of burying her in excrement, destroying the last redoubt of her dignity. The masked figure came up to her and uncovered her sexual organ. The Old Woman was struggling, with her last remaining energy, against the fetters and shackles that prevented her from altering her position. She felt pain before her soft flesh was cut with the old silver scissors, before her loving lower parts were snipped with a terrible click that shot up her spine and hammered her head, plunging her into an insufferable sea of steel, unbearable pointed centres. She could still see, among bloody rags, pierced by green knives, rage like horses, beneficent shadow on its way, she could still see the knobbed crook, with the iron point, directed towards the hole of the womb, and then nothing.

When the Guardian of the Security Ritual decided to move on to the last stage, which consisted in the injection of drugs to remove the Old Woman's resistance and force her to confess the whole truth, he knew that the prisoner was about to die, was almost dead already. And so he was not exposed to risk if, after giving her the treatment, the official again asked her the question, as she would not be able to answer it coherently, and the episode's standing as an exemplary punishment, a warning to strike terror into the Retarded Caste, would remain intact, without his subordinates ever finding out that the Old Woman really was ignorant of the whereabouts of Partisan 4. This would be extremely constructive, as his subordinates would form a very high opinion of the stubbornness and capacity for silence of the members of the Retarded Caste, even those who were weakest and most obsolete, as in the case of the Old Woman, and tortures would be applied with redoubled zeal after the next, similarly functional arrests that the Guardian had planned. Nevertheless, when the Old Woman — her face broken, ashen, and her body, which seemed to have shrunk, wrapped in brown prison rags — half-raised her eyelids under the effects of the injection as if they were made of lead, and slowly let a crack open up between her lips to say I will speak, to say I know where Partisan 4 was last week, but her voice weakened while the Guardian of Security's smooth, round face shook with fear, his cheeks of watery flesh quivering in horror as he witnessed what he had not foreseen, that the Old Woman was speaking again, she could speak again as the tape-recorders registered even the slightest parasitical sounds of her vocal chords, she was speaking again, she was saying that Partisan 4 had by this time changed his hiding place knowing by now as he did that I, she, had been arrested and tortured and would speak, that if they wished she would tell them where Partisan 4 had been hiding before, it was right there in my own, in the Old Woman's own rooms, and as she lay there dying the feathers on the Guardian's helmet swayed in a colourful cyclone for he knew that Partisan 4 was a tactical-operational invention of the Security Ritual and did not exist, had never existed. Not yet.

(From *Elipsis e outras sombras*, 1974)